SPY
FAMILY

JAMES
RAHFALDT

This is a work of fiction. The characters and events in this book are used fictitiously or are a product of the author's imagination, and any similarity or resemblance to actual persons, living or dead, events, business establishments, locals or incidents, is coincidental and not intended by the author.

JAMES RAHFALDT'S SPY FAMILY

First Edition: December 2011

ISBN: 978-0-9849278-0-7

Matcole Publishing a division of Matcole Properties, LLC.

Matcole Publishing
117 South Cook Street, Suite 147
Barrington, IL 60010

Printed in the United States of America

For my twins, Matthew James Rahfaldt and Nicole Elizabeth Rahfaldt, we all had a great time researching the locations for this book.

Chapter 1   Vacation Time

Some heroes are born, some are created, and yet others only realize they are heroes when they are faced with challenges.

It is the bottom of the 9th inning, the score is tied, 2 outs, with runners on 2nd and 3rd in the last inning of the championship game. James Ward is up to bat, this could be a lot of pressure, for a 13 year old boy, but James doesn't even think about it. He is more concerned about getting Tommy home from 3rd base. All he needs to do is make a hit and their team, the Tigers, will win.

The first pitch comes across a little inside, James backs out quickly from the batter's box, but the ump calls a strike. The second pitch is also inside, if James had stayed standing where he started he would be walking to first base right now, but again he jumped back out of the way, ball 1.

The third pitch has James looking and at the last second he swings, a line drive down the 1st base side, but it hits the ground hard on the foul side of the line before reaching the first baseman's glove. Good thing because it would have been a sure out if it had been over an inch or two to the left. A couple of bad pitches later and we have a full count, 3-2.

James needs to make a big decision in a short amount of time. As the ball comes hurdling towards the plate, he decides he is going to take a big swing. His muscles start to tense, his hips start the move around, as he starts a step forward, his shoulders, arms and hands bring the bat in an arc to meet the ball. At the moment of truth his wrists rotate to transfer the most power possible and still keep control.

James hits the ball; it is going to right center. A great place to hit it in Little League, most coaches put their most challenged players in right field. The right fielder never saw it coming, probably because he was looking at the cloud formation he thought looked a lot like an elephant at the time.

With a solid double the winning run comes in and Tommy is mobbed by his team mates, then comes James' turn to be mobbed when he cuts from 2nd base to run home, almost knocking the pitcher over on the way.

James is very happy, and he should be. He just drove in the winning run in an important game, but he is still waiting for one thing, the Manager, his father, to congratulate him. Luke Ward is James' Dad, baseball Manager, and the person whose respect he most desires.

Luke comes out onto the field and high fives every boy he sees. The last one he comes to is James. James has a killer smile on his face, almost a smirk. Luke says, "Nice job James," gives him a high five, then grabs him around the shoulder and pulls him in for a big hug.

"You did it, I am proud of you," Luke said. Now James has a real smile on his face and pulls away from his Dad to join the other boys in celebrating the win.

After the game, James' Mom, Bianca Ward, congratulated her son. She made it to every game, good weather and bad, which in the Chicago Suburbs was guaranteed. She was a striking woman who looked younger than her 45 years of age. Bianca had black hair, dark brown eyes and tanned easily. It was hard to believe that almost 13 years earlier she had been in labor delivering boy, girl twins. Elizabeth, James' twin sister was also in the stands every game.

The family went to Hill Street, a local restaurant to celebrate with the team. A great time was had by all, pizzas for everyone, beers for the parents, and soda for the kids. What a great season the boys had. Luke had been a coach for James since the boy was four. The coaching back then was closer to herding wild cats, than really coaching, but Luke was there for James all the same. The twins were tall for their ages, close to 5 foot, Luke was sure that within a few years they would both be taller than he was at 6 foot tall.

John O'Malley, one of the coaches on the Tiger's team, said to Luke, "So now that baseball is finished, what are you going to do with all your spare time?"

"We are doing a family vacation in Italy; Venice, Florence, Sorrento, Rome and also visit some of Bianca's extended family."

"That sounds like a fantastic vacation, how long are you going for?"

"Two and a half weeks, almost three. It should be a vacation to remember for the kids, really… for all of us."

"Have you been there before?"

"Bianca has been there multiple times; I have only been there once before with Bianca, about 15 years ago. The last time we went, we had a great time, the history and the buildings are like nowhere else on Earth. We really wanted to go back and enjoy it with our kids."

"When are you going?"

"Next week, we will be there for Bianca's birthday in mid July."

The group finished their pizza, said their goodbyes and talked about how great the season was. The Wards got in their silver Acura MDX and drove to their home in Barrington, IL, still considered a suburb of Chicago. Everything within an hour or so drive was considered a suburb of Chicago.

Their house was in a nice neighborhood. Years earlier when they were shopping for a house, they liked the area, but couldn't find a home that met their needs, so they decided to build, and this was one of the few places close to the village that still had some buildable lots.

Luke Ward had done well for himself and his family. He was an entrepreneur. Luke Ward really liked his house, not because of its size or cost, but because it was one of those things that he and Bianca had done together. Even though it was a good sized house, it was designed to be cozy, a home to live in, raise a family in.

The Ward family house was designed and decorated in an old European style, arched entry ways and windows, Tuscan colors and wrought iron designs throughout. The kids each had their own rooms as well a spare bedroom for when the Grandparents visited.

The family was going to Italy in the next week and not everyone was packed. Luke knew he was mainly bringing shorts, because the long range weather forecasted for Italy was heat and more heat. No rain was in the cards, but it was going to be in the high 80s and 90s for most of their time there if the weather websites were right.

Luke and Bianca had decided that they should take about 7-10 days of clothing and do laundry over there. Luke knew that they were taking trains and that luggage should be limited, for his sake. After all, he will be the one really lifting every bag on and off of the trains, usually quickly. They got down to four large pieces of luggage, all of them with rollers. This was amazing to Luke who remembered the last time they went to Italy as a couple they had four bags. With the twins in tow, this really was compact packing for Bianca.

The week before the trip to Italy was uneventful except for having to put the family dog in a kennel. The Ward's dog, Bingo, was on his way to a home style kennel, where he would be with about 12 other dogs in a home as opposed to a full kennel where the pets are in cages and you have to pay extra to have the dog walked and played with "x" amount of times a day. Bingo is a 20 pound, highbred dog, a Cavapoo, (a Cavalier King Charles Spaniel and a Toy Poodle.) The dog was really cute; he had reddish fur with a white chest and a little white tuft of hair under his chin, a beard, like Colonel Sanders' from KFC. The family would miss Bingo very much.

The limo arrived for the airport about 7:30 pm for a 10:30 pm flight. The limo was about the same price as a taxi to O'Hare International Airport from the Northwestern Burbs, so why not start in style Luke thought to himself. The kids were very excited about the trip. They couldn't wait to go on a gondola ride through the canals of Venice.

Using the internet, the twins had researched some of the places that the Wards were going in Italy. James had recently seen the Bond film "Moonraker" and wanted to see where James Bond had driven the gondola out of the lagoon and into Saint Mark's Square.

The Wards were taking a Lufthansa flight that had an hour and a half layover in Frankfurt, Germany, before continuing on to Venice, Italy.

On the way to Germany James and Elizabeth slept most of the time. About an hour before landing, the airline served a breakfast that they all ate. The fruit cup must have been a little off because multiple kids that ate it were starting to get sick and vomit, James unfortunately was among this group.

He must have vomited 4 times before landing and was still looking green when they were taxiing for the gate. When they arrived in Frankfurt Luke and Bianca were hoping that James would feel better once on solid ground. They bought him a roll from a bakery/café in the airport and some water. He started eating the roll but could not keep it down. Now he was physically shaking and moaning while lying across a couple of chairs by the boarding area. This kept all but the most adventurous people away from this sitting area.

Luke said he was going to go to the gift shop to see if he could get something to calm James' stomach. Luke went to the store, but was informed that only pharmacies can sell over the counter medications in Europe. Luke had to leave the secure area of the terminal to find the closest pharmacy. Once there, he described what his son's symptoms were and they recommended two medicines, one to stop the upset stomach and one to help stop the dehydration. Regardless, about 40 Euros later and he had the medicine.

Then he had to go back through security. They questioned him because he didn't have any baggage. He showed them the medicine and even asked them to verify what it was for since all of the writing was in German. Luke was mainly German by heritage, but was a 5th generation American and had not been exposed to the German language. He had blond hair and blue eyes, not exactly your terrorist type.

The airline counter person saw that James was ill and said that he had to be able to walk on the plane himself or that he would be considered too sick to fly. Hearing this, James suppressed the pain in his stomach long enough to walk on the plane, sit in his seat, and then vomited again. It was a short, bumpy flight from Frankfort to Venice. James still felt ill while flying but, he had pretty much purged his system by the time they landed in Venice.

After arriving at the gate in Venice, James started feeling a little better. The Wards had arrived safely in Venice; hopefully their luggage had made the trip with them. Going through Italian Immigration should normally not be an issue, they let whole families traveling together go up to the counter at one time.

Bianca handed all of the passports to the agent. He scanned the passports and looked at each person in turn. The last one he scanned was Luke's. The agent immediately got a serious look on his face, held the passport up so as to see both the picture and Luke's face at the same time. The agent nodded his head a little, then said, "Bianca, Elizabeth and James you may go on," as he handed their passports to them, "Luke Ward you must stay where you are because my supervisor must speak with you."

Luke said, "What seems to be the problem?"

"Mr. Ward, please stay where you are, my supervisor will explain everything shortly."

Moments later, the supervisor showed up, along with two armed agents. Luke is a little surprised, but tells Bianca, "Go ahead, get a porter and our baggage, I will be there shortly."

The supervisor said, "Mr. Ward, Mr. Luke Ward of Illinois, United States of America?"

Luke, "Yes"

The supervisor said, "Mr. Ward, please come with me, there is an issue with your passport that we need to clear up before you may enter Italy." The supervisor then walked Luke to a door that lead into an interview room. The room was well-lit by bright florescent lighting, which helped show that the beige room contained exactly one table and two chairs in it, no windows and two doors, including the one he just came through.

The all metal table had a metal ring attached to the top. One of the armed agents removed a set of handcuffs from his belt and hand-cuffed Luke to the table. Up until this point Luke had assumed that this was a simple misunderstanding with his passport, but now he was starting to worry. Without saying a word, the supervisor and the two armed agents left, one minus his handcuffs.

Luke was left alone to ponder his supposed crime. He was only in Italy once before, 15 years earlier with his wife, Bianca. Had his passport not been cleared correctly the last time he was there? He knew from business travel that Italy will let American's in country for 90 days without a special type of visa, could that be it, did they not check him out of their system 15 years earlier?

The other door in the room opened, it startled Luke, simply because he was deep in thought trying to figure out why he was there to start with.

The first man in the room looked American, about 6'1", muscular build, had close cropped black hair, and was wearing a navy blue suit with no tie. The second man in the room was someone that Luke had met the year before when the Wards were on vacation in Washington, D.C., his name was Tom Howard, Assistant to the Special Agent in Charge of the Vice Presidential Protective Division. Luke was surprised to see him here in Italy.

Tom Howard closed the door and walked over to the table. He laughed as he took out his handcuff key, "These Italians sure wanted to scare you a little." Tom unlocked Luke's cuffs. With Luke's hands now free, Tom reached out for a handshake, "Let's start over now, … Luke it is good to see you again."

Luke shook his hand while still in shock. Tom said, "Luke Ward meet Edwin Grey, CIA Station Chief in Charge of Italy." Luke and Edwin shook hands. Edwin's eyes were the same color as his name. With the lighting in the room, they looked more like orbs of steel, lifeless steel. Edwin's handshake was very firm, but not overbearing. He now had Luke's full, undivided attention.

Edwin said, "Luke, Tom has been working a special case as a liaison between the Secret Service and the CIA to help stop a counterfeiting ring that is mainly in Italy, but is looking to expand in the U.S. Your name came up as a person that could assist us while you are here, in Italy, with your family."

Luke hardly heard what Edwin was saying, he was thinking back to the last time he had helped Tom Howard out, and how they had met each other in the West Wing of the White House almost a year earlier.

Chapter 2   Washington D.C.

Luke Ward was thinking to himself, "What a great day today, we went up in the Washington Monument, climbed the steps of the Lincoln Memorial, walked along the Viet Nam War Memorial, WWII Memorial and the Korean War Memorial, and now we are going to the West Wing of the White House."

Luke and his family were able to get a very exclusive tour of the West Wing of the White House. Some of Luke's best friends, the Bridgeworths were going to visit Washington at the same time that the Ward family. Mrs. Bridgeworth's secretary's son was a Secret Service Agent in the White House and was able to get a West Wing tour arranged up for all of them.

The Secret Service had required a two month lead time to do a background check on the visitors. In April, the Wards and the Bridgeworths provided their vital information to the Agent, full name, date and place of birth, passport and driver's license numbers. Everyone cleared the background check and they scheduled the tour for their second day in Washington D.C.

Everyone dressed up for the big event, gentlemen in sport coats, ladies, including Elizabeth, in summer dresses. Because of security requirements after 9/11, Pennsylvania Avenue is closed to motorized vehicles, so the groups' taxi van dropped them off on H Street, in front of Lafayette Park also known as Presidents Park. This seven-acre park is located directly in front of the White House and gives a great view to the majestic building. An amazing statue of Andrew Jackson caught the groups' attention and pictures were taken.

The grounds of the White House are bordered by a black wrought iron fence, the outside of which is as close as the general public can get without being on a tour. Most tours were done in the East Wing of the White House, in the public spaces where dignitaries are welcomed and the State diners take place. Those tours still need to be arranged months in advance through one's local Congressmen.

Today the Wards and Bridgeworths had an amazing treat, they were going to see the working end of the White House were the Pres-ident, Vice President and all major Cabinet meetings take place, the West Wing.

The tour was much anticipated and was scheduled to start at around dusk on a day in early August. The excited tourists first had to clear through the security check point at the Northwest Appointment Gate, on Pennsylvania Avenue, just shy of West Executive Ave, where the Old Executive Office Building resides. The security staff diligently checked passports and ran all items and people through metal detectors.

The security check point was basically a one room building about 25 by 25 feet square with a metal detector conveyor belt system off to one side, similar to what you would see at any airport screening point and a security guard with a wand to verify that no person carried anything bigger than a gum wrapper that was made of metal without being personally checked.

The group was told that no photography could be taken inside the West Wing with the exception of the press room. A personal tour guide was provided; actually he was an intern that was a little nervous because this was one of his first tours he was guiding by himself. Luke thought that he was nervous because he was worried he would say the wrong thing and get himself in trouble.

The tour stared on the lawn of the White House where pictures were takes of the group with the White House in the background sans the wrought iron fences. This picture was already earmarked for the Ward's 2009 Christmas Card.

Next the group moved up the driveway towards the West Wing. To the right, facing the West Wing was the permanent outdoor sets used by the major network news organizations. At this time all of the cameras and lights were covered with thick green and brown custom made tarps, and looked similar to covered patio furniture in the Midwest. The Wards and Bridgeworths would note the camera angle and noticed that every time a story from Washington was on the news the White House shot was done from here.

Entering through the main entrance of the West Wing was surreal for the group. The façade of the West Wing also had four columns, similar to the main entrance of the White House, but once through the doors it was slightly anti-climatic. It seems that the West Wing was built to an old standard before people were 6 feet tall on average. The ceilings seemed very low compared to today's standards. The carpeting was not very plush beneath their feet, and the walls were covered with recent photos of the President and Vice President, taken by the White House Staff Photographer.

After Entering the Lobby they went down the hallway leading to the Cabinet Room, the largest room in the building by square feet but not by volume, that went to the Oval Office, which actually had a much higher ceiling and felt as grand as it appeared on TV.

The Cabinet Room had a very large table running down the center with grand leather chairs around it. Each chair has a brass name plate attached to the back of the chair. Any person with a named chair can purchase said chair at the end of their service with the White House. Luke chucked when he heard this, he thought, "They spend Trillions on dumb projects, but on this one point they are frugal and make the person purchase the chair, instead of just giving it as a perk."

Next on tour was the Oval Office, and like its name, it is indeed oval, with four doors, some of them hidden from immediate view. The tourist were able to lean into the room but not actually step into the office, the velvet rope and more importantly the 6 foot tall, 220 lb Secret Service Agent saw to that. Next to the Oval Office James saw that there was an open crack in the decorative molding, a secret door.

"Dad, look a secret door; that must be where the Secret Service watch the President from."

Luke took a second look and saw that indeed it was a door without a door knob, but had what looked like a key hole for an internal locking mechanism. Just as James was making his find public to his Dad, Tom Howard, Assistant to the Special Agent in Charge of the Vice Presidential Protective Division, was walking by after finishing a meeting in the Vice President's Office down the hall. Tom, was deep in thought, they had just had a meeting discussing how they wanted to find a Washington outsider to help gather information at a fund raiser that was happening the next night.

Tom saw young James and said, "Son you are right, that is a secret door used by us to watch and protect the President, you are very observant. Hundreds of adults pass by there a day and never see the door. You may have a future in the Secret Service." After this praise, James started to get a little color in his cheeks and quickly day dreamed what that would be like.

James exclaimed, "Thanks, but isn't that a secret?"

"It is one of the worst kept secrets, also take a look at the roof of the White House when you go outside and you will see agents moving around on the roof."

"Just like James Bond movies, cool."

Tom said to Luke, "Good boy you have, wish more people were so observant."

Luke proudly boasted, "My son loves this stuff, he ate up the *National Treasure* movies and thinks that he can find something that everyone else has missed to solve some mystery here."

Tom pauses, then he asked Luke, "Do you have a second, I would like to ask you something in private."

A Secret Service Agent asking Luke to talk to him in private was both exciting and scary, what did he want? Why did he want to talk to Luke?

Tom pulled Luke into a close by office station that had multiple copy machines and supplies in it.

"Luke, believe it or not, we were looking for a couple that is not from D.C. to help us gather some information at a big party tomorrow night. Your country would be obliged if you and your wife could help us out."

This caught Luke by surprise; this was like a movie, how many people get asked to help the Secret Service? At first Luke was going to say yes immediately, then he mulled it over for a second or two and wondered if this would be dangerous, why him and his wife, then he thought, they didn't have a sitter and didn't have dress clothes with them.

"Sure we would like to help, we do have a couple of issues though." Luke explained the sitter and clothes issues and Tom promised that neither would be a problem.

The Wards were really not told much about their first assignment. The party turned out to be a fundraiser for State Senator Gray Feeds at the Hilton McLean in Tysons Corner. The President would be delivering remarks at this event.

They were asked to sign NDAs, Non Disclosure Agreements, which said they couldn't tell anyone that they were doing a project for the Secret Service. They also signed an agreement that showed that they would have to pay taxes on the value of the clothing that they would be wearing and got to keep. They would get monetary compensation to make up for the taxes. The 1099s would of course come from a shell company that was incorporated in Las Vegas, NV and impossible to track back to the U.S. Government.

Tom Howard of the Secret Service explained that they were doing a great service for their country and that citizens like themselves were used all the time for gathering information to help out Government agencies when an actual Agent was not available or up to the task at hand. Sometimes it was a scientist, sometimes it was fashion designers, and sometimes it was simply rich people that travel around the world for pleasure.

Tom also told them that these information gathering tasks usually were not dangerous; they reserved those for the James Bond types that actually were trained for field work. No, this was the easiest type of mission; simply put, the volunteers were using very sophisticated micro-sized audio/video recorders and asked to engage the target in a certain line of questioning.

For the Wards' first assignment they were simply to engage Silvano Rosito, an Italian Businessman in conversation about Italy and his work. They shouldn't be obvious; the questioning should be seen more as inquisitive instead of an interrogation. Luke and Bianca were shown pictures of Silvano and his wife Elena. Silvano had dark, olive skin with jet black hair. He appeared to be in his mid 30s. His wife was very good looking but not exceptional compared to Silvano's looks.

What Tom Howard failed to mention to the Wards was that his running into them in the White House wasn't really by chance. The Wards, as does everyone, needed to submit their personal information and be cleared by the Secret Service before being allowed to go on the West Wing tour. While checking their backgrounds the Secret Service verified which schools they attended, general information from the IRS, such as job descriptions and income, criminal background and credit checks, and pulled their passport information from The Bureau of Consular Affairs, Department of State.

The Secret Service was always looking for "normal" people to help them gather information. The theory was that the Chinese could honestly track and eavesdrop on all 600+ US employees at the U.S. Consulate in Beijing, but it was much harder to keep tabs on the over 400,000 tourist coming through on a monthly basis.

The Wards had a great combination of intelligence and travel to merit a closer look. The Secret Service agents gathered more detailed information about the Wards, actual school transcripts, government information including traffic and parking tickets, children's information, i.e. names, ages, schools etc. They even looked at their parents' information and that is when they hit gold. Bianca Ward's parents were born in Italy, there was a good chance that she had relatives in Italy and that she herself spoke Italian. By checking Bianca's college transcripts, the Agents were able to verify that Bianca took Italian in College and got A's.

Tom Howard was informed about the Wards two weeks before their scheduled visit to the White House's West Wing. He had made sure that no one else toured the West Wing for the same time slot; this would make it easier to bump into them by accident and isolate Luke Ward to ask him to help serve his country.

Chapter 3   The Party

The Wards told their children that they got a special invitation to go to a party in Washington, D.C. through one of Luke's work contacts. It was a fancy affair that didn't allow children. The kids looked at each other. James said, "Who is going to watch us?"

Bianca said, "Your father and I didn't want to use some teenager we didn't know, so we went through a babysitting agency that is the same one used by Congressmen when their families were in town. The sitters have had their backgrounds thoroughly checked and are all over the age of 24. We asked for a young woman and got Samantha to watch you, she will be here at 5 pm. She can take you to dinner and a movie tonight."

The kids sang out together, "Yeah!"

Elizabeth said, "G-Force, I want to see G-Force." James agreed.

A limo was waiting for them at the entrance of the Hotel as promised by Tom Howard. The trip was a short one. During the daytime D.C. took a long time to navigate through, there was no easy way to go from one side of town to the other, but at night it was a piece of cake.

The Wards were dressed impeccably, thank you Uncle Sam; Luke in a Christian Dior tux and Bianca in a Dolce and Gabbana three quarters length black party dress with purple high healed multi-strap shoes over black nylons. Luke's bow tie coordinated with Bianca's outfit by being black with a thin outline of the same in your face purple of her shoes. Bianca completed her look by doing her black hair up and wearing a deep red lipstick.

Luke could hardly feel the microphone disguised as a tuxedo shirt stud with another stud doubling as a camera. These as well as Bianca's audio and video recorder in her dress were being captured on a micro memory card instead of being transmitted live. It allowed for much lower power requirements and was not easily detectable, basically someone would have to see the device or it would not be detected, even with a metal detector wand which was in use at the door. The guards would expect that Luke's tux studs would beep and that Bianca's shoulder design made of metal and rhinestones would cause a "verp, verp" sound as the wand passed over it.

The Wards were turning some heads. They didn't know if it was because they looked good or because no one knew who they were. Most of these events where the President talked were expensive affairs and this was no exception, $10,000 per plate. The event was in the Hilton Grand Ballroom, but it was starting with drinks and hors d'oeuvres in the Pre-function Atrium. This room was large with areas of ceiling that would best be described as a modern glass cathedral. The carpeting had many shapes designed into it, but with hundreds of people standing on it, the Wards couldn't tell what the pattern was supposed to be, if anything at all.

Luke had a Woodford Reserve Bourbon on the rocks and Bianca had a glass of Mumm Brut Rose Champagne. After they had a lobster puff pastry and a mini shrimp cocktail they decided to start meeting other people to get an idea of who was there.

The first couple they met was from the D.C. area, a car dealer. He was grateful to still have his dealership after the government took over GM. He was more than willing to part with the $10 K a plate to have a chance to meet the President and thank him directly. Luke, thought this guy was already a little too tipsy on the free drinks, there was no way the Secret Service would let him by the President if he hadn't already parted with the 200 Benjamins to get in the place.

The next couple they met, the Andersons, was from Kansas, they owned one of the largest wind farms in the country. It supplied power to about 85,000 homes and was built by an Italian Energy Company that has customers in over 46 countries. The green revolution had hit the plains of the US and was generating real power.

As it turned out, this couple would be sitting at the same table as the Wards. The Andersons introduced the Wards to Antonio Turnelas, the North American representative for Evoluse Energy headquartered in Rome, Italy. In turn, he introduced his wife, Amy, who could have easily been mistaken for a super model. In fact, Luke, thought to himself, she could be a super model, he wouldn't know it, he didn't stay up on those things anymore, not since the times when Cindy Crawford was a household name.

There were roughly about 30 tables that sat 10 in the spacious Grand Ballroom. There were no big chandeliers, but instead the coffered ceiling was high and had indirect lighting. The President dined at the head table on the main floor the same as everyone else. A raised dais could be seen behind the President's table and would be used later for his speech.

The fund raiser would also function as a general meet and greet for the guests, they would meet the President and his wife, the State Senator and his wife, and get an official picture taken. A physical picture would be ready to take home as the guests left later. As a nice touch, the guests would also get a card identifying a website, log in and picture number to download the digital image. The background for the picture was a simple blue background with the American flag behind the Presidents left shoulder.

The whole process reminded Luke of how they did the pictures with Mickey Mouse and friends at Disney World. Luke chuckled to himself, "If I hold out my hand palm up, I wonder if they can superimpose Tinker Bell on it?"

The smooth Jazz background music was interrupted to announce that dinner would be served and that everyone should head to their table. As the Wards walked towards their table, they noticed another couple that they recognize. It was Silvano Rosito, and his wife. Of course, they have not been formally introduced; the couple looked just like the pictures that the Secret Service had shown them earlier that day.

The Italians sat together, the Wards sat across from them. Everyone went around the table and introduced themselves, as was proper. Besides the two Italian couples, the couple from Kansas and the Wards, the last couple, the Smiths, was from the Washington, D.C. area. Luke said, "Mr. Smith goes to Washington," out loud before he thought to himself that this guy must have heard it a thousand times before. Mr. Toni Smith simply smiled and acknowledged the attempt at humor with a nod of his head.

Multiple servers came over to offer white or red wine with dinner. The Italians all had red, the Wards also had red, but the other couples preferred white wine. After everyone had received their wine, Luke proposed a toast, "here, is to new friends, from close by," nodding towards the Smiths and Andersons, "and from far away," nodding towards the Italians. "May all of our paths cross again, in another place, at another time,… soon."

After taking a sip of the Red wine, Silvano said to Antonio in Italian, "Il vino non è difettoso per un vino di California." Bianca said in perfect Italian, "Penso che sia molto un vino di andata della frutta." Silvano said, "Ah, how rude of us to speak in Italian. The lady is right the wine has a bold fruit flavor." He went on to ask,

"Bianca, with a name like that, I should have guessed that you have some Italian blood in you. What part of Italy?"

"The Calabria region; my parents were from the town of Cosenza or specifically Moreno, on the mountainside away from the water."

"Do you still have family there, do you every go back?"

"Yes, I still have some aunts, uncles and cousins that live there. We are planning a family vacation there next July." She went on to ask, "What area are you from?"

"I am from the town of Sorrento, but I now live in Rome, doing business in Venice, Florence and Rome regularly."

"What is your business?"

Silvano paused for a second or two, as if to compose himself, "I am in the import business, mostly fashion items."

"How interesting, Luke has his own software business and sells items worldwide."

"Luke, what type of software do you sell?"

"We sell software that is used on Smartphones for personal security. Basically, if you think that you are in a questionable area, like at night on a college campus, or on a train platform downtown, etc, you start the JTrek application and it sends video, audio and your location instantly to a secure website. If you think you are in immediate danger you hit the "panic" button and JTrek will send a text and email to your emergency contact list saying, "I need help" and include a link to the information you uploaded on the website. For example, your family, friends, Campus security, the police etc. can view the video and determine if you really are in trouble or hit a button by accident."

Elena Rosito said, "How wonderful, I think I would like to have that on my phone."

Mrs. Anderson said, "Our daughter is at Notre Dame and I want her to use this."

Luke then took his phone out and demonstrated how easy it was to use. Everyone at the table liked it.

Luke put away the phone and said to Silvano, "What brings you to Washington, D.C.?"

"Antonio and I were at lunch last week in Rome, when he mentioned he was going to be attending this fundraiser and that the President would be here. We had been talking about how my wife and I should come visit him here in America. Elena wanted to come and shop in New York.

Elena said excitedly, "Yes, we took the train to New York yesterday and shopped for dresses on 5th Avenue, took a carriage ride around Central Park and even went to the big Apple Store."

Silvano said to Bianca, "When you come to Italy next year, please look Elena and I up, we will share a dinner together with our families."

Bianca said, "That would be fun. Do you have a business card with an email on it?"

Silvano fished out a business card that had Italian on one side and English on the other. The card listed Silvano as President of Roma Imports, S.A.

As the group was being served dessert, The President started his talk. He was very charismatic and spoke well. There was a standing ovation when The President finished, then the Secret Service whisked him away to some "undisclosed location," probably the White House.

The Italians excused themselves and the Wards left soon after. The Wards then returned to their limo and the limo driver took the eavesdropping devices and the memory cards from them. He dropped them off at their hotel. Samantha, the babysitter gave them a report.

Samantha said, "The kids loved the movie, they especially loved the spy gadgets."

Luke said, "If they only knew."

Bianca said, "We will tell them when they are older, they will get a kick out of it."

Chapter 4   First Night in Venice

Edwin Grey said, "Luke, I read the report about your intelligence gathering in D.C., you and Bianca did a great job."

Luke said, "To be honest with you, I didn't think that Silvano revealed much useful information."

Tom explained, "Luke, I need to level with you. That party was more of a test. A test to see if you and Bianca had what it took to talk to a real person of interest and not act nervous or give away your mission as you knew it. To be honest with you, we mainly observed Bianca via your video recorder and you with Bianca's."

"What!"

"I don't blame you for being a little upset with us, but how else could we test you?"

"If that was a test, what are you looking for now?"

Edwin said, "Silvano is a criminal leader here in Italy. We believe he heads up a large counterfeiting operation. The selling of purses, shoes, watches and other luxury knockoffs is huge business here in Italy, especially amongst the tourists. On top of that, Silvano brings in illegal aliens from Kenya to sell the items on the streets. They are virtually indentured servants. They can't go to the police to complain because they are illegal. They learn enough English and Italian to sell their items and don't know much else.

The CIA is interested because we were able to track some dirty money through Silvano's group that ended up going to an Al Qaeda Terrorist group in Kenya."

Tom said, "As you may remember in 1998 the US Embassy in Kenya was bombed. The terrorist planners were Osama bin Laden and other members of what became Al Qaeda. My brother, Paul, was killed in that attack. The CIA has never stopped following the leads discovered after those attacks. The enemy wasn't as sophisticated as they are now, they learned from their mistakes, as we have. OBL first got on the 10 Most Wanted List after that attack and has been on it ever since."

Luke had that "deer in the headlights" look, licked his lips a couple of times, then said, "What is it you want of us again, these guys sound dangerous?"

Edwin stated, "These guys are dangerous, but we are not asking you to do anything that is dangerous. We want you to contact Silva-

no and let him know you are in the country. See if you can get together for the dinner he talked about when you met in Washington,
D.C. At dinner you simply mention that you have been looking to
diversify your business and were thinking about starting to import
items into the US and maybe he could give you some advice.

We know he is looking for a distribution channel that is larger
in the US. The Chicago area would be perfect for him. This time
there will not be any recorders, nothing to make them suspicious.
After all, you would have your family with you, he wouldn't suspect
that."

Luke said, "That's all, just have dinner with him, tell him I
would like to expand my business ventures, finish our vacation here
and wait for his call in the US? Anything else like ask him who really killed Kennedy or if Aliens really visit the Earth and abduct hu-
mans for tests and let them go?" Luke often used humor when he
was nervous or thought that a situation was almost unbelievable,
such as this one was.

Tom said, "Luke, this isn't funny, we really need your help,...
your country needs your help. Silvano would sniff out one of our
people in a heartbeat. You and your family would never be suspected. We will be monitoring you from a distance, any sign of
trouble and we would jump right in there and get your family out of
there."

"I don't know ... this seems a little dangerous to be getting involved with. What if I say no?"

"Luke, we already sent an email to Silvano from Bianca's email
letting him know your schedule in Italy to see if you can get together
for dinner. He already wrote back and said that tomorrow night
would be great, he is in Venice on business, and he still would like to
meet your whole family."

Luke was shocked, "Bianca didn't tell me she got a response."

Edwin said, "We did everything on our end, she never saw it.
Are you in?"

Luke was really conflicted, he liked the excitement the last time
he did an assignment for the Secret Service, but he didn't want to
endanger his family, but Silvano was expecting them, it might look
weird if they didn't show. "We will do it, just have dinner with him
and offer up the business questions."

Edwin said, "Luke, your country thanks you, Tom thanks you
and I thank you. Now you better get going, Bianca is probably start-

ing to worry about what is taking you so long. To help, we have a private boat for you and your family; the captain will take you to your hotel. We will contact you tomorrow with the information about where to meet Silvano for dinner. Dinner will be at 8:30pm, so please be ready to leave your hotel by around 8. Also, please fill Bianca in and wish her a happy Birthday for us."

Luke looking inquisitively, "How did you know?... Never mind, I know how you know her birthday; I forgot who I was talking to."

Luke went out to meet his family. Bianca looks concerned and angry. After all, she has been waiting with a porter that wasn't too happy to be sitting idle, in addition to the two kids that just finished flying for over 10 hours.

James was starting to feel a little better, but Luke was still worried about how he would fair on a small boat. The private boat ride turned out not to bother James' stomach. The kids loved to be out on the water, especially after being cooped up on the plane for half of a day. The Captain moored his boat in front of their hotel, the Monaco & Grand Canal Hotel, right next to Piazza San Marco.

After checking in, the Wards went to their two rooms that have balconies overlooking the Grand Canal. Even though it was rated as a four star hotel, by US standards it was closer to a 3 ½ star, but with these views it brought the rating up considerably. The whole family was anxious to get out and roam around Venice.

James reminds everyone, "It is Mom's Birthday today and we are going to go on a gondola ride, after we have dinner, to celebrate."

Luke said, "Let's go eat, does anyone feel like Italian today? It is your Mother's Birthday, so she can pick."

Bianca always prepared, answered, "I really want to go to St. Marks Square and eat at one of the overpriced restaurants and listen to a band play."

Sure enough, as the sun was setting, there were four dueling band/orchestras turning out music all in close proximity to one another. Bianca choose one of the closest restaurants to St. Mark's Basilica, mainly because she loved the very brightly colored yellow chairs, they nearly glowed. St. Mark's Square was pulsating with people. Luke was surprised there were hardly any pigeons, the last time he was here, 15 years ago, there were thousands of pigeons. He asked the waiter about the pigeons.

The waiter said, "The Police don't allow people to sell pigeon food anymore, the city realized that the pigeon droppings added a great cost to keep the buildings clean, let alone it was not very healthy for the dinners at all of the nearby restaurants."

In fact, St. Mark's square didn't look like itself at the time. Due to the global recession, the city of Venice used sponsors to refurbish the facades of the buildings on the Square. The sponsors then got to advertize on the largest billboards Luke had ever seen, basically scaffolding was built 3-4 stories tall and the width of the whole Square on two sides with ad images of people listening to music with headsets and talking on cellphones etc. In other words, it was a very modern look in a very old city. Luke was not happy that his kids would not be able to picture the Square as it really should look.

The bell tower was also being refurbished and part of the Square around the tower was also behind a one story shroud to hide the heavy equipment and scissors lifts used for that project.

After a great meal, the family was ready to walk around and go for a gondola ride. There are multiple gondola stations along the entrance to St. Mark's Square, but Luke decided that they should walk to a less crowded area; he wanted to work off some of the heavy pasta he just ate. They took a right turn out of the Square, towards their hotel. Where one could walk no further without running into the Grand Canal stood both a water taxi and gondola station.

Luke wanted the kids to learn how to negotiate in the real world and explained, "James and Elizabeth I want you both to go ahead and ask one of the gondoliers what the price was for a ride for 4 and then tell him it was their Mom's Birthday and see if he could do better on the price."

James said, "Do we have to?"

Elizabeth being a little more courageous said, "Come on James, it will be fun."

The kids ran up to the gondolier asked their question, heard the answer and tried to negotiate. Then they ran back to their parents.

James said, "He said it is €110 and they don't negotiate."

Luke looked around and the area was almost deserted, few people rode gondolas at night, the canals and buildings were not well light. Luke noticed that the Gondolier was starting to pack up his boat. He said to the kids, "Go back and say to him that he is about to close, doesn't €75 sound better than nothing."

With that, the kids ran up to the Gondolier and tried again, this time they came running back with smiles on their faces. Elizabeth said, "He will do it for €100 but not any less"

Luke smiled, the kids were learning a valuable lesson. He asked, "Do you think he will come down in price more?"

James said, "I don't think so he said that is as low as he can go."

Luke pointed out, "He originally said he couldn't go below €110, but you got him down." Luke took €90 out of his pocket and handed it to James. Luke said, "Go and say this is all we have and we want to take our Mom on a gondola ride for her Birthday."

The kids ran off again with their new offer, the gondolier laughed out loud and nodded his head yes. The Wards loved their night time gondola ride, the gondolier gave them a great history lesson about Venice, the views were unbelievable and the family was together for Bianca's Birthday.

She asked the gondolier, how he knew English so well. He said that he had spent 7 years in Texas working in construction and met his soon to be wife there. After a few years of marriage they decided to come back to where he was born, Venice. He was already part of the gondoliers union. It turns out that pretty much from the age of 6, the fathers take their sons out and teach them how to handle a boat. Most boys learn fast how to handle a boat and some progress to being a gondolier. In a city that has streets of water, being able to handle a boat is a necessary skill.

At the end, Luke tipped him €30 and said, "Thanks for the great tour and thanks for helping me teach my kids how to negotiate."

The gondolier said, "They drove a tough bargain. Have a great vacation and enjoy our beautiful cites in Italy."

Chapter 5   Dinner with the Man

The next morning was nice, but hard to wake up to, the Wards' internal clocks were all messed up. James was feeling a thousand times better than he did on the trip over. The sun was shining and the view was still amazing. The group headed down for their breakfast.

One item that both kids loved and Luke and Bianca also, for that matter, was the Blood Red orange juice that was popular in this part of Italy. It kind of looked like cran/orange juice, but tasted like very sweet orange juice. The kids found it strange how there was a lot of anti pasta at breakfast, multiple types of sausages and cheeses, olives etc. There were also traditional American breakfast items; cereals with milk, oatmeal, muffins, bagels with cream cheese and breads. Everyone found something they could enjoy.

After breakfast the family headed back to their room to freshen up and get their cameras, water bottles and put on sunscreen. As they walked through the lobby of the hotel, the person at the front desk said, "Mr. Ward, I have an envelope here for you."

Luke took the envelope and opened it. He simply saw a name of a restaurant and the time 8:30 pm. Luke asked the front desk man, "Do you know where this is located?"

The man took a paper map off of the counter and showed Luke where they were now and then where the restaurant was, "It was about a 10 minute walk," the front desk man said.

Elizabeth asked, "Dad what is that about?"

Luke said, "We are having dinner with a person that your Mother and I met last year in Washington, D.C. You and James are invited as well, you must both promise to be on your best behavior."

The Wards made it back to their rooms, gathered their things and started out into Venice, Italy, one of the most unique cities in the World.

First on the tour schedule was the Doge's Palace. The family learned that the Republic of Venice was its own country and the center of the maritime trade world for quite a while back in its day. The Black Death killed about half of the population two different times and it never really recovered, later becoming part of the Italy. Another gondola ride during the day, a walk to, and over the Rialto

Bridge, the largest bridge over the Grand Canal, and many gelatos, Italian ice cream –only better, later and the Ward family was pooped.

Back at the hotel they all showered and changed for dinner. The July weather in Venice was hot during the day, but very comfortable at night. The girls wore light, flower pattern dresses, the boys wore light kakis with short sleeve shirts; Luke's was a nice dark blue silk Tommy Bahamas with a textured pattern of palm leaves in the same color thread.

The Wards decided to walk to the restaurant. It took them about 15 minutes of walking when they got to the Ponte Academia, one of the three bridges that crossed the Grand Canal. They had allowed for a 20 minute walk so they had time for a few pictures of the family on the bridge. The pictures looked good, they were all recently sho-wered and had on fresh dressy, casual clothes; with the barber pole stripping on the gondola moorings in the background anyone would recognize that the Wards were in Venice. A few more minutes of walking and they spotted the restaurant for their meeting with Silva-no.

Silvano was waiting in the bar area. He seemed to be talking to two men at the bar, but didn't introduce them to the family, so Luke figured he was just killing time waiting for the Wards. Bianca no-ticed that Silvano was alone, not with his family. After seeing the Wards enter, Silvano stood and walked toward them.

He said, "I am sorry that my family couldn't be here. We live in Roma, but I was not going to be in Roma when you were sche-duled to be there, so I thought I would meet you here in Venice by myself. Next time, if you give me more notice, I will arrange for our families to get together."

He then told the hostess that his party was all here and that they would like to be seated.

The table was ready; they were seated in the outdoor section, which was just about the perfect temperature right now, 75 degrees with a slight breeze. The area was covered by shadows as the sun would set in about 30 minutes and the surrounding buildings blocked out the Sun that was now low in the sky.

A young man approached the outdoor area; he was carrying a musical instrument case. He opened the case and produced a flute. As the young musician assembled his flute, the restaurant manager said something to him in Italian. The boy put his case down and left it open, then walked away from the restaurant, crossed a bridge over the small canal and stood across the water from the restaurant.

He began to play. Beautiful music filled the air, it was not overwhelming or loud, but instead just the right volume for background or dinner music.

Silvano order a bottle of red wine, a Chianti Classico for the adults and Bianca ordered limonatas, a sparkling lemon soda that is not overly sweet, for the children. Silvano also ordered an anti-pasta platter with various air cured meats, cheeses and an assortment of olives. Luke and Bianca could live off of this stuff, it was so good.

About 15 minutes later the waitress came to take everyone's order, there never seemed to be a hurry in Italy, dinner was a time to relax and enjoy the company of who you were with as well as the ambiance of the restaurant and its location.

With the formality of ordering out of the way it was time for more small talk. Up to now the small talk was more about the restaurant and their specialties, both the waitress and Silvano took turns explaining how the chef prepared unique dishes.

Silvano asked, "How is your trip so far?" He directed his question at Bianca.

Bianca said, "It started out a little poorly with James getting sick on the airplane, but was great once they actually got to Venice and got to their room." She went on to describe their hotel and about where they had already visited so far.

Silvano said, "You should go to the island of Murano and get a custom made glass piece. In fact, I know a water taxi guy that owes me a favor and will give you all a free ride there and back. Do you have time to go tomorrow?"

Luke deferred to Bianca; she had planned the trip with the travel agent and knew the schedule the best.

"We did have it scheduled around 10:30am and have a boat voucher as part of a tour we are taking tomorrow."

"Those are quick trips to the island that try to hurry you to buy something fast, and then send you back. You use my guy Samuel, he will take you when you are finished with your tour. I will set up a special glass factory tour, you stay on Murano for a lunch, you come back when you want."

Silvano then took one of his own business cards out and wrote Capitan Samuel and a phone number on the back. He handed the card to Luke.

"You call him when your tour is over around 10:30am, and he will be waiting to the left of St. Mark's square down about 3 blocks past the Bridge of Sighs."

Silvano then turned to Elizabeth and said, "Such a beautiful girl, you must like to sing or dance or play an instrument, tell me what you like to do."

Elizabeth was not shy and she kind of liked how Silvano was getting us a boat so she answered, "I like to dance, play soccer, what you call football, I don't really sing, but I do play a little piano and just started playing the viola."

Silvano smiled then turned to James, "And you, what do you like to do?"

James was a little shyer but answered, "I like to play baseball, golf, soccer, video games and chess."

Silvano said, "Ah, an athlete and a thinker that is a great combination."

The food came and there was a hushed silence as everyone dug into a great Italian meal. Luke asked, "Silvano, I have been thinking about diversifying my business, when you just handed me your card it reminded me that you have an import business, I was thinking that I could import Italian wears to the U.S. and maybe you wouldn't mind giving me a few tips?"

If Luke and Bianca had really known Silvano a little longer, they may have been able to pick up on his quick look of surprise, followed by an insincere smile.

"Of course I can help you, but you are on vacation, let us talk again when you are finished. I will be happy to share all that I can to assist you in your new endeavor."

As the plates were cleared, the server brought out a platter with pieces of tiramisu and cannoli. The men ordered espressos; Bianca didn't care for coffees so she simply drank sparkling water. Coincidently, as the meal ended, so did the flute player's playing. He walked back over the bridge.

James asked, "Can I have some money to tip the music guy?"

Elizabeth chimed in, "Me too, I want to give him some money."

Luke reached in his pocket and gave them each a 5 Euro note to put in the flute case. The musician saw the children put the money into the case and said "Gratzi."

Elizabeth said, "Prego."

All of the goodbyes were said, and all of the cheek air kissing given, the meal was now finished.

Silvano excused himself and left the table, walking over the same bridge that the young musician had crossed almost an hour earlier.

It was now dark and getting late for the kids. The Wards were going on a walking tour in the morning and to Murano in the afternoon. They were bushed and all decided to simply go back to the hotel and sleep.

As Silvano walked, he slowly shook his head. About two blocks from the restaurant, Silvano was joined by the same two men that were in the bar area from earlier.

The first man said, "Well, were they trying to get evidence like our contact said? Were they working for the US government?"

Silvano answered in a low guttural voice, "I am afraid so. They seem like such a nice family, but they must be stopped. Our contact said that the CIA can turn a simple meeting with the Wards into a case for an international crime. He also told me that they are working for the US government and that we need him, the inside guy, more now than ever if we want to continue the shipments into the US."

The second man said, "What about our friends from the Middle East, they could take care of them?"

Silvano said, "The Wards are in Italy, they are our responsibility. We will question them first, and then hand them over to our Middle Eastern contacts."

Chapter 6   Murano Glass

The next morning Elizabeth was the first up, she then woke the rest of the clan to start their adventure. After a continental breakfast, they all were excited about the days tours and rushed off to meet the tour group at their offices by the Corner Museum on St. Mark's Square. They toured St. Mark's Basilica, the Academy, the Rialto Bridge and many sights in between. At the end of the tour the Wards were glad that they would soon be on a private boat and could sit down for 20 minutes or so.

Luke called Samuel, they found him and his boat docked where promised. 20 minutes later they arrived at Murano. Not surprisingly, they arrived directly at the dock of a glass company. The Ward's personal guide introduced herself as Mary. She was wearing a colorful, pretty flower print dress with a white belt. She reminded Luke of a young Sophia Loren.

The items lining the walls of the entrance hall inside were unbelievable. The craftsmanship was apparent. There were various blown glass items of great detail, such as animals, flower arrangements and etc. There were also glass bowls, platters, cups and decanters of various bright colors.

James was attracted to a whole custom glass chess set. The pieces were amazing; the knights in particular had fantastic looking horses they were riding. The King and queen pieces had to be 6 inches high. The board was also interesting. It looked like marble at first glance, but it was all colored glass that was cut and set in a frame. The lighting in the case practically made the whole set glow.

James said, "I don't think that the chess club guys at home had ever seen such a board."

Mary said, "I doubt they have, this chess set is priced at $25,000 US and this is only one of two made."

"Who owns the other one?"

"It is at the Louvre Museum in Paris, France. It is on loan for an exhibit on Venetian glass, antique and contemporary."

Elizabeth said, "I would like to go to Paris, maybe for our next vacation."

The tour of the glass factory was a private one. The small group wound their way to the back of the building where the sales shop was housed. They then entered into a simple concrete structure and walked down a dark hallway. The temperature climbing with every step forward they took. The severe heat of the furnaces was obvious simply by entering the room, it had to be about 100 degrees in there.

A man came out; our factory guide introduced him as Manny. "Manny has been with us for over 30 years, he is one of our master glass blowers in our factory and in fact, is one of the top glass blowers in the world. Most of the items you saw in our display cases in the hallway were created by Manny."

James asked, "Including the chess set?"

"Yes, Manny made the chess set."

Mary also translated to Manny what James had asked. Manny smiled and walked over to the furnace to check on some glass they had been heating in there. Another man came out to assist Manny.

The group sat down in the first row of the stadium seating. The area normally held about 50 people, so this really was a private tour.

Manny was not a tall man but was very muscular; especially when one considered that he looked to be about 50 years old. Manny went over to one of the ovens and pulled out what looked like a long metal rod with a glowing red/orange hot blob on the end, which obviously was molten glass. He spun it continuously and kept peering into the glass as if he was communicating with it, what did it want to become?

Suddenly, he took a breath and then blew into the long metal tube. A glass ball appeared at the end of the tube. Manny rolled the tube back and forth while at the same time he held a tool that looked like a giant set of tweezers and started squeezing the ball into a different shape. He used various tools and blew multiple times until at the end he had made a beautiful vase. He broke the bottom off of the vase and the blowing tube and set it down on a tray that went into what looked like a pizza oven.

Mary explained that you didn't want the pieces to cool too rapidly; they would form cracks, so the oven would gradually cool the piece over the next few hours.

Manny started on another smaller piece of glass. He used some different tools and started squeezing the glass into a shape. At the end it was a horse about the same sized as the knight on the chess board, he spoke to Mary in Italian. Bianca smiled.

Mary said to James, "He has made a special piece for you because you liked his chess set so much. No cost, it is his special gift to you. We will send it to your hotel tomorrow."

James beamed, "Thanks, it is beautiful."

James whispered something into Bianca's ear, then she into James' ear. James then told Manny, "Manny, il cavallo è bello." James continued, "I told him the horse is beautiful."

Elizabeth, being a twin, wanted something as well. Manny saw that and told Mary something.

"Elizabeth, Manny will now make you something special. He wants to know what your favorite animal is."

Elizabeth thought very hard on this, because she was truly an animal lover. She liked all animals, even imaginary ones like unicorns and friendly dragons, but she decided that she missed her dog Bingo and would love a dog. Elizabeth said, "I like dogs the best, I miss our dog Bingo and would like a glass dog."

Manny must understand some English, because he nodded his head and started to work on a piece of glass. The glass was a pretty golden color, not unlike Bingo. He blew and shaped, and squeezed until about 2 minutes later there was a dog that was laying down with its head looking up at you.

Elizabeth didn't need a translator, she exclaimed, "Grazie! Manny"

"Prego."

Bianca asked if Manny would be in a picture with them, he agreed. Luke thanked him on the side and also slipped him a 50 Euro note while they shook hands. The group said thank you and good bye to Manny and headed back outside. Even though it was about 85 outside, it felt cool compared to the glass blowing room. They headed back inside to see the other glass objects for sale in the store. It was air conditioned inside and felt even better.

Bianca asked Mary, "Can we purchase the vase he made to start with?"

"I believe so, I will check on the price and get back to you." Mary left the shop while the Wards looked around.

Elizabeth noticed other glass animals on a shelf. She looked but there were no dogs similar to what Manny just made and said so to James. A sales lady overhead Elizabeth and commented.

"Manny usually doesn't make animals anymore; it was something that the apprentice glass blowers start with. Any animal Manny made would sell for about 100 Euros compared to the 20 Euros listed on the nearby shelf."

Hearing this made James and Elizabeth excited that they have a special glass piece made by a real artist.

Luke was worried because he knew that the vase was not going to be inexpensive. As he was thinking this, Mary entered the shop with a smile on her face.

"I talked to the owner and they said that the piece would normally sell for about 800 Euros, but that because you are friends with Silvano you could have it for 200 Euros. They will also include a letter of authenticity with Manny's signature and a picture of Manny holding the completed piece, which usually adds another 20 Euros, so this is quite a deal."

Bianca said, "Thank you for the great pieces, we are very excited to display them at home and show our friends. Also, thank you for the great tour. We will have to thank Silvano again for his helping with getting us the tour."

"No problems, we were happy to meet your family. Are there any other pieces you would like to look at?"

Bianca and Luke felt a little guilty about getting the kids pieces for free and their vase for such a good deal that they purchased many gifts for their relatives that day.

Luke asked, "Can we have this all shipped to our house in the States, so we don't have to worry about it getting broken on the rest of our vacation?"

"Of course, we will ship all of your items to your house, when do you want it to arrive?"

"Three weeks from now would work well; we will be in Italy for the next 2 weeks or so."

"Great, we will ship it to arrive then. Your boat is here if you want to follow me I will show you back out to the dock."

Elizabeth said, "I need to use the restroom first." The rest of the family agreed it was a good idea and they all went. Inside the restroom the lighting fixture was all hand blown glass and was very colorful. The whole factory had wonderful glass objects.

The boat was waiting as Mary had promised. The Ward family said their goodbyes and was on their way back to Venice. About half way back to Venice, Samuel got a call. He didn't say much; just saying he understood a couple of times.

The Wards didn't notice that Samuel was taking a different route back to Venice until they turned into a canal that wasn't by St. Marks, after all their hotel was right off of the Grand Canal by St.

Marks and was very recognizable. Luke noticed and was just about to question it when James said out loud, "We are going the wrong way, what is up?"

Samuel said with a smile, "There are some cruise ships in the Lagoon that would slow us down, so this route will take about the same amount of time and let you see more of Venice."

Bianca looked at Luke with some worry, but the kids were enjoying the ride, so Luke didn't really object too much. Luke also would have thought that this was just a case of a taxi, albeit a water taxi, trying to increase his fare, but they had already negotiated a fixed price, free, so he doubted that.

After a few more turns in smaller canals Luke started to fear the worse. The area they were in was not touristy at all, in fact there were very few people around and the buildings looked to be more like storage warehouses instead of housing or hotels etc. Just as Luke was about to object to this route, Samuel turned around with a gun in his hand. This took a few seconds for Luke to register, but Bianca got it in a hurry and let out a little scream.

Samuel said, "One more scream and the little girl will be hurt," as he pointed the gun toward Elizabeth.

Chapter 7   We are Spies?

Samuel was not really looking where he was going but was very familiar with this canal and his boat. He maneuvered the boat to the side of the canal just as a few men came out to tie the boat down. One boarded the boat, he also had a gun. This man was huge, 6', 7" and had to weigh about 300 lbs, most of that muscle.

Big man said, "Everyone off the boat and follow Morey into the building. Do this without talking or someone will get hurt." After the Wards exited the boat, Morey with his gun drawn, pointed towards the building. Big man pushed a wad of Euros into Samuel's hands and said, "You dropped them off at St. Marks and that is the last you saw them. The boss said now you are even for all of your debts."

The Wards were herded into a building that looked and smelled as old as any they had seen in Italy, which means it dated back at least 400-500 years. Inside the building, they saw lots of construction materials; this building was being renovated, not unlike hundreds of buildings in Venice. There were a series of temporary lights strung in the building's interior. The lights were in yellow plastic cages with thick yellow extension cords running between them.

Most of the walls had been gutted in the entry area they first came in. Sheets of plastic separated the rooms from one another. In the hallway, they were walked through, only a dull glow emanating from the construction lights and windows on the outside walls.

They all marched along quietly through the middle of the building where they descended down a set of stairs that wiggled and vibrated slightly under the strain of the group's weight. Once on the lower level, there were very few lights to be seen. The stone floor looked to be a little shinny and it was due to being damp or just downright wet. The lower level on many of the old buildings becomes unusable as it sinks, unless the whole building is lifted up and a new floor built, this level would be claimed by the canal within years.

The group was taken toward one of the lights in a plastic defined room where there were 5 chairs. The Wards were each tied to a chair. The Big man said, "Don't scream or we will have to use gags, which will be very unpleasant. We will be back soon to give you some water." Before leaving the Big man took Bianca's purse, and Luke's phone and wallet.

Elizabeth asked, "Who are you, why are we here?"

The Big man said, "Mr. Rosito will be here shortly, he will talk to you all."

The two men with guns left. James said, "What is going on, why would Mr. Rosito put us in such a crummy place?"

Luke answered, "James, Elizabeth we need to tell you something. Your Mom and I were asked by our government to get some information about Mr. Rosito. He is not a very good man. He works with people that give money to terrorist groups. Like the ones that did nine-eleven. All we were supposed to do was meet him and ask him some questions; it was not supposed to be dangerous. We would never have done anything to put you both in danger."

James looked at Elizabeth then back toward his parents and said. "We are spies, and this is a Spy Family vacation. Did you get any cool spy stuff like from "Q" in James Bond?"

Luke said, "This is very serious, those men have real guns with real bullets, this is not like the movies. If they are trying to scare us, it's working."

Bianca said, "I can almost get loose of these ropes, how about anyone else?"

Elizabeth said, "Mine are so tight they are almost cutting my hands off."

Luke said, "My hands are turning blue, the ropes are so tight I can't get away."

James said, "I think my left hand is loose enough to squeeze out." James worked his hands back and forth, twisting and pulling at the same time. After a minute he said, "It is hopeless, I am stuck also."

Elizabeth started crying.

Luke said, "We are not giving up, we just need to keep our heads and we will get through this."

As Luke was finishing, they heard footsteps coming down the stairs, then steps across the wet floor to the area where they were sitting. It was Silvano and the two guys with guns, which were now tucked in the waist of their pants, in plain sight.

Silvano said, "I am not happy that this is happening. You seem like nice people, a nice family. But, you come to harm me, must I not defend myself? You come to stop me, must I not stop you?"

Luke said, "There must be a misunderstanding, please let my wife and kids go, they are innocent."

Silvano said, "I wish this was simply a misunderstanding, but I need to figure out what to do with you and your family. You see it is not up to me, the group that I help doesn't like loose ends."

James said, "You mean the terrorists? You are a bad person."

Luke said, "Quiet, don't say anything."

Silvano said as he shook his head side to side, "So the kids do know what is going on, I am sorry to hear that." He went on to say, "My business associates will come and get you, I don't want to guess what they will do to find out all that you know, but it will not be pleasant. Do you want to tell me now what you know or do you want to tell them later?"

Luke said while fighting back tears, "We were told to meet with you and have you contact me back in the U.S. Also, I was told that your group helped launder money for the terrorist group responsible for the bombing of the US Embassy in Kenya in 1998. They said this was not a dangerous task, in fact, we thought we were done after yesterday. Now please let my family go!"

Silvano said, "I can tell you are no professional, and I tend to believe you, it is my associates that you will need to worry about now."

Luke asked, "Why did you bring us here, why did you suspect that we were helping the government?"

Silvano took a second as if to think, then said, "I have to admit, at first, I didn't think much of our first encounter in Washington, D.C. I forgot about you for almost a year and then Bianca's email came mentioning you would be in Italy soon. I thought to myself, I will have dinner with you and hopefully it would simply be a nice night, but you, Luke, had to go and ask me, out of the blue, about me helping you with an import business and then I got very suspicious.

I called someone I knew at Italian Customs and he said that they had a special flag on your passport entry placed by the US government. He asked around today and one of the other agents remembered a US man being taken into one of the holding rooms and other Americans meeting with him. I got this information confirmed about an hour ago, when you were riding back from Murano with Samuel. That is when I called him and asked you be brought here."

What Silvano didn't share with Luke was how his U.S. Government insider told him that Luke Ward had come to kill Silvano and that the family was just his cover, that Luke was really an assassin.

Luke just held his head down.

Bianca started crying, "Please, let my children go."

Elizabeth and James started crying when they saw their mother crying.

Silvano took a long look at the family, stood up and shook his head and started walking away with the gun men without saying another word.

James said, "Can we at least have some water, I am very thirsty?"

Silvano nodded to the Big man who brought a water bottle over to James.

"My hands really are tied too tight can he loosen them a little and let me drink some of the water?"

Silvano, nodded again and walked away. The Big man untied one of James' hands and James drank. Then the man tied his hands again, but James had remembered a trick about being tied up that he learned on the History Channel from a story about Houdini. One had to expand whatever part of their body that was being tied up so that later in a relaxed state, one could escape. So James put his hand into a fist and squeezed as tight as he could the whole time he was being tied up. The gun men gave the others a drink and then left.

James now relaxed his hand and started wiggling, pulling and twisting his hand to try and remove it from the rope that was still tied tightly around his wrist. After about 30 seconds James was feeling pretty confident that he would be able to free himself, his hand was past the point where it was stuck last time. A few more pulls and one arm was free. He bent down and freed his legs that were also tied to the chair. Once his legs were free, he was able to get out of his seat and untie his other arm from the back of the chair.

James jumped over to his father's chair and started to untie his hands. Just as he started, they all heard footsteps coming down the steps.

Luke told James in a whisper, "Go and get help, now, leave us."

"No, I want to help you first."

"You are our only hope, please go now and get help."

James ran off in the opposite direction of the stairs as quickly and quietly as he could. It was a virtual maze and very dark in the basement of this building. James thought he could hear a boat motor and hurried in that direction. He came to a set of doors that were located by a set of partially submerged steps. The doors were very rotten with the bottom of the doors actually in the water. Between the doors was a gap of an inch or two where James could see the canal on the other side. He almost started to yell out of the door for help, but thought better, he didn't see any people around when they arrived and his yelling would surely bring the two gun men in his direction. He was sure they were already looking for him.

James thought that he saw a little light peeking under the doors through the murky water. He slowly climbed down the stairs, not wanting to make too much sound. He reached the doors and realized that when he pushed out on the doors that they had some give, a chain that was a little slack was holding the two doors closed and locked. The doors moved about 10 inches then stopped.

James wasn't sure if he could fit his head and body through it; he was very close to getting through but it was just not working. He then realized that the bottoms of the doors were also swinging out and that towards the center where they would meet was rotted away from being underwater for years. A plan formed in his head, he had to push out on the doors and squeeze out under the water.

One floor up Silvano's phone rang; it was his insider from the US Government. The Insider wanted to know if he had the Wards and whether they were still visiting Italy or a permanent part of Italy. Silvano understood the not too deeply coded language meaning were they still alive or dead at this point. Silvano said that they spilled their guts and told him they were working for the US Government, but that they thought that they only had to meet with Silvano to set up a future meeting, they didn't say anything about being ordered to kill Silvano as the Insider had suggested.

Silvano told the Insider that he planned on letting his Middle Eastern friends question them to find out the full story. The Insider immediately said; no don't do that, if they get caught with the Wards the whole organization could be torn down. It was best if Silvano's people took care of the family and made it look like a boating accident or a robbery gone bad, something that the police wouldn't have to investigate too closely. The police were on the payroll, but the US Government would put pressure on them if the crime looked too questionable.

Silvano said, "I really don't want to kill children, can't we just beat up the father and tell them that if they go to the police or the government that we will kill them?"

The Insider said, "Think about it, they can put you away for kidnapping right now, with your history, the Italian government would throw the book at you for that alone, you need to finish the job, the sooner the better." The Insider hung up.

Silvano knew what he needed to do. He called his men over and told them to take the family, in a boat, out beyond the Lagoon, weight their bodies down with cinderblocks and dump them where the water is deep.

One floor down, as James was looking over the doors, the two gun men arrived at the set of chairs where the Ward family was tied up. The Big man noticed the boy was missing immediately. He asked Luke, where he was, and how long he had been gone. Luke chose to not answer, he thought, why give them any information that could help them capture James.

The Big man didn't like the silence and back handed Luke pretty hard across the face. A trickle of blood was seen on the corner of his mouth where his lip got caught on his teeth from the slap. Luke just spit the blood out and remained silent.

The big man said to the other gun man, "We need to find the boy and fast. Mr. Rosito will not be happy with us. You go that way and I will go this way." He said as he reached for his gun and pointed toward the stairs and away from them.

The Big man thought he heard something up ahead, he hurried his pace, and he remembered that up ahead there was an old set of doors to the canal, but they were always kept locked to keep out simple thieves from steeling the construction supplies.

James held his breadth and slid under the water, pushing the doors out as he got his head and shoulders under the door. He then lost some of his grip on the doors as his arms came through. The doors came back in toward the center and closed around his middle and waist, he was stuck. He was going to die right here, his hopes to save his family would also.

All these bad thoughts flashed before him quickly, but then he thought to himself, I am not going to die; I can do this and save my family. He calmly, pulled on the doors and somehow got his foot on a step to help him push through. His left leg ended up scraping along the door, but it was a simple cut not a gash.

Once James struggled free of the door he burst up above the water and took a big breadth of air. Thank God, he got out; he made a promise to God to go to Church more. He looked around and like earlier, there was no one to be seen. The canal water was about 4-5 feet below the wall across from the building he just escaped from. James was going to have to swim until he could find an exit route.

He swam down the canal as fast as he could, after about 100 yards, he saw a set of steps next to a bridge over the canal, these steps were used by boats that docked there to pick up supplies etc. James climbed out of the water on to the steps and then he was finally on solid ground again. He ran down the road, which was really not much more than a 4 foot wide alley until he found someone.

"I need the police, my family is tied up and they are going to kill them!"

"No capisce Inglesi, Poliziotto?"

James said, "Si," but kept running to find someone that spoke English. The man followed James.

James came upon a small shop and pleaded again, "I need the police, some guys with guns have my family tied up!"

The shop lady screamed, "Oh, let's calls the police right away, where are they?"

James described the building on the next canal over down to the left. The shop lady dialed the phone and got them on the line, she explained what was going on and which building it was. Within a minute James heard sirens coming toward them. James ran towards the sirens, towards the canal with the building that had his family in it.

Just as James got to the bridge over the canal he saw two police boats coming up to the building from the far side. He started shouting. "It is that building! The one with the black doors!"

The police must have heard him because they pulled up to the right building. One police boat stopped by the dock area that the family had used when they arrived and one stopped by the door with the chain and lock on it. A police man used bolt cutters to cut the chain and pulled the doors open. He then jumped out of the boat with three others; they ran into the basement of the building with guns drawn.

The Big man heard more sounds up ahead, he was sure it was the sound of water and of a chain rattling on the doors that lead to the canal. He ran faster, almost knocking himself out as he ran into a support beam that was hard to see in the darkness of the basement. Just as he got to the partially submerged steps he saw the door heave outwards and some splashing at the bottom of the steps under the door.

He jumped into the water but just missed grabbing the boy by the ankle. The Big man decided that he better get out of there because there may be people outside for the boy to talk to. He climbed out of the water, up the steps and quickly made his way back towards the tied up Wards.

The Big man called out to the other man who showed up 30 seconds later. They discussed in Italian about how the boy got away. Bianca held her smile, she didn't think these two realized that she understood Italian and wanted to hear more about James. The gun men talked about how the boy would surely get help and that they needed to decide what to do with the family.

The second gun man said we should kill them, no witnesses. The Big man said in Italian, "No, they didn't have time to wipe everything down and he wasn't going to get caught for murder of a woman and child. No he thought that they should just leave them and get away as soon as possible." Bianca couldn't hide her excitement from that decision she winked at Luke. Just at that moment they all heard the police sirens.

The two gun men ran toward the stairs. A minute later the Wards heard a loud noise in the same direction that James had run off in earlier. The sound they heard was the police entering at the basement level off of the canal. The Wards saw a few flashlights running towards them, it was the police, and they were saved.

The Police asked while looking at Luke's bloody mouth, "Are you all healthy and where are the guys that tied you up?"

Luke explained, "There are two men with guns that just ran up the stairs." One of the police men stopped to untie the family while the other three forged ahead to the stairs. The police man with the Wards pulled out a knife and started cutting away the bonds. When he finished, his radio went off. He said that the building was cleared and that the Wards could go upstairs. The police man led them up the stairs and out to the front of the building.

Luke and Bianca were frantically looking for James, and then they saw him talking to a police man about 20 feet away. James saw them at the same time and they all ran towards each other and ended up in a huge, wet hug. Bianca said, "James, thank God you are alright. We figured you were safe once we saw the police."

Elizabeth said, "Thanks for saving us, but you really need a shower, because you smell like Bingo after he goes out in the rain." And they all laughed.

About 10 minutes later Edwin Grey showed up. He said, "Luke, Bianca, James and Elizabeth I am so glad that you are all safe. We had no idea that Silvano would do such a crazy thing as kidnapping you."

Luke was about to punch Edwin, but realized that he was ex-military and that it would end up being more symbolic than smart and decided against it.

"How could you put our family in such danger?"

"Really, we didn't think he would stoop to this level. There must be something big going on. We need to see if you heard anything that could help us."

James said, "Mr. Rosito said that his business associates, the terrorists were coming to pick us up to see what we knew."

Edwin kind of looked off into the distance and said, "I see, there must be a large deal happening if they are here in person. The local police rounded up Silvano and a few of his thugs. Within the hour they should all be in jail, I think it will be hard for them to get out of the kidnapping charges so easily."

James asked, "If we are helping you can we get some cool spy gadgets?"

Luke said, "I think we may want to cut our vacation short and go home, this has been pretty stressful."

Edwin stated, "All the more reason to continue your vacation. I will make sure we have one of our people with you at all times. We want you to be able to enjoy what is left of your vacation, we owe you that much."

James said, "I still think that we should get something cool."

Edwin said, "We will have to play that one by ear." He said to Luke and Bianca, "Our man will pick you up at your hotel tomorrow morning and come with you on your train ride to Florence."

The Wards' needed to provide statements to the police that Silvano and his guys held them against their will. The Venice police department was in a very old building, but the inside had been recently remodeled. Luke had described Captain Samuel, his boat and how he had really kidnapped them and turned them over to Silvano's crew.

The police were able to get confirm his identity from the glass factory and they picked Samuel up within an hour. The Wards also had to pick the men with guns out of a lineup of sorts. It was basically, are these the men that harmed you and they were the only men there.

No one slept well that night, especially Bianca, she was thinking about how if the men in the basement had decided to kill them that the police really would have been too late and they would all have been dead right now, except for James of course. Bianca really wanted to go home. But, Edwin Grey explained that they really weren't in much danger now, they will have a CIA officer with them to insure their safety.

What Edwin didn't tell the Wards was that they really would be the bait to see who else was involved with Silvano.

Chapter 8   Trip to Florence

The next morning at around 9:30 am CIA Field Officer Frank Brenan met the family in the hotel restaurant. Frank said he wanted to go over some things in the privacy of their room before they left. They all climbed in the elevator and went to one of the Ward's rooms.

Frank said as he was pulling out some phones from his pockets, "These are for you to use while here in Italy."

James and Elizabeth squealed, "iPhones, cool!"

Frank pulled out the four phones and gave one to each family member.

"These phones have a couple of unique features. First, they are tracking devices, so we know where you are at all times. Second, if you type the code *911 enter into the phone it will send a distress email and text to my phone as well as Edwin and a few other officers in Italy. Third, if you need me I am on the speed dial as Uncle Frank. I will also automatically get your location from the phone when you call me, so I can see where you are. Fourth, if you punch in code *111 enter; it will turn into a voice recorder. We can retrieve the recording remotely"

James asked, "Does it have any weapons, lasers or poison gas?"

"No, just the tracking etc., but for Luke and Bianca we do have a couple of simple devices that could help you get away if something did happen."

Frank then pulled out two silver pens. He held up a pen in his hand and said, "One click, it is a pen, black ink, one more click it retracts, like normal, but if you click it out, then depress the spring pocket clip on the side, the pen has now turned into a onetime use stun gun. Simply jab the ballpoint end into the person and the shock will incapacitate them for a few seconds to 30 seconds depending on where you stick them. There is only a small insulator between the tip and the barrel of the pen, so don't do it in water etc."

James asked, "Can I get a pen?"

"No, the charge could really hurt a small body like yours, you would best stay clear of it."

James said while holding his phone up to his ear, "Ward, James Ward." Everyone laughed.

The Ward family took a final boat ride around Venice with Frank to the train station. The family said their goodbyes to this magical city on the water. The Wards certainly would have some memories of their vacation. Arrive, celebrate a birthday, see lots of sights, get kidnapped, almost get killed, get saved, you know the usual.

The Euro Rail train ride was like nothing the Wards had experience before. The train was modern, quiet and smooth as flying. Luke noticed that the train tracks were laid on cement railroad ties and were shiny to boot. Most of the US rails looked rusty, with old oiled wood railroad ties and were not nearly as smooth.

When Luke uses the Metro to go downtown Chicago, one could feel the bumps every few seconds, the Euro Rail tracks were a smooth as newly laid asphalt roads while driving with a new Mercedes Benz S Class. No wonder the Europeans liked using the rail system to get around their country.

The first class rail tickets were 53 Euros per person to go from Venice to Florence, a 2 ½ hour trip. Time was flying by, when Luke noticed that at the first stop the lady in the seating group in front of them got up for the whole time the train had stopped.

Luke thought about it and finally realized that he should get up and make sure that no one took his bags off the train, or stole them when it stopped. Luke had to stow the heavy bags they were traveling with in a small open compartment by the train doors. He had to really stack them in there like a puzzle to fit the four bags they were traveling with in Italy.

When the train made its second stop, Luke got up to watch their bags. Frank asked him where he was going and Luke explained he thought that he should watch the bags. Frank said that made sense but stayed seated where he could keep an eye on the whole family.

Luke noticed the lady from the seats in front of them by the baggage area. He tried to engage the lady in conversation while they stood watching their bags, "My name is Luke, we are traveling to Florence, I noticed you watching your bags and thought it was a good idea, do many get stolen?"

The lady looked at Luke and said, "No capisce."

As the train started to pull out of the station, one of the Ward's bags shifted and started to fall. The lady caught it and put it back in place.

Luke said, "Grazie."

The lady said, "Prego!"

The lady then said in English, "Where are you from?"

"Chicago. My wife's parents are from Italy, Calabria Region."

"Ah, Calabria, how beautiful, we have a summer home there by the sea."

Luke chuckled, "Your English is pretty good."

The lady laughed back, "I don't think so, I am embarrassed to say the wrong thing. My name is Louisa."

She held out her hand and they shook hands.

Luke explained, "This is the first time I traveled by train in Europe where we didn't have our own private car for first class, I am glad I notice you watching your luggage."

"Yes, like anywhere you need to watch your bags. Gypsies sometimes wait on the train platforms and will jump on a car and take a bag. There is usually only one conductor, and so if he or she isn't nearby, then it is free time."

The train doors closed and the train started moving, Luke said, "See you again at the next stop."

At the same time Luke noticed a man standing on the other side of the doors to the next train car. He might have been watching his bag, but Luke realized that there were only five bags in the compartment, four were his and one was Louisa's. Luke then thought that the man was probably just stretching his legs, but filed away his description in case he saw him again.

Luke returned to his seat. The Ward family had a seating group in first class, which consisted of four chairs with two facing the other two and a table in the middle. Frank was sitting across the aisle from them. James and Elizabeth wanted to play Angry Birds on Luke's iPad. Luke also liked making the birds fly into the pigs and take out their buildings.

But, Luke liked the iPad for reading his eBooks on. Currently he was reading a book about how all life was a game and all people played the game as a job and in reality they would accomplish real work while playing games. The world was basically one big mega multi-player on line game. Neat concept, not too far from reality when one looks at how the drone planes used in the Iraq and Afghan Wars were flown remotely by people in the U.S., like a game.

The other day Luke ran into a high school kid that wanted to fly helicopters for the Army, but wanted to do it remotely. Luke was amazed because that didn't even exist yet and here this kid was determined that he was going to do it and be the best at it. This also was part of the problem, a person that didn't really want to invent or create or manufacture something, but use a skill to do something.

The skills being developed by kids now were more down the services avenues. What Luke thought that we really needed were more kids in high school that want to invent the helicopter which could be flown automatically versus the kids that want to fly it via video game.

Luke had high aspirations for his two children.

Elizabeth was amazing at using her brain for creativity. She could tell you a story you swore was from a book, but instead was just made up by a thirteen year old that was bored. She also was very well coordinated; she could dance tap, jazz, or ballet equally well and enjoyed all of them.

She was a very determined person at whatever she decided to apply herself at. He just wanted her to always do her best.

James was very bright also. He took after Luke in doing math in his head quickly. Always calculating what someone might do or say. He was good at chess for this reason. James liked sports but was not a sports fanatic. He liked baseball, golf, soccer, running, riding his bike and most of all video games.

James was the best of his friends at most all games that he played. He took a lot of pride in his abilities. At times, his friends would have him over just to help them advance past a certain level.

The train was pulling into yet another station; Luke got up to watch his bags again. This time Luke looked for the man, but didn't see him. Luke arrived at the bag storage area just as the train was stopping; the last little jolt made the bags shift a little and one almost fell from the top of the others. Luke thought that was strange, the ride for the most part had been smooth as silk, so what would have made the bags shift now, he had restacked them last stop. Louisa was there again and she talked with Luke for the ten minutes it took for the train to get moving again.

After returning back to his seat, there was an announcement on the train about the dining car, what it offered and where it was. It turned out that it was in between the first and second class sections of the train. Luke walked back to see about getting some bottled water and maybe a sandwich for the kids and Bianca. Luke needed to go through 3 cars before getting to the dining car.

He was thinking about the man he saw at the first stop and looking for him in each of the three cars. But, Luke didn't spot him until
he got to the dining car; he was at a small stand up table drinking an
espresso. Luke and the man locked eyes for a few seconds, the man
actually nodded to Luke, like they had known each other from
somewhere.

Luke looked at the sandwiches behind the glass by the espresso
bar and decided it was best to wait until they arrived in Florence to
have lunch. He did get waters for everyone and decided to get a
double espresso for himself.

The man behind the counter didn't understand what Luke was
asking for and made Luke two espressos. No problem, Luke just
poured one into the other, added sweetener and drained the little chi-
na cup. He loved the little cups that had a little fin like handle with
no opening in it.

When Luke looked up again the strange man was no longer
there. Luke figured he would see him as he went back to his car, but
didn't see the man. Luke was thinking that maybe he had gone to the
bathroom or maybe he was really in second class and was simply
going for a walk on the train earlier, quite a few people were walking
on the train.

Florence was the next stop. The Wards would need to all be responsible for a piece of luggage, not for actually carrying it, because
Luke would bring each piece down to the platform, but everyone was
responsible for watching a bag. Almost instantly there are people
that ask to help you with your bags, the only problem is, many times
they are not really porters, but vagrants looking for tip money. Some
of them haven't showered in weeks.

Now, Luke understood why people watched their bags on the
trains during the stops until they got to their destination.

Frank was going to act like he was not traveling with the Wards,
he was going to be nearby, but let them enjoy the rest of their vacation in Italy.

In Florence, the Wards now headed for the taxi stand. They
waited on cue for about 10 minutes. As they became first in line, the
next couple cabbies didn't have enough room in their cabs for the 4
family members and their luggage. The cabbies were insistent that
they should take two cabs. Luke wasn't born yesterday, so he said
no he needed a station wagon or van taxi. There was one further
back in the cue.

Luke left Bianca and the kids for a few moments while he secured the taxi van. The driver beeped and made multiple cars get out of his way. One of the original cab drivers swore in Italian at Luke. Luke looked at Bianca and she said he called you a very not so nice name; she didn't want to repeat it in English with the kids there. Luke simply smiled at the cabbie and flipped him the big number one with his middle finger, which was internationally known from the look on the cabbies face.

As Luke was going back to help with the bags, he noticed the strange man from the train about 10 people back in cue. This time he didn't catch his eyes, but he was positive it was him.

After a short cab ride, the Wards arrived at their hotel, a four star hotel from the description and according to the embroidered entrance rug. The front of the hotel was nice, the entry way and small dining rooms off of the entrance looked quaint, with antiques and old Persian rugs, a little worn but authentic. That was supposed to be the theme of this hotel; the antiques in every room were unique.

The Wards were supposed to have one big multi-room suite, but the front desk man said that the air conditioning was not working properly in that room and offered two individual rooms to make up for the suite. The rooms were on the same floor, but were not attached or next to each other.

Right after entering the first room, Luke knew that the four star rating must have been from the time that the antiques in the room were considered modern, because this was no four star hotel, not even a three star. The bathroom had a bath tub that was older than Luke, no shower curtain and had a rickety shower head somewhat haphazardly nailed and/or affixed to the wall in the middle of the long side of the tub. There was no drain on the floor of the bathroom, with no way to really take a shower without it going all on the floor. The toilet seat was literally held on by only one screw and that one was stripped and about ready to fail.

After about 10 minutes in the room Luke realized that it was about 90 in the room and the air conditioner was not cooling the room properly. He sat on a chair to take his shoes off and realized that one leg of the chair was about an inch shorter than the other one; he looked around and realized that what the hotel called antiques; Luke would have called yard sale finds. Luke and James were to share this room; Bianca and Elizabeth were to share another.

He decided to go and check Bianca's room out. The first thing he realized was that her room was 10 degrees cooler, not cool mind you, but a lot more tolerable than Luke's room. The second thing he noticed was Bianca's furniture was better and she had a newer bathroom, something that had been updated in the last 20 years and was closer to what an American would expect to find. The tub was modern, with a curtain and had a real shower head built in the wall.

Florence hotels are expensive and the closer you are to the tourist area the more so. This hotel wasn't close or far and was located across the street from the Arnot River and three bridges from the Ponte Vecchio Bridge that crosses it.

The Ponte Vecchio,("Old Bridge" in Italian) is the oldest bridge in Florence because the Germans destroyed all other bridges when they were retreating in 1944, but saved this one bridge because of its beauty.   The Ponte Vecchio, today, mainly has jewelers located on both sides of the pedestrian bridge.

In the mid 1500s the Medici family didn't want food shops located on the bridge, because of their smell.   The Medici's lived across the river from the business district. They had a private walkway/corridor built above the shops on one side of the bridge, so that they didn't have to walk with the common people to go to work.

Luke told Bianca that his room was unacceptable. They called their travel agent to complain. She wasn't available but someone else was supposed to help them. When the Wards went downstairs to go out for dinner, the manager asked how their rooms were. Luke didn't pull any punches and told the manager that his room was unacceptable.

The manager simply said he was sorry Luke was not happy and that if the suite would have been worse. Luke said that it is too hot and that they were trying to change hotels, but that was proving to be tricky because the Wards had prepaid through the travel agent.

The hotel manager knew that they had prepaid and were not going to find last minute accommodations for the same price at a better hotel. He did offer another room, that he said should be cooler because it was smaller and on the North side of the building, so it didn't get direct sun. Luke didn't want to take the room, he really wanted to go to another hotel, but he knew he couldn't sleep in a room that was in the 90s let alone the other problems, so Luke agreed to change rooms.

He went up with a bellman and James and they changed rooms. Now they were one floor higher than Bianca and Elizabeth. This new room was remodeled in the last 5-10 years and was much cooler. The room was much better than the last one, but still not a 4 star. Luke opened the bathroom and it was 100 in there. He left the door open figuring that the air conditioning unit should be able to handle the small room and bathroom.

The Wards finally were going to get out and see Florence. Luke and Bianca had been in Florence on their trip 15 years ago and they loved it. The combination of large stone block construction, open air restaurants, historical buildings, museums, and the stone paved streets all made it a city to remember.

Right now though it was too hot, around 95, and it was feeling very humid on top of it all. Another aspect that Bianca really liked about Florence was they were known for their leather goods, coats, shoes and purses. Luke could use a new leather coat, so he was OK with Bianca wanting to go shopping right away. They had about an hour or two before the kids would be hungry.

On the edge of a covered market the kids found a brass fountain of a wild boar. A guided tour group was going through and the Wards overheard that if a coin was dropped from its mouth, where the water was coming from, and fell through the drain grate it meant that you would come back to Florence. It must have worked because Luke and Bianca had done it 15 years earlier and here they were.

Elizabeth went first. She rubbed the snout of the boar first, everyone did, and it was shinny from hundreds of years of rubbing. She posed for a picture then dropped her coin, it went in the grate. James was next and he was also successful. Another kid went after James and his coin bounced off the grill on the bottom part of the fountain, so he wasn't going to come back.

As the family moved on, Luke caught sight of Frank about 50 feet back. Frank was good, he blended in, and his clothing wasn't American. He was wearing some plaid shorts that were a teal color and a salmon shirt, it was hideous and still he blended in. Oh, and he was wearing yellow Crocs.

The funny thing was, he wasn't the only one dressed a little unusual when compared to Luke and James' khaki shorts and loose fitting button down shirts. Bianca had on a sun dress and Elizabeth was wearing a scooter skirt with a white sleeveless lacy cotton shirt.

The girls looked lovely, especially with the heat the way it was. After a stop at a gelato stand, everyone was feeling better.

They were drawn towards the Duomo. When they got there they were amazed at how huge the Duomo and the Baptistery were. Both have octagonal domes. The Baptistery has huge golden doors with scenes on them. The Baptistery was open and only cost a few Euros for entrance, with the kids being free. Once inside it was amazing how the temperature was so much lower than outside and how the ceiling was just beautiful. The kids even thought it was amazing, but were ready to leave within 10 minutes.

After exiting the Baptistery, the Wards started to cross over the court yard to the Duomo. They were going to walk around it, because the next day they were going on a tour inside. Just then, the crowd started making noises. Luke looked towards the ruckus and saw the crowds parting as four men on motor scooters were making their way through the walking only plaza. These scooters were the large ones that were basically motorcycles that you didn't have to straddle; they were very popular in Italy. The lead man looked familiar; he was the man from the train. Luke put two and two together, these men were after them.

"Bianca, James and Elizabeth, these guys on scooters are after us, we need to run and get away from them. Let's go for the Duomo, there have to be police around here somewhere."

The lead man was quickly closing in on the family. He looked like he was going to try and snatch James. James veered off to the right, Luke was yelling for everyone to stay together, but James couldn't hear him. The other men chased the rest of the Ward family while the man from the train veered off to follow James.

James formulated a plan as he was running; he noticed a few portable gift shops up ahead. As he passed the first one, he looked for anything substantial that he could throw at the scooter man that was gaining on him, but didn't see much. The scooter was only 15 feet behind him now and James could see a gun in the man's waistband. James was running as fast as he could, but as he passed the second gift cart, without missing a step, he grabbed a statue of the Duomo, it had some heft and was a solid heavy plastic type material.

Just as the scooter man was about to pull up and grab him, James sidestepped allowing the scooter to pass him. As it passed he shoved the Duomo statue in the front spokes of the scooters wheel. The statue swung around in the wheel and jammed on the fork causing the scooter to flip the back over the front, with the man and scooter ending up about 10 feet further up. The man lay on the ground motionless, his head was turned too far towards the back of his body; it must have broken during the fall.

Without thinking about it for 2 seconds, James cleared the statue from the wheel of the scooter, which was surprisingly not too damaged. The scooter was still running, so James climbed on and gunned the throttle; just like a video game he played on the Xbox 360. This was no video game, with one very real dead guy and the other scooters now approaching his family.

James found the horn on the scooter and started pressing it like crazy. Luke saw James driving the scooter, but didn't have much time to think about it as another scooter was closing in on him. Just before Luke was run over by the scooter, a man came running out of the crowd and tackled the man off the top of the scooter in one fell swoop. Luke saw a flash of yellow go by, Frank's crocks.

He was there to help the Wards. He hit the man a few times until he stopped moving. Frank then put zip tie handcuffs on the bad guy. The scooter guy chasing Bianca just saw his buddy get tackled and Frank was running towards him with the same look of determination in his eyes.

The scooter guy was next to Bianca but paused to take in the scene unfolding before him. His mistake; Bianca clicked the stun pen, pressed the side clip in and plunged the pen into her attacker's bare upper arm. The man's eyes rolled up into his head and he shook violently, falling off of his scooter.

Frank turned around when he heard another scooter coming up behind him, but it was only James. James never slowed, he saw that the last scooter guy grabbed Elizabeth and was driving away. Elizabeth was putting up a fight and then she wasn't, he must have threatened her with something.

James was not going to let her out of his sight. He was hot on her trail.

In the mean time, Frank picked up the scooter from the man he had tackled. He asked Luke to stay with the guy he cuffed and told him to let the police know what was going on.

The guy driving the scooter noticed that James was behind him and laughed to himself, perfect, they were supposed to get the kids and here they are. His plan was to lead the boy back to the warehouse where they stored the purses and then he would turn on the kid. The boss would be happy.

This scooter man was not the brains of the outfit or he would have realized that as he rounded the corner of the backside of the Duomo there would be about 20 policemen waiting. They came everyday at the end of the tour cycle to close the area around the Duomo down and make sure that the shops closed when they were supposed to.

The police saw a scooter with a flopping girl almost falling off. Ten seconds behind her is a boy riding way too fast for the area, beeping his horn, and yet another man on a scooter chasing them all? The police jumped into their cars and started chasing the scooters.

James heard the sirens and is glad they are coming, but he is not stopping until his twin sister is safe.

The scooter man realizes that he can't get away with the weight of the girl, let alone having to drive with one hand while holding her, so on the next sharp corner, he slowed down and tossed the girl. She landed by the garbage that was out at the curbside, waiting to be picked up for that day.

James screamed when he saw Elizabeth being thrown to the curb. He stopped to make sure she was OK. Frank never slowed; he kept pursuing the scooter guy. The police car right behind Frank also saw Elizabeth being thrown to the curb. The first car stopped by Elizabeth and the second police car continued chasing the scooters.

One of the police men knew basic first aid and had brought a kit from his car. Elizabeth looked pretty bad; there was a lot of blood on her face. The ambulance came minutes later. While they checked out Elizabeth and cleaned up her bloody face; Luke and Bianca arrived in a police car.

They jumped out of the car and ran over to Elizabeth, Bianca started crying. The blood on Elizabeth's face had been mostly cleaned up; it was just a bloody nose. Once Elizabeth saw her Mom and Dad, she started feeling better.

The police wanted Elizabeth to go to the hospital, but she said she was fine and was talking about the harrowing ride she just took.

Luke said, "What did the guy say that made you settle down?"

"He said he had a gun and he would kill me and you."

James explained, "He probably did have a gun, the guy chasing me had one, but he is dead now."

Bianca asked, "How can you be so cavalier about a man dying?"

James coolly explained, "It was him or me and I am still here, I wouldn't change a thing."

By this time, Frank had caught up to the scooter guy and ran him into a curb, sending the scooter and its passenger on a short ride with a quick stop ending at a stone wall. The police came with drawn guns making Frank get face down on the street. He quickly explained that he was with the US CIA and to check his identification in his pocket.

They told him that he was supposed to register with their office if he was going to do any official business there. Frank pointed out that the Italian Central Security Office was aware that he was in country and was cooperating on a mission of interest to the Italians but that he couldn't say more than that. The officer took down Franks name and badge number and asked which hotel he was staying at; he promised to follow up on his statement and would come visit him if it didn't clear.

The man from the train was dead; he had no ID on him. The police had the other three scooter guys, two that Frank restrained and one that Bianca got. Bianca wisely didn't tell the police about the stun pen. She wasn't sure if they would approve of the weapon; which was a good call because she was not an official CIA operative and the weapon was illegal to carry in Italy.

Frank made a couple of calls, one to his superiors and one to his contact with the Italian Secret Service. He explained how the police will be verifying he was with the CIA; the person on the other line understood and said he would take care of it. Secondly, he wanted to be updated on who the scooter men were working for.

Frank returned to the Wards after finishing his calls.

"My best guess is that they are local group associated with Silvano's gang. He wasn't too happy about being in jail the last I heard. These guys were not professionals, professionals wouldn't have been so easily stopped and would not have chosen one of the busiest areas of Florence to try and capture you. Professionals also never would of left Elizabeth go. These guys were just simple street thugs."

Luke said, "This is a pretty dangerous vacation for us so far, I really do think it is time for us to go home."

Bianca agreed and shook her head up and down.

James said, "I think we should stay and make sure that they capture the people that sent those guys after us today. Otherwise they may just find us in our house in the States. We don't even have an unlisted phone number; they probably already called and left us a message. "We know where you live," then James made some heavy breathing sounds." Elizabeth laughed.

Bianca said, "This is no laughing manner, Elizabeth could have been hurt."

James said, "I think that Elizabeth and I just need to get a pen that shocks or some other cool stuff and we will be fine."

Frank explained, "James is right, not about the weapons, but about the bad guys knowing where you live. It might be better to travel a little more and let us mop up these guys."

Luke said, "You mean we should continue acting like bait so you can reel them in after they bite? No thank you, I think we should go home."

"Luke, Bianca, I am serious when I say we will increase our protection of your family here. Either I or another CIA Officer will be with you at all times when you are out in public. We will stay at the same hotel as you and have people following us to watch our perimeter. We would never put children in danger on purpose, you must believe me."

Luke liked the adventure of the chase, but was really worried about his children. They were smart for their age, one might even say cleaver. James had definitely thought on his feet quickly and saved himself from the scooter, train guy. The police did recover weapons from these men so they were in immediate danger.

Luke was mulling this all over when James cut in, "Let's keep vacationing, this will be the most memorable vacation we ever do!"

Frank said, "You all look tired, let's go back to the hotel and relax in the pool."

Luke said, "There isn't a pool in our hotel, there isn't even cold air in our hotel."

"We already started moving you into a new hotel with a three bedroom suite, it is east of the Ponte Vecchio across the river, it has a pool and is fully updated to meet your needs. The US government is very appreciative for your help so far and is picking up the tab for the rest of your trip. You need to rest any way, so let's discuss this again tomorrow. We should eat dinner at the hotel tonight."

Luke and Bianca talked it over and agreed to think about it more once they had a chance to shower, relax, eat and drink something. They knew they couldn't get out of Italy until the next day anyway and maybe longer depending on how booked the flights were.

Luke said, "OK, we will stay tonight and decide tomorrow."

Elizabeth said, "Good, I want to see the rest of Italy, but I could use a dip in the pool right now and maybe some chocolate gelato."

Frank said, "That's a deal."

Chapter 9   The Big Decision

The Hotel was fantastic, now this was a four star hotel from this century. Up four steps to the entryway, the check in desk was straight ahead with a salon on the left and a dining room on the right. The decorating was European classical contemporary. Not too many antiques, but it wasn't all chrome and black either, but instead was a great mix of classical fabric French chairs and tufted leather chairs. The floors were tiled with large two foot Italian Carrara white marble veined with grey that were set at an angle with Black Italian marble dots at the corners. The check in desk was also made of marble, with the computer screen set lower behind it to keep the old world look.

The suite was a dream compared to the Ward's last room. With three bedrooms each of the kids got their own room. Luke and Bianca's room had a King size bed, private bathroom, all marble, and a private balcony overlooking the back gardens and pool area. The living room area of the suite also had a large balcony with a table and chairs overlooking the same gardens and pool area.

Bianca said, "Looks like we can have our own private dining room tonight," pointing to the table and chairs on the balcony, "Then it is off to bed to get some sleep." She then thought to herself, "And decide if we are going to continue our vacation."

They ordered a simple meal, Margarita pizza, pasta with red sauce, Italian sausages with grilled peppers and Tiramisu for desert. The adults shared a bottle of Chianti and the kids had a Sprite. After dinner, the family all read a little to unwind and then everyone went to bed around 9:00pm.

In Luke and Bianca's bedroom they didn't fall asleep immediately. They were discussing whether or not they should continue. Luke's thoughts were to go on, especially with the government providing the protection and the great hotel's gratis. Bianca was worried about her children, but did recall how James defended himself well and how Elizabeth was ready to go shortly after being abducted and threatened with a gun. Her kids were tough.

Luke and Bianca thought about the pros and cons and they decided to continue the vacation. Luke did point out that they needed to get a better agreement with the CIA and get a few more weapons and contacts. Bianca used her one use pen, she needed that replaced and they thought that the kids were also responsible enough to handle the pen stun gun and maybe other devices. They would check with Frank the next day to see what was available.

Luke pointed out to Bianca that they should probably join the CIA as part time operatives so that if something happened to them, the CIA would feel more compelled to get them out of trouble. Bianca also put in her idea of the whole family getting some self defense training from Frank.

After a nice long sleep, the Wards went down for a Continental breakfast in the Hotel. The kids filled up on French Toast with Elizabeth adding a roll spread with Nutella, a popular Italian spread that was like a hazelnut and chocolate peanut butter without the peanuts. Everyone also enjoyed the blood red orange juice.

Luke and Bianca each had two eggs over easy with some seasoned fried potatoes slices. Frank had obviously already eaten but joined the family with a coffee.

Frank asked, "So, are we still on vacation or?" This perked the kid's ears up and stopped their small talk about who was in more danger this trip so far.

Luke started, "Well, we gave this a lot of thought and we really don't want to put the kids in more danger than need be. So, we decided to continue on vacation with your added security."

Luke added, "There are some conditions we would like to discuss, maybe up in the room." Frank agreed that the room would be more appropriate for any further discussions.

Before heading up to the room Luke called a woman over to their table, but she wasn't a server. He introduced her as CIA Officer Olivia Brown. They all said their hellos then headed up to the room. As they neared the room, Frank told the family to stay in the hall for a few moments. He took the key from Luke and opened the door. Olivia then slipped in the room past Frank.

Luke noticed that both CIA Officers now had their guns out. Frank stayed by the door, to make sure the hall stayed clear and to be able to help Olivia if she needed it. Frank kept his gun pointed down in front of his black pants. From a distance the gun would be hard to see. Olivia checked each room to make sure it was clear, and then came back by the door to tell the family to enter.

Bianca said, "Was that necessary?" She was a little concerned but at the same time relieved that the officers were doing their jobs.

Olivia said, "You are under our care now and that is just standard operating procedure for places like hotel rooms."

Olivia was a petite woman in her late 20s, with tanned skin and dyed blond hair with highlights. She dressed conservatively, hiding a firm, toned body that could do a ten mile run in less than 50 minutes, was an expert marksman, could swim and bike well enough to win an Ironman triathlon.

Bianca said, "Speaking about standard operating procedures, Luke and I think that we should have something in writing with the CIA about our helping you. In case we were harmed or captured it might carry a little more weight to help us."

Frank said, "I don't know about that, but we do need to get you registered to carry the weapons that we gave you. If the police had questioned you about the stun pen, we all could have been in trouble."

Luke asked, "Speaking of the stun pen, Bianca's is used now, she could use another one and we think that the children are responsible enough to have some also. In addition to the pens do you have any other weapons that we could have to help protect ourselves?"

Frank reached into his pocket, grabbed a new pen, and handed it to Bianca. The pen was identical to the last one she used. He asked for the old one back and got it from her. He then plucked from his inside jacket pocket a black metal rod that was about 8 inches long.

"This is a onetime use weapon, but its best used for defense. Look on the bottom of the "Power Rod", there is a recessed switch," he flipped the switch, a red dot was now visible by the switch, "the dot shows it is armed. This is very dangerous, watch."

He pointed the rod away from the group and pressed a button on the side of the rod. Immediately, a crack bang happened and the rod was now about 30 inches long.

Olivia explained, "There is a highly compressed CO_2 cartridge in the handle, when the button is pressed it opens the valve and the compressed gas forces the sections to extend and lock. They can't be closed down once fired. The force of the rod will drive the rod through a person if held tightly, but can be very dangerous to use as a weapon because if you don't hold onto it tight enough it could pop back and snap your wrist. Once the rod is locked in the fully extended position it is a great defense tool for blocking an attack. The rod is made of titanium and is very strong but very light, so you can't really use it like a club."

Frank passed the rod around and all commented on how light it was for its size.

Frank stated, "Bianca, we think that you should carry one of the "Power Rods" in your purse. Luke you will mainly be wearing shorts on the trip, so you really can't conceal something like this easily. The power rod is great for blocking blows from someone's hands, a gun or a knife. Because of its lightweight it is easy to swing it around while fighting. We will show you some moves with this one that is already extended."

"Speaking of which, we wanted you to teach us and the kids some basic self-defense moves. Better prepared than sorry, especially after with what has happened the last few days."

"Fair enough, we will work with you the next hour and then you can go out and have lunch and do some touristy things. Also, I will get the kids some stun pens."

Frank left the room to get the pens. Olivia started working with the group to show some basic blocks, how to swing elbows, gouge at eyes and hit and kick at groin areas.

He returned about 30 minutes later with some sheets of paper and the pens as promised. The paper was a printed agreement between the Wards and the CIA.

"I have been authorized to offer you both a Special Field Officer position, contingent on you passing a full training and physical exam back at the Farm in Langley."

Olivia was a little shocked at this. She never heard of this happening in the field before. Sure the CIA recruited people to use once in a while but never a field assignment like this.

Luke and Bianca looked over the contract. It was basically a non disclosure agreement so that they couldn't tell anyone they were working for the CIA and additionally an offer of employment with the contingencies Frank outlined. There were also a couple of lines acknowledging that the Wards gave permission for their kids to hold and use pre-approved CIA produced weapons.

Luke chuckled when he noticed that there were four signature lines on the contract. Even though the kids could not legally sign for themselves, the CIA wanted them involved enough to realize the risks and to keep the secret. All signed the forms.

It was official now; the Wards really were a Spy Family.

Chapter 10   Training

Frank said, "We have some time booked at the local Kung Fu Club of Italy here in Florence. The master is available in 30 minutes, he and his apprentice will teach you some of the most important moves of Hung Gar Kung Fu and Tai Chi to get you started. You will continue your studies back in the States. The Master is originally from the US, a former Special Ops guy, he lets our locals use his place to train and helps out once in a while, like today."

"Cool, Kung Fu, now we are talking. I started Tai Kwon Do and am a yellow belt," said James.

"This will be a little different, but the structure of obedience and respect is the same."

The group took a couple of taxies to the Kung Fu center. The place was spacious enough, with two main rooms for training. Hung Gar Kung Fu is a derivation of the original Shaolin Kung Fu and this Kung Fu Club specialized in the Tiger and Crane methods. The Tiger method is a lower body based technique that strengthens the skeleton and the main muscles while the Crane tends more towards speed and agility, strengthening the tendons and improving responsiveness.

The Master greeted the Wards and started right away with training. He showed them the "Horse Stance" and asked them to hold it as long as possible. Basically, it is standing with ones legs shoulder width apart, hands in fists with the pinky side of the fist touching the hip bones and the knees slightly flexed.

The kids didn't have the patience to do this for more than 45 seconds at a time, but Luke and Bianca did it for over 10 minutes before getting tired. The Master told them to practice this stance whenever they had a free moment, to build up to being able to do this for 30 to 60 minutes at a time.

After the 10 minutes of doing the Horse Stance, Luke and Bianca had a sweat going. Luke was laughing, he wasn't even moving and he was working. Master explained that the energy of their bodies was flowing into the Earth and back out and this was the original meaning of being "well grounded."

The Master told them that he normally will teach exercises for a month or two, before teaching any real moves, but that he understood the rushed time he had available. He showed some basic blocks with arms and did some basic punch, block, and kick combos to help them feel empowered.

He also showed them how to stretch and that being flexible was the secret to being able to get your body to help match what your mind was possible of.

One final very advance set of moves he taught at Frank's suggestion was some ¼ staff moves of defense. Luke realized it was for using the Power Rod, but the Master didn't seem to realize why he was being requested to teach such an advanced topic to obvious novices.

Two and one half hours later the group was ready to go back to the pool at the hotel. That night they decided it was OK to go out for dinner in Florence. The group went out to a normal tourist restaurant and had a great meal. Everyone had increased appetites because of all the training earlier. They had pasta and meat dishes for a first and second plate. Gelato at a nearby shop capped off the dinner.

The schedule for the next day had them at Kung Fu training between 9-11, lunch, and a tour of the Duomo with a climb to the top of its dome.

The 463 steps climb to the top dome of the Duomo was nothing short of amazing. The first few flights were normal, and then came spiral steps, passages Luke could hardly fit through and more steps. They got to go on the inside of the top of the dome, what a view; they could see the great ceiling Frescos up close. Then they still needed to go up 3 plus flights of stairs, ending in a vertical ladder climb through a hatch to the roof of the dome.

At the top of the dome, one could see for 30 miles in all directions. It was a great overlook of the city of Florence. Many pictures were taken, but none of the pictures could do the actual experience justice, one had to be there, after climbing the steps, to truly appreciate the experience.

The Duomo was actually built as two domes, an inner and outer dome; this allowed the support for the domes to be hidden between the domes. While climbing, the patrons were really climbing between the two domes, an engineering feat not easily reproduced even with today's modern tools and machinery.

After the Duomo tours, the Wards had a private tour guide set up for a tour of the Statue of David at the Academia Gallery. This was definitely a good place to use a tour guide. By using one they bypassed the general admission line which was easily 2-3 hours long.

As it was, the Wards, Frank and Olivia waited 45 minutes for entrance, but it was worth the wait. The tour guide pointed out the relevant facts about how long it took Michael Angelo to create this masterpiece out of a huge single block of white marble, how it was moved to this location, and how it was closely monitored now using video cameras and seismic sensors.

The Wards had another night out on the town and were finally starting to enjoy their vacation.

Frank found out that the scooter guys started to talk; they worked for a local criminal who reported to Silvano. Apparently, Silvano got word out to his network that the Wards were working for the US Government and should be dealt with as a favor to him. The train guy that broke his neck worked directly for Silvano in Venice and must have got the other three local boys to assist him. The police had a warrant out for the boss of the three they had in custody. Frank would feel better once he was arrested.

The next morning the Wards did Kung Fu training from 8-12 and then had a scheduled tour of the Uffizi museum. Some great artworks in the Uffizi, which are not to be missed, include one of Luke's favorites, the Birth of Venus by Botticelli. After a few hours in the Museum, the kids were begging to leave. They could only take so much history in one day. Elizabeth wanted some Gelato and James agreed; they were all pretty addicted to the small ice cream treats.

The group headed down the street where they found a giant three dimensional gelato cone sign as tall as Elizabeth. Bianca had the kids hug the giant ice cream cone with three scoops and took a picture.

"Now, that will be a great picture for our Christmas cards this year."

Before heading back to the hotel Frank had some more "presents" for the Wards.

"I have some more gadgets for you."

James and Elizabeth perked up. Frank pulled four key chains from his pocket.

"These have a super loud alarm that is hard to stop once it is started." He demonstrated by twisting a circular locking piece by where the chain attached to the fob, then pulling out the chain, which ended in a pin in the fob. A very loud, piercing alarm sounded.

Frank calmly reinserted the pin and it stopped. He then twisted the locking piece and the key chain was ready to go again.

"If it is inside, the noise is so loud; it is hard to think clearly, that is when you would need to make your move. These alarm key chains can be found on the internet, except ours also happens to have an emergency beacon transmitter that we can monitor and find your location. Once the unit is activated, even putting the pin in doesn't stop the beacon transmitter."

He then took a small device out of his pocket the size of a cell phone and showed them how there was a push pin symbol blinking on a map showing them their present location. He tapped some buttons and the push pin turned solid.

"I just turned off the transmitter so it doesn't drain the batteries. You would only need to use this if we got separated for some reason."

The next day the family was headed to Naples, Pompeii, and Sorrento so they all wanted to get a good night sleep. Tomorrow would be a full day.

Chapter 11   Pompeii

The Ward family left their hotel around 8 in the morning. They needed two taxis because Frank and Olivia were along for protection. The group was traveling via the Euro Rail system to Naples. Once they arrived in Naples, two private cars picked them up at the train station to take them to Pompeii.

The area around the train station in Naples was a little scary for the Wards. There were dozens of street people that looked like they were living out of bags, trying to sell junk and old food to one another. Some of the people just looked blankly into the windows of the nice cars the Wards were now in.

Elizabeth said, "I feel sorry for these people, some look like they are sick and there are even little kids running around the sidewalks with no shoes, but there is broken glass and garbage everywhere." Elizabeth was starting to choke up a little.

The driver said, "This is a dangerous part of the city, you don't want to walk around here at all by yourself. When you come back here you want to go right in to the station once a car drops you off. Even inside the station you must always be alert, the police try to keep them out, but there are too many."

A similar conversation was happening in the other car that held James, Luke and Frank. In less than an hour the cars were pulling up to park at Pompeii. Mount Vesuvius was in the background, it seemed to have a steam cloud over its peak, an eerie reminder of the volcano that lies beneath.

After meeting their private tour guide, Linda, in front of the ticket window, they all proceeded in to the national treasure. Frank and Olivia said they would scout around and would always be within shouting distance, and went up ahead.

Linda explained that where they were standing used to be underwater, she pointed to a boat mooring at a lower level than the entrance. It looked strange, because it was all solid land now and they were quite a way from the sea. When Mount Vesuvius erupted in A.D. 79, it covered everything in 12 to 18 feet of ash and pumice, which also filled in much of the water canals that had made this city connected to the River Sarno and to the Gulf of Naples.

As the group hiked up through the Port Gate, they were already amazed at the detail of the entry way. There were really two entrances side by side, one for people and one for carts and animals.

Once inside the city walls, for Pompeii is known as one of the oldest Roman Walled Cities that hasn't been changed for almost 2000 years, the Wards took in the still standing walls of shops, restaurants and homes. They walked up one of the main streets and noticed how it was intricately paved with multisided stones.

There were also raised stones in the middle of the streets in places, with a raised sidewalk on either side of the street. The stones were for people to cross the street without getting muddy or worse. Animals pulled carts in the city and when it rained the water would flow through the streets via gravity and would make a slimy mess of things at street level. The people used the elevated walkways to cross the streets.

Linda explained how the crossing stones served another purpose, they had openings that would allow only a certain width cart or wagon through the streets. The width and height of the wheel tracks was still evident to this day. Wheel ruts and cart tracks were still present in the paved roads and between the openings in the stepping stones at crossing points. She went on to explain how the gauge or opening width seen in the streets later was used as the same width that Europe used for its first trains and tracks.

The most interesting places to James were the bakeries where one could still see the ovens and grinding stones to make the flour for bread. Elizabeth really liked the restaurants that still had stone serving areas with areas where hot pots of food would be lowered in and used the stone like an insulator.

Bianca really liked the homes; some of them still had frescos that had amazing color and detail that were created almost 2000 years earlier.

Luke, being an engineer by trade, was amazed at how this ancient city had plumbing and water supply for the entire town with water fed via aqueducts. In fact, the family refilled their water bottles from public water fountains in Pompeii.

One creepy place was where the archeologist finds on site were being kept. Also stored there were some plaster casts of actual people and animals that tragically got buried alive under ash and pumice. When the archeologists were excavating the Pompeii ruins, at times they would come across air pockets in the ash and rock.

One archeologist realized that each time they found one of these air pockets they would also find human or animal bones in the same area. He deduced that people and animals were buried under the ash and that through the years their bodies had decayed, leaving an air pocket and their bones behind. This archeologist devised a plan.

When testing areas to excavate, if one of the diggers found a pocket they would let him know and he would have them drill a few holes down to the opening. Then they would pour plaster down the holes to fill in the cavity. After a few days, the plaster would cure, and the diggers would remove the material around it.

The people frozen in time are surrealistic, the ash and pumice was so firmly compacted on the bodies after the eruption, that some level of detail can be seen in these three dimensional plaster casts. The Wards saw three of these on site; they saw a man, a pregnant woman, and a dog. The others cast could be found at a Pompeii museum in Naples.

Towards the end of the tour, the group headed towards the amphitheater, this was going to be the last stop before exiting the ruins. Frank and Olivia had joined the group by this time.   Linda described how the amphitheater had been rebuilt and pointed out some of the original stone seats and hallways.

It looked like there were some sets on stage for a play, with music stands and chairs in an orchestra pit area directly in front of the raised stage. Linda said there were public restrooms nearby and asked if anyone needed to use them beside herself. No one had to go. She said they could look around the amphitheater while she took a break.

The top of the amphitheater seating was a story up from ground level where the Wards stood. The stage was about 40 feet lower. The kids already started down the stairs towards the stage. Luke yelled out, "Don't touch anything."

There were only a few people in this part of the ruins, which was kind of strange, because the rest of the day there were hundreds of people around. It seemed like the tour guides all had a set plan because the Ward group had run across the same tour groups multiple times that day, yet none were here now. Frank also noticed this.

He had been shadowing the group most of the day, but now they were practically alone. The hairs on his neck were about to stand up, not easy to do considering it was about 85 degrees and Frank was sweating. He looked back towards where the group had entered the amphitheater area and saw a man standing in the main road leading into the area directing people to another place. A quick glance ahead and he saw another man at another entrance doing the same thing. He immediately reached for his gun. Olivia seeing Frank do so, reached for her gun in her purse as well. Both officers started to bark out orders.

Frank yelled to Olivia, "You go get the kids!" as he waved his free arm towards the kids.

She started down the stairs towards the kids, who by now had turned to see what the yelling was about. As they turned to look back towards Olivia, they would miss the two guys, with guns in hand, that stepped out from behind the stage and started running towards them.

Frank grabbed Luke and Bianca by the scruffs of their shirts and practically threw them into a small hallway under the upper grandstands, just as the bullets started to fly. The bullets bit heavy into the old parts of the amphitheater, sending down large chunks of rubble after each hit. Frank knew about the two guys, who were redirecting foot traffic, what he didn't know was if there were more than the two guys out there shooting.

He realized that they were badly pinned down where they currently were and he needed to draw off their fire and terminate them. He decided to go with the plan that they were the only two up on this level, he couldn't worry about the children, which was Olivia's responsibility right now.

Frank dove out the open arched doorway, hit the ground, did a military somersault, then sprung to the right side behind a half wall, bullets hitting around him the whole while. Frank thought to himself, "Good, there were only two shooters, or at least only two people shot at him just now."

He crawled to the other end of the wall. They wouldn't know for sure what he was doing and that would give him the half second he needed when he was going to pop out of the other side. Frank stopped for a second when he got to the other end of the wall, he was listening for footfalls, "Got him," he thought to himself.

Frank did a side roll to the right, came up to a one knee shooting position and shot three times. He hit one guy dead center in the chest. Later the forensics guy would find all three slugs in the bad guy's chest. Frank couldn't stop to admire his work or feel anything, because the other guy started shooting again at him, just as his last bullet had left the gun. Anticipating this, he immediately rolled back to his left behind the half wall where he started from.

The other shooter stopped and took cover. Frank still hadn't heard or seen any other shooters up here, so he had one left. About this time, he also heard some shouting and gunshots coming from the stage area. Frank hoped that Olivia and the kids were OK, but right now he was starting to worry about his own safety.

He was really pinned down and didn't have many options. The shooter had a slight height advantage over his position. Frank's only advantages were the element of surprise and that he was a crack shot. He was a trained marksman with both pistols and rifles.

Olivia started towards the kids at a run with her gun drawn. She saw the two men coming from out behind the stage. She also saw they had guns out. Olivia then heard the gunshots behind her and realized that these guys were more than armed and dangerous; they wanted to kill the Wards. The kids were only about 20 yards away from the gun men.

Olivia, while still at a run down the aisle in the amphitheater shouted, "Kids, get down now."

At the same time, she fired at the gun men who only spotted her after she started to fire. For one of the gun men that was a second too late. He was struck in the chest and his gun went flying out of his hand.

The other gun man ducked back behind the stage, which was good because that put the children out of direct line of sight. Olivia continued to fire her weapon at the man's location. Unfortunately, he was able to outlast the ammunition in her gun. When he heard the click of an empty chamber, he sprung out from behind the stage and fired 4 shots in Olivia's direction.

She had started her crouch down to get another clip out of her purse, when one of his bullets hit her in the left leg. Olivia fell down to the ground with severe pain. Unlike how the movies show people with multiple shots in them keep going, many people go into shock from the immense pain of just one gunshot wound. Unfortunately, this was Olivia's fate, she went into shock and became unconscious.

After disarming the female officer, the gun man turned his gaze and gun to where the children had last been and realized they were no longer there. He spotted them running past the other side of the stage and out the back. The children ran towards the gladiator's apartments. This area was where the gladiators for the original games were housed two thousand years ago.

There was a training yard that was ringed by small rooms. The children made a break for these buildings; it was the closest thing they could see that might offer some form of shelter. As James and Elizabeth ran towards the buildings, bullets were raining down around them.

Thankfully, this man was not trained for shooting while running and most of the bullets missed their mark by many feet. His gun ran out of bullets.

The man was starting to gain on the children, if this foot race had been another 100 yards, he would have caught them, but it wasn't, the kids made it safely to the first apartment.

James and Elizabeth ran into the first room that they came to. Thankfully, it was a larger suite of rooms that had an internal hallway to the right, away from the direction the man was coming from. They ran into the last room and noticed a window opening. James helped Elizabeth through the opening, and then jumped through himself. He landed on the other side of the window on his feet. Funny thing was, James did a perfect Pommel Horse mount and dismount over the window sill, without knowing what a Pommel Horse even was.

Once on the other side of the building, the kids continued to run in the opposite direction of the amphitheater. The gun man reached the building. He also ran down the short hallway to see where the kids could have gone. As he got to the last room, he thought he heard a noise out back. He climbed through the window and stood in the back walkway behind the building to listen.

In a few seconds he could hear the kids' footfalls on the crushed volcanic stone path down the way. He knew he was faster and could catch them in a foot race, which is what this had turned in to. He only had a few minutes before the police would show up. Someone would be sure to report gunfire in the park.

He knew that the unarmed local park security would wait for the police.

Luke and Bianca had heard gunshots from outside where they were standing and now from down in the amphitheater, where the kids were. Bianca took out her stun pen and Power Rod, handing the compressed rod to Luke. Luke also made sure he knew where his pen was, inside his front right shorts pocket.

Frank and Bianca now stood and went deeper into the dark hallway they were in under the upper seats of the amphitheater. They followed the contour of the wall back, it was curved, and they really couldn't see very far up ahead. It got darker as they progressed, this area definitely wasn't for general public use, there were parts of stone moldings and small piles of rubble and cracked stone pavers along the way.

Once they traversed into the hallway about 25 feet or so, it got darker. James remembered that his iPhone had a free flashlight app on it and turned it on now. The glow from the screen helped them see ahead and saved them from a few spider webs they would have walked through. After another 25 feet they could see light up ahead, the other side of this hallway.

They walked quickly toward the opening. Bianca was about to run out of the hallway, when Luke's hand on her shoulder slowed her to a stop. He didn't talk, but put his finger up to his mouth to make the "shush" sign. Bianca understood now and nodded her head, he wanted to take the lead and make sure no bad guys were waiting for them outside.

Luke now put the rod in his left hand and took out his pen and held it in his right hand. He was ready to click it, in a moment's notice. He slowly edged up to the end of the hallway and looked down the one side, then slightly moved only his head out into the opening to look down the other way. He figured a small part of his head and one eye would be hard to see from far away, compared to his whole body. The coast was clear. He told Bianca so with a wave of his hand and by him stepping out into the new corridor area.

Bianca and Luke wanted to find James and Elizabeth. They walked quickly to the top edge of the amphitheater and were shocked to see Olivia on the ground, not moving. More shots fired, the couple looked to see their kids running from a man. Luke said, "Bianca, you go see if you can help Olivia, call the other contact numbers we have, I thought that there were supposed to be more CIA people around. I am going to help the kids."

Luke dashed down the aisle toward the stage. That is when he saw the other bad guy on the ground; he wasn't moving and from the looks of it never would again. In that instant, Luke saw the gun on the ground and picked it up, putting his pen and power rod back in his pockets. Luke hadn't shot a pistol in a while, but he was a great shot when he was in college. Luke saw that the safety was off, so he was careful when he picked it up. He removed the clip, saw there was at least a few bullets in it, he knelt down on the ground and slowly pulled back on the slide, the live round plopped out. He put it in the clip, put the clip back in the gun and pulled the slide back quickly and released. The gun was now loaded with one in the chamber, the trigger was live. Luke did this all in about 10 seconds. He stood and ran as fast as he could towards the buildings next to the amphitheater.

James and Elizabeth were starting to get winded, but knew that they needed to keep running. Their adrenaline was pumping through their blood and it heightened James's senses. As they were running James heard someone running behind them, he had no illusions that this was Frank or his Dad, he knew the gun man was quickly closing the gap. James realized that they couldn't out run this guy; they needed to either hide well or confront him.

Looking around there were no great places to hide. This section of the building was pretty decrepit, mostly collapsed, no roofs, not even whole walls in places, no great place to hide. Then, up ahead he did see a full corner of a building still standing that he couldn't see past well, he knew that if they hid there for a while, the guy wouldn't see them right away either.

James formed a plan; once the bad guy came past the corner, he would zap him with the stun pen. It was risky to jump a guy with a gun, but James felt there was no other choice.

He grabbed Elizabeth as she was going to continue running past this corner. As soon as he pulled her in he said, "Shush" putting his finger to his mouth. He then pulled his pen out of his pocket. He told Elizabeth to stand back into the corner. If the guy got off a couple of shots while James rushed him, he didn't want her to get hit.

James pulled his keychain with the alarm on it out of his pocket and twisted the locking piece on the chain. James thought that if he could surprise the guy with the alarm, he may have a chance of getting the man before he shot.

The gun man was running, but stopped when he realized that the walls were starting to have gaps in them and the kids could have peeled off in any direction. He stood still and listened, but didn't hear anything. He thought to himself, I will come find you, and then you are dead. He then remembered that he used one full clip of ammunition, changed clips and chambered a round.

Frank needed to flush the other guy out. He came up with an idea. Frank gathered a bunch of rocks, the size of pool balls, and threw one without looking over the half wall towards where he thought the man was crouching behind a tree. The rock hit the tree and bounced through a few branches before hitting the ground. Frank threw another rock, and another one, and another one, and another one. As the last rock left his hand Frank popped strait up in the middle of the wall, not exactly where the gun man would expect him to stand up.

As Frank had hoped, the gunman was busy watching the incoming rocks, trying to make sure not to get hit as one came down the tree branches towards the area where he was standing. The guy didn't see Frank until it was too late, it was the last image he would have. Direct hit and the second bad guy went down. Frank ran over to this guy to make sure he would stay down; he then verified the other guy was permanently down, he was.

Frank cautiously checked out the rest of the tree lined area and ran back towards where he left the elder Wards. They were gone. He now ran towards the amphitheater and saw Bianca by someone on the ground. As Frank came up on them, he saw it was Olivia.

Bianca was on the phone talking to someone. Frank heard her say, "Frank is here now, but my husband went after a man with a gun chasing our children. ...My husband picked up a gun from another guy."

Frank simply asked, "Which way did they go?"

Bianca pointed and said, "They went into the buildings over there."

Olivia started to moan. Bianca said into the phone, "She is still alive; she just started to moan, get an ambulance here, fast."

In the distance Bianca thought she could hear sirens, but she was thinking they were probably police cars responding to the gunshots, not the ambulance that Olivia needed. Bianca took Olivia's purse strap, disconnected it from the purse and used it as a tourniquet above the wound on Olivia's leg. Bianca knew that if the tourniquet was on too long, Olivia would lose the leg, but if she didn't use one, she would bleed to death.

James was ready to spring his trap. He could hear the man coming, slowly; he must have been looking in the broken rooms for the kids. James was starting to worry he may come around the corner and look right where he was crouching, then the plan wouldn't work and he would probably be shot and killed, not a very positive image. He physically shook his head to get that thought out.

After another few long minutes, James could tell the man was within 30 feet, then 20 feet then 10 feet. James had to time it in his head; he wanted to get the man when he was about 2 feet short of the corner. James had the chain for the alarm in his teeth, the alarm in his left hand ready to pull and the pen in his right hand. James clicked the clip to fully activate the pen. The man must have heard the slight click and stopped.

Now James wasn't sure how far he was, probably 5 feet away, close enough for James to cross the distance in one second, also about the same time it would take to pull a trigger. Hopefully the alarm will disorientate him. It was "go time."

James sprang around the corner, he pulled the alarm with his left hand, the chain and pin stayed in his clenched teeth, the piecing alarm almost stopped James in his tracks, but he half dropped, half tossed the alarm at the guy's feet, he just had to get it away from himself. At the same moment that the man heard the alarm, he started to raise his hands to his ears; this is what James had hoped for. James didn't delay; he leapt forward and thrust the pen towards the gun man.

The gun man recovered from the alarm a little faster than James thought he would and was able to block the pen with his gun. The gun being metal conducted the shock and sent the gun flying and the man to his knees. A startled James looked down as the man simply shook his head and got to his feet.

He located the alarm and stomped on it a few times until it stopped. The man then looked for his gun and found it about 6 feet away on the ground. James followed the gun man's eyes and saw the gun also. He realized that if the guy got to the gun first he and Elizabeth were as good as dead.

Without thinking about his own safety, James started a few quick steps towards the man and did a flying kick to his chest. A little Kung Fu will go a long way when the other person isn't expecting it. The man went down to one knee. James quickly followed up with a couple of solid hand strikes, punches to the face. The man simply blocked his face, shook his head and stood up with the gun pointed at James.

The man's head must have been a little fuzzy but, he was still functioning enough to now have a tremendous advantage over young

James. James started to back up at a slow even pace. He figured the further away he got the smaller the target he would make, while at the same time drawing the gun man away from Elizabeth's location.

The gun man realized his target was trying to get away and decided he better shoot him soon. He raised the gun level at James' head. James wanted to run but didn't want to prematurely have this guy pull the trigger. James heard a loud bang. His head was still attached and he didn't feel any pain, did the man miss?

In that instant James dropped, hit the ground and rolled to one side. As he scrambled to get behind a partial stone wall he looked towards the gun man and realized that the man had been shot. The guy dropped his gun to the ground and collapsed next to it. About 25 feet behind the man's body James saw his Dad, then he saw the gun in Luke's hand.

James ran to his father. Luke put the safety on the gun and put it on the ground. James practically jumped into Luke's arms. He hugged his Dad and said, "Thanks for saving my life."

Then he remembered Elizabeth was still hiding. She must have heard James thanking their Dad because Elizabeth came out from hiding. She ran to her Dad and the three of them had a big hug. About a minute later, Frank came upon this wonderful site.

Frank looked over and saw the bad guy down and the gun at Luke's feet. He thought to himself, "This is going to be a lot of paperwork."

He picked up the gun from the ground and said to the group, "Let's get back to see how Olivia is doing, she was losing a lot of blood the last time I saw her."

They all started jogging back to the amphitheater. Frank told them to all stick together, he didn't think there were any other gun men, but you couldn't be too careful.

By the time they arrived back at the amphitheater, the police had showed up. The police came down the aisles with their guns drawn. Frank had his ID out and his guns were on the ground by his feet. The police asked him to get down on his knees, which he did. The nearest police man came up and grabbed Frank's ID from his hand.

He took the ID up the stairs to show to another man. The whole time police still had their weapons drawn, mostly aimed at Frank. The man who looked like he was in charge walked down the aisle toward the group, Frank's ID in his hand. As he got closer, he told the officers to put away their guns.

He signaled to Frank it was OK to stand and pick up his gun. Frank handed the other gun to the nearest police officer, indicating it came from the bad guy by the stage. The man handed Frank back his ID. Frank then went over and picked up Olivia's gun.

The man in charge said, "I am police sergeant Mario Rofino, what has happened here?" He directed his question to Frank and waved his hands around the area as he talked.

Frank said, "This is Officer Olivia Brown, she has been shot and is losing blood, she needs an ambulance immediately." Olivia moaned for good measure, she was floating between conscious and unconsciousness.

A nearby officer talked on his handheld radio, he said, "the ambulance will be here in 60 seconds, they will be able to pull up behind the stage there," as he pointed to the back of the stage area where the ambulance was starting to pull in. Within another 60 seconds, two paramedics were tending to Olivia, to stabilize her wound. They started an IV. A minute or so later she was on a stretcher going into the back of the ambulance.

Frank quickly told Sergeant Rofino about what had transpired, that there were four dead, two outside the entrance way, one by the stage and one behind the buildings, he pointed as he talked to help clarify the situation.

Sergeant Rofino said, "We just got notified that you were going to be in our area this morning, but no one said anything about guys with guns attacking people in a national park. I will find out who these guys work for and let you know, do you have a card?" Frank handed him his card that had his cell phone number on it.

Frank said, "If it speeds things up I am pretty sure they work for Silvano Rosito's organization.

At hearing this, Sergeant Rofino winced and said, "I heard he is in jail now, was that your doing?"

"Yes, he and his group in Venice kidnapped the Wards. He should go away for a while."

The Sergeant shook his head in agreement.

"Will you be staying here, locally?"

"We will be in Sorrento for a few days."

Frank didn't mention the name of the hotel on purpose, too many people standing around that didn't have a need to know. Frank was already wondering how anyone knew they were going to Pompeii, unless they were simply followed, but no; it seemed like a planned ambush.

Speaking of which, where was Linda, the tour guide. She conveniently had to use the facilities before the shooting started. Frank looked around and couldn't find here. He asked a few policemen and no one had interviewed her or seen anyone that fit her description. Frank could check on that, the Rome office had set up the tour. He also wouldn't question her running away once the bullets started to fly; she may not have stopped until she got home.

After the police interviewed everyone, they were released. Frank then called the CIA Rome Office for more support and to report what had happened to Olivia. He also asked them to look into Linda the tour guide, explaining how she disappeared earlier.

Another two officers from the Rome Office would arrive in Sorrento within a few hours. Frank requested that the Ward's hotel be changed. He told them not to cancel the original one, but to set up an additional reservation with a suite and a few rooms for the officers. The hotel should have a restaurant in the hotel, so they wouldn't need to eat out.

The Ward's were targets and the bad guys were not pulling punches now; that hit team had some organization. They almost succeeded, had Luke not been there, the children would have been killed.

Frank led the group back to the parking lot, where their drivers were waiting for them. They were very curious what was going on, because of all the police cars and ambulances. They didn't hear the shots; they were listening to music in the car.

Frank pulled Luke aside and secretly gave him Olivia's gun.

"Obviously you know how to use one of these. The safety is on and a new clip is in it, there is not one in the chamber, you need to pull the slide back to load one and cock the trigger.

You will take James in your car; I will go with Bianca and Elizabeth. I will call you as we approach Sorrento to tell you which hotel to tell the driver to go to. Don't tell him now that we are changing hotels, we will tell him at the last moment. If he reaches for his phone before we get there, distract him so he can't make the call, ask him about the town etc.

On the trip to Sorrento, there is a great overlook where we can stop to see the fishing port and the city on the cliffs, it is beautiful and the kids will love it. I will tell your driver now."

Luke slipped the .38 caliber snub nose gun in his front shorts pocket; he gave Bianca back her power rod. With his shirt untucked and hanging loosely over his shorts, it was hard to see the gun bulge in his pocket.

Chapter 12   Sorrento

The drive to Sorrento was uneventful, but then again most things would be in comparison to the last hour or so.

James thought to himself, "It isn't everyday that my family gets shot at, that I attack an armed gun man with only a pen, albeit a stun pen, but still a pen, and that my Dad shoots the guy that is about ready to kill his son.

Oh yeah, and one CIA officer is shot after getting one bad guy, while another CIA officer shoots two bad guys."

An uneventful ride to the hotel suited James and his family just fine.

The two cars stopped on the side of the winding SS145 road, just south of Montechiaro. It overlooked the town of Piano de Sorrento, which is just east of Sorrento. The views were amazing. The winding road had a pull off area for vehicles and a wide sidewalk area for sightseeing. There was a frozen lemonade truck there and everyone enjoyed one.

With the sea breeze, the water and the city on the cliffs filling out the view, Luke grabbed his wife around the shoulders and said, "Happy vacation."

Bianca smiled, and then looked towards the children that were fighting about who got a bigger serving.

"I hope that they can bring their children back here someday…" Bianca didn't finish her thought, she didn't need to, Luke understood that she was worried about the safety of their children.

Frank volunteered to be the photographer of the Ward's family picture. The vista behind the Wards was fantastic. They now had another picture suitable for the family Christmas card.

The road through Piano de Sorrento was narrow with many turns. It was a maze of a road, at times Luke thought that there was no way this was the biggest road or the fastest way to Sorrento, but it was. There was one bend that was so sharp that the car couldn't make it with one try, they had to actually start the turn, spin the steering wheel, then back up, spin the steering wheel and go forward again.

Just as the cars were approaching Sorrento, Luke's phone rang, it was Frank. Frank told him the name of the new hotel. Luke relayed the name of the new hotel to the driver. The driver paused a few seconds, and then said he knew the hotel, it was very nice; they would like it better than the other hotel. The driver considered charging more, but realized that was probably not a good idea.

Luke watched to see if he was going to use his phone, he didn't. What Luke didn't realize was that this new hotel was only a block away from the original hotel. The new hotel was grand and right on a cliff overlooking the water, about 150 feet below. The cars pulled up in front of the hotel in its private auto port and the bell staff hopped to.

Frank jumped out of the car first and told the bellman to take the bags directly up to the rooms. They already were assigned and paid for, but the front desk still needed their passports. Frank collected the passports from Bianca and handed them to the bell captain, while saying, "Please have them check these quickly, because we will pick them up after dinner." The bell captain said, "Yes sir, of course sir." Frank slipped the Bell Captain a 20 Euro note. Frank also signed for the drivers charges and gave them each 40 Euros as a tip.

The rooms were amazing. There were private balconies overlooking the water for both the master suite and the guest suite, which had two beds in it for the kids. Frank had checked out the room before hand and was still there when the bellman finished unloading the Ward's bags.

Frank told Luke, "You should all get ready for dinner. Tonight we will be eating in the hotel restaurant, which really is one of the best in town with a view over the water. Luke, lock the door and don't let anyone in for any reason. I have to run a quick errand and will be back in 20 minutes, shower and gather you all for dinner around 7 pm."

Luke locked and dead bolted the door after Frank left.

Frank hurried out of the hotel, but was not in such a hurry as to miss noting who was in the lobby. One always had to keep a lookout for suspicious people, especially in this line of work.

He walked briskly out to the street and then down a block. He now slowed his pace as he approached the hotel they were originally going to stay at. The lower level was all glass walls and modern sliding doors. This hotel was newly remodeled and had just been completed earlier that year. On the second floor was a bar, all chrome, mirrors, crystal light fixtures and leather. It too was behind a wall of glass.

Frank walked past on the side walk and casually glanced inside the lobby. Just as he suspected, two men sitting on a couch, one was reading a newspaper; the other was playing a game on a smartphone. And, another guy for good measure was sitting back further by the elevators.

The sidewalk was climbing the hillside along the hotel and the bar was only about 6 steps up from the sidewalk at this point. Frank peeled off the sidewalk and went into the 2nd floor bar. There was a bartender, but no patrons. Frank asked for one bottle of water. The bartender asked him for his room number, but Frank put a 5 Euro note down and walked away. In the background Frank heard the bartender say, "Gratzi." Frank said, "Prego," over his shoulder.

The second floor had a restaurant and a few meeting rooms in addition to the bar and a large lounge area where there were a dozen or so white leather couches and dozens of tufted back chairs in a navy blue pattern. Frank walked towards the elevators; he saw a large open stairway to the left of the elevators that went down to the first floor lobby. Between the two elevators was a small table with a house phone on it. Frank picked it up and dialed the front desk.

"Please tell the gentlemen waiting that Luke Ward is sitting at the bar on the second floor."

He then hung up the phone and went over and had a seat where he could see the stairs, elevator and the bar entrance, he also removed his gun from its holster, but kept it under his jacket. He didn't want to bring it out in the open and alarm the bar tender. Frank was guessing that the three guys downstairs were the welcoming committee for the Wards. If they didn't come up, he may have been mistaken, but he didn't think so. His guess was that two would come up the stairs, and one in through the outside bar entrance.

Almost on cue, two men came up the stairs. Their guns were not in the open, but Frank recognized the bulges under their jackets, and who wore a jacket when it is over 90 outside? People who carry guns wear jackets when it is over 90 degrees, people like them and people like Frank. As he predicted, Frank saw a third man outside the bar's glass door, he paused slightly after he entered, to see where his associates were. He also had a look of confusion wondering where the target had gone.

The three guys came together in the middle of the bar, spoke to one another, and then started to look around. They had been so focused on looking for Luke Ward, the person they had a picture of, that they hadn't notice Frank sitting about 15 yards away with a smile on his face. The man that came in through the door recognized Frank first. It was a panicked look, but it only lasted a split second before he reached for his gun. The last thing he did was pull his gun out of its shoulder holster; Frank didn't miss from this distance, double tap to the chest.

The other two heard the noise before it registered, they also reached for their guns a little too late. Two more bad guys down. This all happened within seconds, the bartender didn't have time to hide before it was all over; he just kept cleaning the one glass he had been cleaning.

Frank re-holstered his gun and walked toward the bartender. He pulled out a CIA business card and put it on the bar and said, "Call the police and tell them to call me to discuss what happened here, I have to make a dinner date right now."

The bartender simply shook his head up and down. Frank started walking back to the other hotel. The police cars passed him on the street as he was about to cross to go in the private drive of the hotel they were now staying in.

Frank showered, and then went down to the pick up the Wards for dinner. He would not mention the crew waiting for them at the other hotel; it would just have made them nervous. Frank also checked to verify the other two officers were on their way and where they were. He still had about an hour and one half to wait for his crew.

He found out that Olivia's surgery went well and that she was recovering. He was supposed to relay to Bianca that her quick thinking with the tourniquet saved Olivia's life; she surely would have bleed out otherwise.

Dinner on the terrace was for five. The Sun getting low over the water was beautiful, with great swatches of pinks and oranges and heavy yellow light that painted everything it fell on with surrealistic colors, that were way over saturated.

Frank told the Wards that Olivia was going to be fine and how Bianca's tourniquet saved her life. Everyone was relieved that Olivia was going to be fine. His phone rang numerous times during dinner, he had left it on vibrate, the Italian police were calling. It made Frank feel a little safer knowing that they didn't show up to question him, because they didn't know where he was right now.

What bothered him at this moment was that someone on the inside was leaking information to Silvano's crews across Italy. Obviously, it wasn't one of the car drivers, because they would have had plenty of time to call in the hotel change. No, it had to be either someone in the CIA or Italian police, Frank was leaning towards the later. He knew for diplomatic reasons that the CIA foreign relations desk contacted the Italian police to inform them of CIA officers in their area.

He made it clear to his people to not update his hotel with the local authorities. This way maybe Frank could start narrowing down who is leaking the information. Frank would have to track down the mole. The mess that Frank left at the other hotel would mean a lot of questions. The other officers would be coming soon; Frank could use all the help he could get right now. Once they came, he would go talk with the Italian police; his current job was to make sure the Wards were safe.

After diner, the Wards wanted to take a walk down to the water level, about 150 feet vertically, but hundreds of winding steps to walk down. Frank agreed it would be good for the digestive process after such a fine meal, but they would have to hurry to catch the Sun set. They all headed towards what looked like a glorified alley, but it was a road.

The Italians may have been one of the first to pave roads, but they didn't necessarily think that they had to be big enough for a Chevy to traverse. The group walked about one hundred yards until there was a break in the stone wall on their right, towards the water. It was not much of an entry way, but it was the start of the largest walking path down to the water. The opening was only about 4 feet wide, the winding steps going down started immediately, there were few landings.

After descending about 100 feet there was a beautiful large landing, with a short stone wall, that faced out over the water. Everyone paused to take in the view from a much closer perspective. There was also a little fountain on this landing of two children playing, how appropriate for the twins. Elizabeth was the first to notice the boy and girl in the fountain were the same age. She wondered if they were twins like her and James.

On the side where the steps continued down to the water's edge one could see multiple fishing boats coming in to port for the night. There also was a large, 80 foot wide, paved walk way for people to get around between the buildings, restaurants and the waterfront. On the docks, some people could be seen scurrying around to secure the catch and the boats.

The Sun was now beginning to disappear behind the horizon and a glorious sunset had begun.

The group headed toward a restaurant/bar that was literally built on peers out over the water. Here the group ordered some drinks and sat in silence to watch the last few minutes of the vividly glowing pink sky blend into the water, with the reflection completing the falling, shrinking Sun for a moment.

The kids had lemon soda; the adults had red wine, except for Frank, who had a club soda with a lime. Luke noticed his order and figured that like Frank he should keep his wits about him. Luke still carried the gun that Frank gave him earlier, so just the one wine tonight for Luke. Bianca must have been reading Luke's thoughts because she looked at Frank's drink, then Luke's then looked away and exhaled heavily. Nothing would be the same going forward.

Bianca loved seeing the kids enjoy a simple pleasure like the sunset. In today's crazy world, many people forget to see the beauty around them; too many smart phones, computers, hand held games, iPods and etc. to occupy every waking minute. How many times had she heard their kids say that they were bored with a situation after only 30 seconds or so? They always wanted to be stimulated, and yet here they were enjoying a sunset in Italy, life was good, how she wished she could bottle this.

As if on cue, James raised his glass of lemon soda and said, "I would like to propose a toast." All raised their glasses. "To the best vacation we have ever had and to a great new friend, Frank." They all clinked glasses and took a sip.

Elizabeth said, "Now it is my turn. To great parents, brothers and friends, …also our dog Bingo who I miss and wish could be here with us." They all chuckled at the toast, clinked glasses, and took a sip.

Bianca added, "To the best family one could have and to Frank, for helping us through these dangerous times." Bianca almost teared up on this last bit, but choked it back for her family's and her own sake.

Luke added, "To a beautiful wife and children."

Frank said, "To a great family that I am proud to call friends." Frank really did believe this, and now that it was personal, he had to make sure not to loose his objectiveness. He believed that work and play needed to be separated.

After all of the toasts, the drinks were almost finished, as was the sunset. It was time to walk back up the steps and to the hotel to meet the new officers assigned to them. Again, the group paused on the large landing with the twin's fountain.

The little port area now looked different. There were no people on the boats or the docks. Night life was starting to begin, there were dozens more people dressed for fun instead of work around and loud music from each outdoor patio was starting to blend together in the slight sea breeze.

Frank was a little worried about the Wards safety, he probably should not have let them all come down here without some back up, the path was narrow at places and now was also pretty dark in others. Just as Frank was thinking about this, his phone vibrated, he looked at caller ID and could tell it was one of the agency phones from Rome. The other two officers had arrived. Frank described where they were and asked them to meet him quickly.

The officer on the phone also reminded Frank that the Italian Police were trying to get a hold of him. Frank just repeated his orders and hung up. Frank knew these two officers that worked as a team most of the time.

CIA Officers Jerold (Jerry) Banks and George Mullis were ex marines, each slightly over 6 feet tall with dark hair, good builds; they could be brothers, kind of cut from the same mold look to them. They also looked like CIA men right now, they were wearing jackets and trousers, with Maui Jim Sunglasses tucked in their inside breast pocket, located not too far from their shoulder gun holsters.

They each carried a semi-automatic Glock 23 pistol with a 13 round clip, standard issue for CIA officers around the world. The .40 caliber bullets are a great balance when looking at the size/weight scale of effective projectile impact power in a compact size. The gun is easily concealed when using a shoulder holster and is very lightweight, having a plastic frame.

The two CIA officers came across the Ward party about half way up the stairs. They all shook hands, then Jerry took point, George stayed back to cover their flank. After about 10 minutes of walking the group was in front of the hotel. Jerry and George stayed with the Wards as Frank went ahead to check out the lobby. Frank was good at spotting people staking out places, probably from doing so many stakeouts himself.

Five minutes passed and then Frank came up on the group from the side, an exit from the restaurant they ate at earlier. The two new CIA men went in first to register for the night; Frank took the Wards back to their suite. A knock on the door about 10 minutes later put everyone in a ready state. It was just Jerry and George. They asked the Ward family to add their numbers to their phones and vice versa.

Now that everyone was on the same page, the family would get some sleep. They were planning on going to the Isle of Capri in the morning for a day trip.

With the Wards situated, Frank would have to go talk with the Italian Police about the ambush that waiting for the Wards at the other hotel. He didn't look forward to this; he hadn't done most of this by the book, especially the part about leaving the Wards in their hotel without any protection. But first, Frank would have to talk with his boss, Edwin Grey. Edwin, as Frank had predicted, was not happy with Frank. The police had called the agency offices in Rome after the first time they called Frank's phone number and got no response.

Frank had left his card, so there really was no question that he and the CIA were involved, but how could he have not stay behind to answer their questions? Edwin briefed Frank on the situation with the Italian Police. To say that they were upset was an understatement.

Edwin also told Frank that he personally understood how he could be so upset and also agreed that there was an insider feeding information to Silvano's people.

The Italians were never known for their honesty or loyalty. In the past they showed how the whole government was easily corruptible, down to the local police that looked the other way when the Mafia enforced the rules in the local towns. At the highest levels one can find amazing amounts of corruption. Some of the top Italian fashion corporations have been accused of bribing Italian tax officials to get favorable tax bills or look the other way when large sales were at stake.

Italy's tax code was a joke for the last 30 years, very recently hitting a low when people realized that everyone lies for sales and income tax as a corporation and that a company's tax bill was more related to how much they paid their government auditor than to the actual amount of their sales. Hence, the tax rates kept increasing to meet the demands of the spending of the Italian government. So, if one was honest they would pay taxes at a rate 2-3 times that of a corrupt payer.

Regardless of the corruption, Edwin said that Frank needed to go talk to the Police Chief of Sorrento to appease him. The Police Chief's name was Eduardo Sargento. Edwin said he would be available if Frank needed some backup, but to play it straight, after all, Frank did blow into town and kill a few of the local boys.

Frank showed up at the Sorrento Police headquarters and asked for Eduardo Sargento. He was expecting Frank, Edwin must of called ahead. Eduardo said, "Mr. Brenan, it seems you had a bad day today?"

"Yes sir, some men were waiting in ambush to kill me and the Ward family."

"How was it that you became so interesting to these men that they wanted to kill you and an American family?"

"As I am sure you are aware by now, this family was kidnapped and about to be killed by Silvano Rosito in Venice a week ago. They escaped and Silvano is now locked up. Silvano didn't like their part of this equation, so he has tried to kill them multiple times since this has happened.

The thing that worries me the most is how the men here found out which hotel we were supposed to be staying at. Obviously, someone on the inside is feeding them information."

"I can assure you it was no one from this office." Eduardo waved his hands around as he said this. He went on to say, "I also can assure you that these are the first murders in our town of under 17,000 in many years. I am upset that you killed these men instead of maybe calling in the Police." He said this as he was curving his hands in toward his chest and lightly thumping them.

"As you can only imagine, I realized that someone has provided the information to these thugs and I didn't know who that was, but I started narrowing it down, when I realized the CIA knew I was changing hotels, the drivers of the cars knew we were changing hotels, the only ones who didn't know were the Italian Police and the Italian Carabinieri. So it appears that you may want to look within your organization to see who had access to our whereabouts."

"I don't like what you are saying, but I will look into this. I don't want people around me that I can't trust. I still want to know, did you have to kill them?"

"Yes, they came fast and hard, they pulled their weapons and had intent. I only had the advantage of knowing that they probably wanted to kill us. There were many of them and only one of me; every shot had to count and they did. I didn't try to hide the fact of who I am and who I work for, I gave the bartender my card."

"Yes, thank you for that, it allowed me the pleasure of talking to Mr. Grey for 10 minutes. He also defended your actions, impressive considering that you didn't bother to inform him of what you had done, ...or did you?"

"No, Edwin didn't know, I just called him 10 minutes before I came in here. I needed to secure the Ward family and make sure that they were safe, feed and felt secure in sleeping tonight.

"Yes, Edwin told me there were a couple of agents coming from Rome to help you."

"Then you know all you need to for the moment. I will leave now, please don't have anyone tail me, I take my privacy seriously."

"I won't have anyone follow you, but please keep in mind that I also don't want you playing God and killing any more or our citizens, our mayor wants to be able to get re-elected. Maybe you would like to contribute to his re-election fund?" Sargento said this last part with a slight laugh in his voice.

"I think I will pass on the contribution at this time, our Government has helped you many times and our Fed has lent you guys billions that the US taxpayer will never see again.

Do you think we will have any other problems with Silvano's guys while we are in Sorrento?"

Sargento explained, "Sorrento is a friendly place Mr. Brenan, we make Limoncello and intricate wood items, we don't breed killers, you should be fine here."

Frank really didn't like the way the Commander said that last sentence, it reminded him of a used car salesmen saying it was a car driven by a little old lady on Sundays to church and back, when really the car had 100,000 miles on it instead of the 25,000 on the odometer.

Chapter 13   Capri

The morning was like the other mornings on this trip so far, very warm and sunny. This would be a better combination for a beach vacation, but today was not far from it. The Wards were taking a private boat to the Isle of Capri. This island off the coast of Sorrento was known for its shopping. Picture a Rodeo Drive in Europe, on an island, but more expensive.

The Wards weren't as concerned with the shopping as they were excited about the trip itself, going on a small boat to the island. The plan was to go to Capri, shop for an hour and a half, then go back on the boat and go completely around the island, stopping to swim and explore some grottoes. They would visit the famed Blue Grotto if it was open, sometimes it closed when the seas were choppy or the tide was high. Either way, they were mainly looking forward to exploring the rest of the island.

That morning the Ward family, Frank, Jerry and George had breakfast on the terrace overlooking the sea at the hotel. What a beautiful sight for all to partake in. Elizabeth noticed the sea gulls; the graceful white birds gliding on the air currents about 50 feet above the water.

Elizabeth also pointed out the public beach below. Well it wasn't public as in free, but open to the "paying" public. There was an elaborate wooden pier system where many chairs and umbrellas were laid out. In the internal regions enclosed by the walkways, hundreds of people were already swimming.

Bianca added, "We will be able to swim in the water along Capri, a much better adventure than what they are doing." As Bianca said that she thought to herself, "I hope that there really isn't too much adventure on this trip, I have had as much adventure as I can stand."

The hotel didn't want the patrons to take towels out of the hotel so they suggested that the Wards purchase some towels from a street vendor before they go on the boat trip. The Wards ventured out into the streets of Sorrento and found hundreds of shops all selling trinkets and Limoncello. Shop upon shop of silk scarves, wooden trinkets and free samples of Limoncello were every 10 feet.

One of the larger shops had beach items, inflatable rafts, swim suites, and beach towels. They purchased 4 towels; the CIA officers purchased 3 towels. The beach towels all proclaimed Sorrento on them somewhere, with the brightest colors Bianca had ever seen, pinks, magentas, oranges, bright blues and greens were all to be found on every towel.

Once the Wards acquired the towels they went back to the hotel to catch the shuttle van to the boat. The van was a tight fit inside for the eight people that ended up being in the vehicle. The route to the waterfront doubled back the way they had entered Sorrento to get down to Piano de Sorrento, a bay area where the boats used to transport people are located. The ride down to the waterfront was unbelievable. The twists and turns were insane.

The final road down to the harbor was basically a switch back that the van could not traverse without doing multiple "Y" turns to get around the corners. There were many scrape marks on the guardrails and all could see why. Luke thought to himself that he could not have driven a stick shift van down this road without plunging off the cliff, let alone make it back up, but here was a young woman navigating the road like it was the path through her garden.

There must have been at least 6 switchback turns before the van was deposited out to the bottom level of the harbor. Frank looked a little uneasy a couple of times, maybe because he realized that if the van plunged off the road, his gun or wits would not be able to protect the Wards. He was a formable foe to his enemies but he was helpless against gravity and sharp rocks.

After they all piled out of the van, they quickly followed the young women through a series of wooden planks, docks and finally a couple of boats tied side to side.

The captain quickly announced, "Take off your shoes and climb over this first boat to the second boat."

Everyone scrambled to undo their shoes or sandals. The Wards with sandals, the CIA men had shoes. At least the CIA guys were dressed more like tourists; they were wearing baggy shorts and loose fitting button front shirts with patterns, not Hawaiian shirts but not far from it. They must have had their guns in one of the two bags they brought on board, because they weren't apparent to Luke or Bianca.

Luke was wondering if the Captain was aware of the CIA men or if he just was a captain on another cruise with a family and some guys on vacation. Luke had left his gun in the hotel safe as Frank had suggested earlier. He said he wanted Luke to feel more like he was on vacation and that now there were three CIA officers, he should feel much safer.

The barefoot captain was about 6 foot tall, with long wavy sandy blond hair. His hands were scared with a bad case of rope burn across his palms. As he asked the dock hands to throw off the ropes, he pushed the throttle forward and quickly navigated the boat out into the harbor. He wasted no time getting the boat up to speed as he left the no wake zone and trimmed the boat at a land speed of about 30 miles per hour.

He then announced that there was a cooler full of beers, sodas, waters and sandwiches for all on board. They could enjoy the sandwiches whenever they felt like it, but suggested that they eat after everyone had toured the village of Capri and had swum a little. Everyone agreed.

About 45 minutes later the Island of Capri and its main port came into view. The Captain explained how he would drop everyone off, but that he could not stay tied down or dock, and would come back to pick them up in exactly one and a half hours.

Luke and the family wanted a picture with Capri in the background and Frank became the photographer of the moment. Jerry took point and said he would go and buy the tickets for the tram that goes up the hillside to the main shopping area of Capri. George also went ahead to scout out the area around the tram. The tram had only three passenger cars, each were set at a 60 degree angle that went up the hillside for the 5 minute trip.

The tram station was a little crazy. An automatic entry system let people gather in a holding area, and then as the patrons inserted their tickets they were allowed through Plexiglas doors, instead of a turnstile. As Luke and James entered through the doors they became the last two allowed. Frank, Jerry, George, Bianca and Elizabeth were locked on the other side of the doors and would have to wait the 10 minutes or so for the tram to go to the top, reload and come back down. Bianca tried to plead with the guard sitting by the doors, but he said, "No more." He pointed to a large red digital readout saying 120 people.

Bianca asked the guard in Italian if her husband and son could come out and go on the next tram, he said that if they left they would have to go to the end of the line, which had now grown to several hundred people, thanks to a cruise ship bringing the masses to shore recently. Luke assured Bianca it would be fine and that he would wait at the top of the tram station.

To say the tram was crowded was an understatement. No, the tram was packed, like a sardine can. Luke saw that James had a few elbows in his face and tried shifting his son between him and the doorway of the tram. It also was over 100 degrees on the tram and many people were apparently not big believers of using soap or deodorant. After the 4 ½ minute ride to the top of the hill, the doors opened and the external temperature of 92 degrees felt like air-conditioning, at least it would for the first minute.

Luke and James exited the car, half falling out of it more than walking out of it after the doors opened. They walked up the last 10 steps to the exit of the train platform. At the exit way they walked over to stand by the railing facing the port. It was a beautiful view of Capri.

After loading up people for the ride down, the tram exited the station. Soon the Ward family would be reunited. Luke had the family camera and started taking some pictures of the view, then of James with the view.

Ten minutes later and Bianca, Elizabeth and the CIA men were all back together. The CIA guys had a plan to again have two of the officers stay in close proximity but not travel with the group per say. Frank was staying with the family, in a body guard kind of way.

He also was great at taking photos of the family. They got a couple of excellent pictures with the hills and water behind them. At least there would be some choices available for a Christmas card this year. Last year there were only a couple to choose from where they were all in focus, smiling or weren't having a bad hair day.

Bianca loved the shops. It was like a great outdoor mall that had the finest clothing, shoes, jewelry and accessories. Bianca got a few pair of shoes. Luke was grateful that she stopped at three pair and equally as grateful that the store was sending them to their hotel the next day.

They looked at some jewelry, but Bianca was pretty well set in that department, and she would rather have other items of equal or greater value. They did however; find one little, out of the way, jewelry shop that caught Elizabeth's eye. In the 6 foot wide front window, she spotted some bracelets that were basically thin, colored rubbery tubes with a charm on them. The owner said he could cut it a little smaller to custom fit it for Elizabeth's wrist. She wanted a pink one. Luke said that was fine and asked if James had seen any-thing he liked. James picked a braided leather bracelet with a silver closure.

The shop owner then took out some tools, a flat piece of leather to use as a work surface and some glue. He pulled one end off of Elizabeth's bracelet, cut a piece off, put the bracelet back together and tested it on her. It was still a little big, so he repeated the process. This time it was perfect. He then took it off of her wrist, took it apart and put glue on the end that fit into the tube. He told them that it would be fine to wear by that night.

He then took James' bracelet and looked to see how much to take off by wrapping it around James' wrist and adding a little gap. He told James that the style was to wear them a little loose, but he could make it however he wanted it. James agreed it should be a little loose. The shop owner then unscrewed a little screw that held one end of the braided leather into the closure. He pulled out the leather and cut through it with what looked like a wire cutter. He made sure not to let it unravel, and then added some glue and rein-serted the braided leather into the open end of the closure. After waiting about 60 seconds he then put the screw back in. As with Elizabeth's bracelet, James' would also be good to wear that night.

He wrapped the bracelets up in little pull string bags and handed them to the kids. Luke paid for them; he then struck up a conversa-tion with the shop owner about getting back down to the port area. The man told him to follow the walkway they were currently on all the way down; it should only take about 20 minutes or so. The kids liked the idea, so they all started to walk.

As they left the more populated shopping area and headed to-wards the waterfront, Jerry casually bumped into Frank and they dis-cussed how Jerry would take point again with George covering the rear. A little further down, the walkway narrowed to be about 4 foot wide in areas, there were also many turns and places for someone to hide without easily being seen. The paving stone path in places re-minded the kids of the Yellow Brick Road in the "Wizard of Oz." They broke into a couple of choruses of "We are off to see the Wi-zard, the wonderful Wizard of Oz."

Some sections of the path were simply steps, dozens of steps, then a landing area, and then dozens more steps. Other areas were more like going down a steep ramp, with few steps. Being Italy or Europe in general, there were only a few places that had handrails, most of the time there was a wall on one side if one needed to regain one's balance.

As the port filled the group's view, the steps made way at times to small road crossings and more traditional wider walkways. At the bottom of the path it was about 12 feet wide and very ornate with each stone place just right. A couple of park benches, one on either side of the path opening framed it well.

The Wards made their way back to the concrete pier, where the boat was already waiting for them. The CIA men talked amongst themselves. Jerry said he didn't see any formal surveillance, George and Frank agreed. With the long walk completed, the whole group was looking forward to swimming soon.

Once they were all safely on board, Jerry pushed the boat away from the pier and the captain pulled away, into the no wake area of the harbor. When they were about 300 yards out the captain gunned it and the boat again seemed to rise a few feet out of the water and easily cut through the waves.

Everyone enjoyed the breeze which helped counter the 90 plus degree day. They had been motoring around the Island for about five minutes when they happened upon a small boat with a man and women that looked to be in their sixties. The man kept diving down into the water, would be gone for about thirty seconds, and then burst back above the water.

The Captain talked to them to see if something was wrong. It turned out that they had put their anchor overboard, but the rope had not been secured to the boat and it sunk to the bottom. The man had been swimming down to grab the rope, but the rope was shorter than the depth of the water so when he swam up he couldn't swim hard enough to budge the anchor.

The Captain then realized that this guy would give himself a heart attack if he didn't help him. So, the Captain threw them a long piece of rope. He told the lady to tie one end to the boat and give the other end to the man. The man swam down and tied the new rope to the anchor. The old man then climbed back into the boat and pulled the anchor in.

He was going to return the rope when the Captain told them to keep it, he had more. The Captain couldn't believe that they would go out with only a 10 foot length of rope on board. "That is how people get themselves killed," he said out loud, to no one in particular.

Luke thought to himself, "I hope that is the closest we get to someone getting killed today."

The sun was shining bright, not a cloud in the sky. There were a few seagulls following the boat, but they broke off after about 5 minutes when they realized there was no food for them. Elizabeth and Bianca already were out on the deck of the boat in only their swimsuits to soak up the sun. James also ended up taking off his shirt; he could burn quickly so Bianca put some sunscreen SPF70 all over his body and face.

Luke tended to burn if he didn't have a good base tan. He had been working on his tan earlier in the summer, but somehow only his face, arms and legs seemed to be tan, or in other words, the only areas exposed while playing golf. So Luke kept his shirt on, but unbuttoned it all the way.

Everyone was once again shoeless, so Luke was worried that he might get sunburn on his feet, he had a bad experience in the past. On his honeymoon with Bianca they had gone to Hawaii and were walking along the beach for about an hour or so. It was the first day of their honeymoon so they made sure to put sunscreen everywhere, they still had a couple of weeks left.

Apparently, walking along the beach is fine as long as you don't walk partially in the water and let you feet sink into the wet moving sand of the tide. This moving sand had the same effect as sandblasting does on brick buildings and it stripped the layer of sunscreen off of Luke's feet. For the next couple of days Luke could not wear shoes and even two days later he almost passed out when they went snorkeling and he had to put swim fins on.

The Island of Capri was rocky. The boat cruised for about 10 minutes when they saw a large cave opening. The Captain told them that this was the White Grotto. At first glance it didn't look very white. The Captain said wait, we need to pull in a little closer. As the boat pulled in further, when everyone looked up, the cave ceiling was almost glowing white. The roof of the cave had stalagmites and everything looked like it was coated with a whitewash, really calcium deposits. The light from outside reflects up, off of the water and gives it a glowing effect because the cave would be dark otherwise.

The Captain backed out and slowly pulled the boat over about 100 meters from the mouth of the cave. He said that we could swim over to a rock ledge and that there was a set of stairs carved out of the rock that led to a place high up in the cave. The CIA men had noticed the stairs before he mentioned them. The group all wanted to swim and the cave made it a great adventure. Jerry stayed on the boat to watch it and the group. The rest, including the Captain jumped in the water and started to swim towards the ledge.

When the group got to the ledge, the waves were about 1 ½ to 2 feet high. When a wave came in, the Captain put his hands up on the ledge and pulled himself up. He then helped everyone else up expect for Frank and George, they had both experienced much harder landing areas under much harder conditions. They all started up the stairs.

The Italians had erected a metal hand rail on the sea side of the stairs. Some sections of railing were missing, as were parts of the stone steps. There were a few concrete patches on some steps where the rock had totally fallen away. This was not Disney World and if one fell, they would be hurt or killed on the jagged rocks below.

They all climbed about 70 feet above the sea. The stairs ended at an opening into the mountain side where a very old rusty gate was swung open. This gate no longer looked functional and seemed a strange place for a gate to start with. After slowly walking through 20 feet of total darkness, only being able to feel ones way along the rock wall, they emerged into the now relative brightness of the inside of the cave above the water. Again there was a metal railing from 40 years ago or more stopping someone from falling off the edge of the ledge they were on.

James commented on how it looked like a diving platform over the water. The Captain said that his original boss, when he became a captain, brought all the new captains out to this cave and made them all jump in. George looked at the height and said, "This is pretty high to jump from if someone isn't shooting at you." The captain laughed and admitted that he and the group climbed down to where it was about 50 feet or so, still an impressive jump. He also admitted that a great amount of beer was consumed by all before the jump.

Luke looked behind them and noticed that the cave continued for as far back as he could see into it before the light turned to darkness. The Captain said that the cave went on for a long way and that some say it was used during WWII to move men and supplies. Luke now knew why there was an old rusted gate on the cave entrance.

The group headed back down the steps. It was a little harder going down the steep steps than it was coming up. There were many sharp small rocks on the stone steps that bit into their feet. Once everyone was down, they jumped into the water one by one. The Captain said to follow him towards the large cave opening. Just before the large opening, they saw a smaller opening, only about 3 feet above the waterline.

The Captain warned them to watch their heads. It was pretty big inside, big enough for all of them. As they entered the cave, they were amazed at how the light reflected up off of the water and made the whole cave look like it was glowing white. They stayed there marveling at the ceiling and walls of the cave for about 5 minutes or so, and then it was time to swim back towards the boat. There was one more cave he wanted to show them.

The Captain led the group towards the rocky cliffs to the left of the White Grotto. He said, "There is a secret cave here, and you need to go underwater to get into it. The rocks on the ceiling are very sharp and there isn't very much head space on the other side. I will guide you, but slowly come above the surface of the water only as far as your mouth."

They took turns and swam under the sharp rocks. This cave was much dimmer, but glowed a blue green that was amazing. A sight that none in this group, besides the Captain had seen before. Luke was worried about the kids hitting their heads on the ceiling of the cave, but they were fine. Luke did put his hand on the ceiling a couple of times when a wave carried into the cave and started to raise them all towards the sharp rocks, he had small cuts on his hands afterwards.

They went back to the boat and took turns climbing on the rear boat deck to spray down with some fresh water, removing the salt water from their skin and suits. The Captain then suggested eating the lunch of simple Italian sandwiches of Mozzarella cheese and tomatoes on hard rolls. The sandwiches tasted great after all of the swimming the group had done.

The adults drank beers and the kids had Cokes. Sometimes the simplest things in life are the best. Right then Luke and Bianca looked at each other and smiled. What a great family experience, floating on the water, exploring caves, eating simple food and drinking a cold beer, life didn't get much better than that.

After lunch the boat started across the water again. They paralleled the coastline about 200 yards out for most of the time. The views of the Island from the sea were wonderful. They were now on the opposite side of the Island from the Marina where they had started.

The boat went through an opening in a stone outcrop. Elizabeth was right in the bow of the boat and she reached her arms up as if she could touch the rocks all around them.

The homes on the coast were massive; it was a very rich area. There were gigantic yachts anchored off shore. One yacht was over 250 feet long; its lifeboats were bigger than the boat the group was on. It had a helicopter on a front deck, and what looked like a basketball court in the rear deck area.

After 15 minutes the boat slowed again. It pulled into a little inlet area. As the boat got closer to the rocky cliffs, the group saw an opening. The Captain announced that this was the Green Grotto; you must all get off here and swim through the grotto to the other side. They all jumped in the water and within seconds the Captain had backed out and started to navigate around the rocky coast.

Once the group started swimming into the Green Grotto, they could see that there was indeed an opening in the back. As they swam through the 40 foot high Green Grotto they saw how the ceiling and walls were glowing green, but only if you looked from the right direction with the sun to your back.

On the other side, there were many other people swimming. The group swam around the area and discovered a couple of other caves. One was inhabited by thousands of sea gulls and the waste they left behind, this was not one of their favorite caves for obvious, smelly reasons.

Twenty more minutes of swimming and they all headed back to the boat. They rinsed off again and settled in for another boat ride, that was their last scheduled swim. If they could make it in time, they would go through the famed Blue Grotto, but the Captain doubted they would make it. The boat ride was fantastic, the wind whipping everyone's hair; they were all dry in a minute or two.

The Blue Grotto was around the next set of rocks, but immediately one could see that it was closed. There were normally small boats outside the Blue Grotto that took groups through it, but there were none there now. The water level was too high, and the boats could not fit under the mouth of the caves.

The Captain told everyone that they had already swam through better grottos and seen more exciting sites. He went on to tell them that it takes over an hour to go through the process of changing

boats, waiting your turn and that you needed to purchase tickets earlier if you wanted to go. Obviously they hadn't purchased tickets;
they didn't know that they needed to so they couldn't have gone
even if it was open.

Minutes later the Capri Marina was in site. The Captain noted
that a storm was coming in quick and that they needed to head towards Sorrento. The skies turned dark. He said that it didn't look
like we would make it back without a little rain, which would be the
first on the Wards' trip to Italy. He radioed back to the docks and
they confirmed that a big storm was heading their way. The water
became choppy, the winds picked up. Now the boat was going up
and down violently.

The Captain pointed out towards the direction they were headed
and they all saw the rain coming towards them. The Captain got
everyone off of the front sunning deck. He unfurled the rain tarp that
would cover the back part of the boat, including the captain's wheel,
so most wouldn't get too wet.

Jerry helped him secure the snaps on the rain cover and just in
time. They got hit with torrential rains and winds. After only a few
minutes, the Captain had to slow the boat almost to a stop; the rain
was so heavy, he couldn't see out of the clear plastic windshield of
the rain cover any longer.

The beautiful day had quickly turned into a dark, rainy day.
Everyone on the boat really was getting tossed around like rag dolls.
Elizabeth and Bianca were scared. Every once in a while the Captain
would stick his head out from under the tarp to verify that they weren't headed into the rocks. He kept the boat going at little more
than an idle, to maintain their heading. Also, he tried to steer into the
waves, one wanted to hit waves head on as opposed to getting hit
from the side of the boat.

Over the pounding rain Luke thought he heard a noise, almost
like another boat. He wasn't the only one that heard the noise. It
was a boat and it was coming at them fast. Frank told Jerry to get the
family below deck in a hurry and to bring up his duffle bag. The
family hurriedly got into the cabin of the boat. It was close quarters,
but there were plenty of seats for all of them. The heat down there
was pretty high w/high humidity now that the boat wasn't really
cruising fast enough to get the air moving through the cabin.

About 30 seconds after they sat down, the Wards felt the boat
lurch out of the water. The Captain had turned the boat away from

the rocky shore line, out towards the open sea. The waves were crashing into the hull of the boat and the Ward family could hardly hang on and stay seated. It was much harder being down below and not being able to anticipate a sharp turn or being able to see the large waves they were crashing into.

Topside, Frank, George and Jerry got out their guns as well as four lightweight Kevlar vests, one for each of them and the Captain. The rain was not letting up much and the men had difficulty seeing where they were going, but could see the boat behind them was gaining on them. Unmistakable, even in the rain, were the muzzle flashes from two guns aboard the other boat. Frank yelled down to the Wards, "Get on the floor now!" To emphasize this, a bullet splintered through the top of the door frame to the cabin.

Bianca grabbed her children and pushed them to the floor of the boat. The floor area was relatively safe compared to anywhere else on the boat at this time. The sound of guns being fired could now clearly be heard by the Wards. They were hearing the return fire from their boat. The wind and rain made it almost impossible to hear the shots being fired at them, just little pops and cracks, like the cereal.

Frank told George and Jerry to fire 5 shots each at where the captain of the other boat would be. There also had to be a gunman very close on that side, or the gunman was driving the boat. All three concentrated their fire on the right side of the boat. After the 3-4 seconds it took for each of them to unload their 5 shots, the boat behind them lurched a little, then regained its course towards them.

On the left side of the chase boat the shooter thought that the lack of fire meant they were reloading and started to fire on Frank and the other men. One shot actually hit George, whirling him around and down to the floor. The shooter stopped for a second as he took in the sight of George going down, that was one second too much; as Frank and Jerry each took 3 more shots at the new target and down he went, gun flailing over the side of the boat and into the water.

Jerry checked on George who had the wind knocked out of him, but was not seriously injured. George now got back up. Frank yelled to see if George was O.K., and he was. Frank told Jerry to aim the rest of his shots at the driver's side of the boat the same time that Frank fired. Frank told George to hold his fire until one of the chase boat guys tried to return fire. Frank and Jerry would then reload and also start firing at the boat, during which time George would reload.

The chase boat was getting closer, but the driver still had his eyes above the steering wheel to see their boat and that was what Frank wanted to take advantage of. Frank called out, "Now." They fired their guns towards the driver, then George waited a few seconds before seeing the muzzle flashes and then he unloaded his weapon back at the shooter.

After the last volley the chase boat veered off away from the Ward's boat. The chase boat was still going very fast it just wasn't headed in their direction now; in fact it was headed almost directly towards the rocky shoreline. If it didn't turn away within the next 30-40 seconds it would surely crash.

The rain let up almost as quickly as it had started and now they could all see clearly. The Captain turned the boat towards the mainland port. Frank told the Ward's it was safe to come topside now. James and Elizabeth leapt up the stairs with Luke and Bianca right on their heels. Just as the group cleared the cabin the chase boat ran straight toward a rocky outcropping.

Right before it hit, a big wave came in and launched the whole boat up onto the rocks. The bottom of the high speed boat was torn to shreds on the rocks, severing the main fuel lines to the dual inboard motors. They were still running full bore when the whole boat went up in a big explosion, flames leapt over 20 feet into the air, then pitch black smoke came from the wreckage that now was a hull and two motors.

Luke said out loud, "How did they know we were going to be on this boat, especially on the return trip?"

Frank said, "I was just wondering that myself. I noticed their boat moored in the marina when we were dropped off on Capri, no one was on it at that time. My guess is it was some local's boat from Capri. Silvano is from Sorrento, so I am sure he has some solid connections here, but I know we weren't followed out to the Island or while we were going around it. They knew where we were going to be and what type of boat."

The next 10 minutes were eerily quiet. The rain had all but stopped, the Sun pushed its way through the clouds and big patches of blue sky were now open above the boat. Frank looked at his weapon to make sure that it wasn't too wet, he would clean it later. He verified that the last clip was full, but removed the ammunition from the chamber and put the safety on. He then refilled the empty clip with ammunition from a box in the duffel bag.

Jerry helped George take his Kevlar vest off. George had a black and blue mark starting to form where the vest had stopped the bullet, but had not absorbed all of the force of the incoming bullet. George's ribs would be a little tender, but fine. Jerry and George also checked their weapons and filled their clips. The ex-military men knew the best time to prepare for a gun battle was before the battle begun.

As the group's boat came in to dock, a couple of police and fire boats were leaving. The dock men said that they heard the explosion. The remains of the boat were still smoking pretty well at this time. Frank knew he would need to explain this to his superiors and the locals, but he would not do it at this time. He wanted to see the Wards safely back to their hotel. Frank also didn't know if the authorities would find the bodies or if the explosion had made them fish food.

Frank didn't plan on being caught without his gun at the ready so when they were disembarking, he kept his gun wrapped in a towel and carried it with him on the walk back to the waiting vehicles. The trip back up the cliff side was just as twisted as on the way down, but for some reason going up wasn't as scary.

As they got up about 100 feet, James pointed out the window and said, "Look the fire boat is there and they put out the fire, it isn't smoking anymore."

The last few wafts of smoke in the air above the boat were white instead of black, a sign that the boat and fuel were no longer burning, just throwing off some steam from the sea water that was being pumped from the fire boat.

The rocks were very wet and slippery at this time from the storm and the waves were still crashing into the coast by the boat. Police would need to get up there and look around soon, before the wrecker boat came to haul away what was left of the burned out hull and its motors.

The cars were silent going back to the hotel. One of the family's best days in Italy was ruined by the attack. James pointed out, "We are all a little tired, but I think tonight we should go out to dinner and see more of Sorrento, before leaving." At first Luke thought about it, then agreed that a night out would be great.

The storm had passed and most likely the bad guys now lie on the bottom of the sea. Frank on the other hand was worried, after all, this was the second hit squad sent for the Wards while they were in Sorrento, even though they still didn't know about the first one at their original hotel. At the same time, Frank realized that a night out on the town would flush out any more of these guys, if there were still some in town.

More importantly, Frank needed to find the inside person that was leaking their travel itinerary.

When they all got back to the hotel, they agreed to take showers and go out to eat around 9pm. That would give everyone a little down time before going out into the streets of Sorrento. There was a festival in town tonight and the streets would be shut down to vehicular traffic and thousands would be walking around.

Chapter 14   Music Festival

The night was perfect, a slight sea breeze, about 78 degrees, clear skies with millions of stars, and lots of people having a great time. The Wards, Frank, Jerry and George all made their way to the beautiful La Favorita O'Parrucchiano restaurant, who claim to have invented cannelloni. They have a giant, lush garden with many lemon and orange trees.

Frank requested a table for 5; he would eat with the Wards tonight. Jerry and George would be eating at a separate table. Both of the tables were in the back garden. Frank requested a corner location. A minute or so later Jerry and George were shown a table in the back area and asked for the corner opposite the Wards. Frank sat facing the main entrance, but still had a great overall view of the kitchen and other dining areas to his right and left respectfully. Jerry and George slightly rotated the table to have a view of the garden, kitchen, bar, and main entrance.

The gardens were really very lush, like being in the middle of a jungle. The branches of the lemon and orange trees actually were growing into the dining area, which was built 3 feet about ground level. It had a greenhouse type roof and partial walls about railing height surrounding the dining area.

The wait staff descended on the table quickly with bread, olive oil, and grated parmesan cheese. They asked which type of water they wanted, i.e. with gas or still. The kids didn't like carbonated water unless there was a flavor and tons of sugar, so they asked for still as did Frank. Luke and Bianca had water w/gas. Luke also requested a wine list. The waiter came back with the wine list and the menus; he was now the fourth person helping them since they had entered the restaurant. Luke picked a light Blanc de Blanc wine to start with.

Yet, a fifth person returned with the bottle of wine. He verified it was the correct vineyard, style and vintage with Luke, then opened it, presented the cork, and poured a little into Luke's glass. Luke examined the cork for any tell tale signs that it wasn't properly stored or leaked, none were found.

Luke swirled the liquid in the wine glass and held it up to check its color, it was very clear as it should be. He then brought the glass to his nose and inhaled. Happy with the bouquet, he took a small sip, simultaneously holding the liquid in his mouth and sucking air past it, almost like slurping a soup. This ran a lot of air past the wine in his mouth and helped involve his sense of smell with the sensation from his taste buds on his tongue. This all took about 10 seconds. Luke then told the wine server, "Very good."

The server filled Bianca's glass, tried to fill Frank's glass, he said no, he was holding out for the red with dinner. The server then asked if the children wanted some.

James stated, "No, we are not old enough."

Elizabeth smiled, "Yes please."

Luke said, "Give them both just a taste."

The server poured just a little in each of the kids' glasses. James was still protesting, when Bianca said, "Don't worry, this is OK in Italy, it is only a taste." The server finished by filling Luke's glass as well.

Luke was about to propose a toast when James picked up his glass and slammed the ounce of wine straight back, like a shot of whiskey. Luke and Bianca were speechless until the wine server started to gently laugh, then Luke and Bianca started to laugh, then the bread and water servers began to laugh. The wine server asked if he should give the boy some more wine.

Luke still laughing waved him away and said, "No I think he has had enough for now."

After the wine server had left you could hear laughter from the front of the restaurant where the server was now sharing what had happened in the garden.

James didn't know why everyone was laughing at him; he was starting to get upset.

Luke said, "James, one is supposed to sip their wine and make it last, it isn't supposed to be gulped. People laughed because you threw it back the same way people drink hard liquor, like whiskey. Those types of drinks have so much alcohol in them that it burns; wine like this is sweeter and can be drunk slowly to appreciate the nuances of all the smells and flavors."

"They still shouldn't have laughed at me. I told you I didn't want the wine, so I thought I would get rid of it as fast as possible. I really didn't like it anyway."

Bianca tapped her son on the hand and said, "James, that is O.K., you are right, children aren't supposed to drink alcohol, but a little wine with a meal and your family is very traditional in Italy. Back home, no kids are allowed to drink at all."

Luke had ordered some anti-pasta for the table; some salamis, cheeses, olives and breads. The kids were famished and dug in, making a meal out of it. The adults at the table had a couple of each offering and the platter was emptied.

A couple of glasses of wine later and they were ready for some red. Luke decided on a Chianti Classico Reserve that the wine server had suggested. This time Frank had a glass, as did Luke and Bianca.

Bianca liked the wine, "This is great Luke, but it is also my last glass, we need to get up early tomorrow."

Frank chimed in, "This is it for me as well, and so it looks like the last glass in the bottle will be yours Luke."

Luke was alright with that, he finally was relaxing; the wine was helping with that. Even as he thought that, he was reminded of the dangers he and his family had faced so far on this vacation, or even just earlier that day.

One thing was for sure, getting shot at now heightened his senses of his surroundings. When they were on the floor of the boat, he had already eyed up a knife on the counter that was used for the sandwiches earlier. If they would have been boarded, he would have taken one of the bad guys down.

The meals arrived and surprise, surprise the kids weren't all that hungry. Well, after about 4 pieces of bread each, not to mention the cheeses and meats, it really was no surprise. As the main meal came the small talk at the table turned to the business at hand.

James asked, "Frank, who knew we were going to be on "that" boat to Capri today?"

"I have been thinking about it today. I called it in through our office in Rome to make the arrangements.

Certain captains are agents of the CIA, they help us when they can. People tend to talk in front of captains and we need that intelligence, so the CIA has some on retainer at all tourist ports. The Captain we had today has provided us with much information over the years and in fact has helped us with Silvano's case with some counterfeiting on Capri at the little shops off of the main drag.

Counterfeit purses that go for 20-40 Euros are good but selling them for 200 Euros is even better. There are a lot of people with cash in their pocket and shop keepers willing to take it. Capri is an island; everything comes and goes by boat. Normally, they would not use a captain or boat like ours to transport the contraband, they would use a larger boat made for that purpose, but sometimes, in high season, they need to use other boats to get product out to the Island."

Luke said, "James asked a good question, who is telling Silvano's men where we are, must it be someone in the CIA?"

"I was getting to that. Originally, I thought it was simply Silvano's men, or the Italian police or someone inside the CIA. But, this last attack leads me to believe it is someone from inside the CIA. I specifically told Carol our Admin not to tell the Italian authorities where we were going or what we were doing today. In fact, I told her to tell them that we were staying low at the hotel today if they had contacted our main office."

Luke asked, "Do you trust this Carol?"

"Well, I have known her for 2 plus years as I have everyone in our office. It could be someone like her, but I am leaning towards someone higher up, that could have more of a motive than a simple payoff."

Bianca asked, "Who do you think it is?"

"I would rather not say at this time, but I am planning a way to test my theory. Let's agree to keep this conversation private, don't mention it to Jerry or George."

Elizabeth said, "Oh, do you think one of them is the mole?"

"I don't think so because we were being fired on pretty hard, but you never know with bad guys, there really is no honor among thieves, it could be Jerry or George, Silvano's guys could have been trying to kill two birds with one stone or bullet as it were.

But, I don't think it is them and I don't want you worrying about them when they are here to protect you. All the same, don't mention anything to them. They are smart and should be wondering the same thing, maybe even wondering about me."

James surprised, "You, how could they think about you? You have saved us a few times."

"Yes, but like I just was explaining, I also have special knowledge about where we are going. But, I doubt they suspect me, as I really don't suspect them."

Luke said, "Then who?"

Frank said almost under his breath, "We will see if my suspicions are right in the next couple of days."

Desert came and the kids magically had more room than they did for their pasta dishes. Even Bianca and Luke enjoyed the tiramisu. The restaurant offered some homemade Limoncello on the house as an after diner drink. It tasted sweet, tart and alcoholic all in one gulp.

Sorrento was known for the specialty liqueur, every shop had Limoncello or a derivative of it for sale in the area. Some had fancy bottles others had it mixed with chocolate, cream, orange and etc.

Luke asked Bianca what she thought of it.

"I think that the homemade Limoncello from the Francesca's restaurant at home was better than this. Funny, how the hostess told us that their Limoncello was better than what we would find in Italy, but she was right."

By the time the Ward's had finished diner, a few of the main streets in Sorrento were closed for the festival. There were street performers on every block. In Italy, one type of common street performer was the statue that only moved once in a while, usually to scare kids and to take a picture for a tip.

There was a lady that was playing water filled crystal glasses. She had some talent, the music was beautiful and Elizabeth asked and received money from her Mother to put in the donation glass. There were also a couple of jugglers.

But, what got the kids attention were a few guys that had a night toy that shot a plastic helicopter, with bright LEDs on it, about 40 feet in the air and let it slowly come straight down. The person would use a rubber band attached to a plastic stick, hook the helicopter toy, stretch it out and release it straight up in the air, 10 seconds later he would catch it and do it again.

The kids had to each have one. Luke and Bianca gave in and the negotiating began with the salesman. He started at 6 Euros each.

Bianca turned toward the kids and said loudly, "These are too much, we will have to get something else."

"For the pretty lady, 5 Euros each."

"No, still too much...how about 2?"

"The lady is funny too, how about 8 for 2."

"Eight toys for 2 Euros?" She was playing with the boy.

"No, you see the quality, I tell you what, for you 3 Euros each, that is my cost."

"2 Euros or we are going to get some gelato instead."

"OK, lady you drive a tough bargain, 2 Euros each."

The kids were ecstatic. The boy showed the kids how to do it and they played for a while, which helped advertise. He must have sold another 10 in 5 minutes, most of them for 4 Euros each. The kids played with them for the next 10 minutes with a few close calls of getting the helicopter stuck in a balcony or awning.

Finally, Luke told James and Elizabeth, "We are getting closer to the town square and there are more people here, please put them away, you can play with them later on the way back to the hotel."

The town square was light up with strings of colored lights. On one side of the square there were horse drawn carriages that the kids begged to go on. Luke said no, that the streets were bad enough in a car, they all laughed. There was also a band playing. The air was filled with festive music, the smell of food and happy people every-where one looked.

There were dozens of portable cart stands selling this and that. Most had some Limoncello or the other item this area was known for, intricate carved wood. The wood pieces intrigued Luke and Bi-anca. They were looking for some small gifts to take to Bianca's relatives that they would see the next day.

The wood items were incredible. They were basically created like a jigsaw puzzle, with different kinds of wood and stain put to-gether to make pictures. They had passed a shop full of these on their way to dinner and would make a stop there on the way back to their hotel if it was still open.

Off to one corner of the square was a giant glowing ice cream cone, a popular way to advertize gelato shops in Italy. Elizabeth and James went running to it and each of them gave it a big hug. Of course, Bianca had to have another picture of them hugging the giant 6 foot tall ice cream cone, one of many so far on this trip.

Frank said to Elizabeth, "I thought you said you were full back at the restaurant." He said this sternly but was holding back a chuckle.

"Frank, I was full back there, but now I have enough room for a gelato, chocolate gelato."

James chimed in, "I like the chocolate chip or cookies and crème gelato."

Bianca said, "Alright, a small one."

The kids each had a small cup of gelato, about the equivalent to one small scoop of ice cream from 31 Flavors back home. They had to eat them using strange looking plastic spoons that had a straight edge and looked like a mini shovel. Again, the silence was worth the price of the gelato for the adults. Or relative silence, the band was still playing and there were hundreds of people walking around.

Frank, Jerry and George were surveilling the area intently. Crowds like these were the hardest and easiest to spot a tail. Hardest from the perspective that there were literally hundreds of people in a small area, but also easy because the tails couldn't fall too far behind or they would risk losing their mark. Once the group cuts down a side street or alley, if there was a tail, then it would be easy to spot using the three team members.

Jerry and George were not walking close to the Ward group, so a tail should not have picked them out, but one couldn't be too sure. It also could be hard for the CIA officers to spot a surveillance team, depending on who was doing the tail and how many operatives they had.

It was more difficult to spot multiple teams; where one team could anticipate the direction the Wards were traveling and another team could be waiting in the expected area. That would give the surveillance team time to start a negotiation with a shop keeper or be standing in line for a gelato or something else that would allow them to blend in seamlessly with the crowds.

One thing that had changed in recent years is with the growing use of cell phones, one could actually use the cell phone to communicate to other operatives without drawing attention to themselves. With the older style ear pieces and microphones in the shirt cuff, it would appear that they were talking to themselves, or to their thumb.

The Wards decided it was time to do a little shopping on the way back to the hotel. They took one of the first streets off of the square by the gelato stand. It ran parallel to the main street they walked to the square on, but now they headed away from the square. There was a little shop or stand every few feet down the narrow street. The street was so narrow, there was hardly room to walk.

Some of the shops had very colorful items; silk scarves, silk ties and beach bags made of woven burlap with silk ribbon embellishments in vivid colors. There also was a common lemon theme at most stands. Lemon shaped bottle openers, refrigerator magnets, coasters, pens, pencils, lights, salt and pepper shakers, shot glasses, cups, mugs, and many more strange items that really were not related to lemons or their shape or color, but were on display all the same.

The women liked the silk scarves and painted wooden hand fans. Elizabeth found a scarf and fan that had the same tone of purple in them and had to have them. Luke told each of the kids they could have up to 20 Euros worth of souvenirs.

Elizabeth also happened across some woven silk bracelets. She found one with the purple in it and she was finished shopping for the night. James didn't see anything that excited him. Luke told him he could save the credit until he found something he liked; he didn't have to spend it that night.

Bianca also found a few scarves she liked and some silver costume jewelry that was fun, a couple of necklaces and bracelets. Luke wasn't really tempted by any items until they came across a wine store. Luke had a particular fondness for Italian red wines.

Luke looked around the wine store, quickly finding a few of his favorites. To his dismay the pricing here was at least 20% more than in the States. It didn't make sense for him to purchase the wine here for more, and then worry about packing it and it breaking on the way home.

James could not find anything that really interested him, even after they went several blocks and went through about 30 stands or shops. He wasn't going to give up, he wanted his own souvenir.

About 30 feet before the road towards their hotel, the group happened upon multiple Limoncello factories. The store fronts were only about 15 feet wide, but deep. The front part of the shops had hundreds of bottles of Limoncello and all of its derivations, in many different shapes and sized bottles. The rear part of the building was where they were manufacturing and bottling the Limoncello.

The first shop had a man out front asking people to come in and sample some of their specialties. The Wards went in and tried regular Limoncello, crème Limoncello, and orange-banana crème Limoncello. They were all very rich and overly sweet, as was true of most liqueurs. The second shop had the same flavors in addition to having a chocolate Limoncello. Even though Luke loved chocolate, he thought that it was a strange combination and he was correct; after one sip, he knew he didn't like it.

Bianca reminded Luke that they needed to get some gifts for her relatives they were going to visit the next day. Luke was rounding the corner to towards their hotel, when he noticed that the wood shop was still open. It was nearly 10 pm and he wasn't sure how much longer the shop would be open.

They all entered the shop and discovered that it was about 20 degrees hotter in there than it was outside. Even with the unbearably warm climate, the Wards looked though the shop, because they had never seen such intricately made woodworks. There were small pieces of furniture, mainly small tables and trays with stands, but what caught Bianca's eye were the beautiful jewelry boxes and the pictures made of different wood types and colors. Luke liked the hand carved chess sets and boards.

James found a few small boxes that appeared to simply have a lid with a design that he liked. When James opened the box, it had a blue velvet lining. He also noticed that there was another picture inlaid, inside the lid, which was also very cool looking. When he picked the box up that he liked, it seemed to rattle a little when he moved it. He looked again at the hinged top, to make sure nothing was loose. He searched inside the velvet lined compartment and checked to see if something was loose inside, but there wasn't.

The owner of the shop came over and said, "You have found a secret box."

James didn't know what to say to that, he didn't understand, after all, he simply found the box on the shelf with the other boxes. This one happened to have an inlaid pattern on the lid that he found very interesting.

"What do you mean secret box?"

James' question caught everyone else's attention now. The shop keeper reached out for the box and James handed it to him.

"I am the owner of this factory; it has been in our family for about 100 years. My father, his father and his father before him all learned the art of inlaid wood working here, in the building behind this shop.

The intricate shapes and the processes to create these useful pieces of art originated with the Benedictine monks over a thousand years ago.

At first, they used many different types of woods that had different grains and colors to make pictures, not unlike mosaic tiles. As the tools of the trade got better through time, more and more elaborate or fine work could be cut from the woods, until today you see what a master can do." He said this as he held up the box that James had picked off the shelf.

The pattern on the box lid was so intricate, with no gaps and smooth to the touch that it looked like it was painted on. This was not a flowery pattern, although there were some small flowers, but instead had a manlier look with a vine border around a picture of a village on a cliff side off of the water, Sorrento.

I made this box and find it particularly beautiful, as I do most of the items I make, but this is a special box, my father made me a box very similar to this one for my 13th birthday, it has a secret compartment."

Elizabeth and James simultaneously said, "Cool."

"I will only reveal how to open it to the owner of the box."

Elizabeth said, "Hey, no fair, I want to know the secret."

"And that is why they are called secrets."

Everyone laughed except Elizabeth.

Luke liked the story, but he was starting to wonder how much this box, made by the master woodworker was going to cost. He had looked at the price tags on some of the items and they were not inexpensive.

James said, "Dad, can I get the box? This is what I want to remember our trip here. Please!"

Luke looked at the box and the price was 150 Euros, about $200 US, this was no trinket or regular souvenir. He had to admit it was very beautiful and almost found it unbelievable that the picture was made from intricate inlaid pieces of wood instead of being painted on. Luke bent to James' continued pleas for the box.

"OK you can get the box, but we need to get some other presents for your Mother's relatives and maybe we can get a better price on them." He said the last part more for the shop keeper's benefit.

In Italy, the pricing of everything in a tourist area was negotiable. Luke figured if the old man realized they were spending some money there, he would give them better deals on the gifts they wanted to purchase.

About 10 minutes later the Wards had looked through the store and decided that they would purchase multiple inlaid wood pictures. Some depicted Sorrento and some depicted Pompeii with Mount Vesuvius in the background. Each picture was unique, a true work of art. Bianca asked the shop keeper how much for 5 of them.

The man pointed to the price and said, "35 Euros each."

Bianca spoke to him in Italian and asked for a better price, especially considering they were getting the box. The shop keeper shook his head up and down, smiled, and said, "Si, for you, 220 Euros for all." Luke wasn't sure what Bianca had said to the man in Italian, but it worked. Luke paid the man.

James said, "Ok, now you need to show me how to get at the secret compartment."

The shopkeeper shook his head up and down again and waved his hand for James to come around the corner of the counter. James looked very intently at what the old man was showing him. The man had held the box below the counter so that no one but James and he could see it.

He opened the lid and turned the box upside down. There were some short stubby knobs that formed 4 feet for the box. The old man showed James how he could twist one of the legs about ½ turn and then the side of the box was able to slide off toward the back. Inside the box was a compartment that held a small square of inlaid wood design that had two patterns, a different one on either side.

The wood was only about one inch square and about ¼ inch thick, but it tapered on the edges to have an almost pillow shape to it. One side had a bird on it; the other side had the Sun.

The old man told James, "This is a good luck charm. When you think that you need some good luck you open the secret panel and rub the wood as you wish for what you want. The wood charm is fragile so you only get so many wishes, use them wisely."

The man then put the good luck piece back into the secret compartment and closed up the box, sliding the end piece back in place, turning the leg at the bottom and closing the lid. James really felt like a secret agent now, he had a special secret box.

The old man took care to wrap each of the inlaid pictures so that they wouldn't be scratched on the trip. He also had a cardboard box with bubble wrap in it for James' box. The Wards said their good-byes and were about to leave when Frank's phone rang.

While the Wards were in the shop, Jerry and George had gone a few doors down to an outdoor bar area and ordered a couple of Peroni beers. They took a couple of swallows, but were not sure how long the Wards would be in the shop. They noticed Frank stayed close to the front of the shop to watch for any surveillance. He saw Jerry and George, but didn't acknowledge them.

Jerry had purchased a few silk scarves earlier and carried the bag containing them to help him blend in with the tourists.

In a way, Jerry was a tourist; he was from the States and had a wife, Michelle, and 2 children Emily, 6 and Susan, 4. They all had made the trek to Italy when he joined the CIA last year. Michelle was worried about Emily going to a foreign school. Jerry reminded her that the American Overseas School of Rome was great. Emily would learn Italian and English right from the start, and she would be exposed to multiple cultures from an early age. In fact, she was currently able to read, write and speak fluent Italian to her age level.

Jerry's cover had him working at the American Embassy in Rome as a Diplomatic Security Counselor for American corporations working in Italy. The department was created in the 1960s to help American companies operate and or perform services in Italy by providing guidance and assistance with security matters, both physical and intellectual property.

Officially working for the US government as a diplomat offered some insulation in case of a run in with local or national police. Diplomats are afforded the protection of Diplomatic Immunity for most crimes and can't be jailed for spying. Everyone in the intelligence gathering business knows that most all diplomats work for one of that country's secret organizations. This is true for all diplomats around the world, working for every country.

The CIA created a cover story for Jerry. His real last name was Shearer, not Banks. He was listed as a former Navy Electronics Technician First Class Petty Officer, instead of a Navy SEAL. He had a California Drivers license in Jerald Banks name. There were electronic copies of his marriage certificate as well as his children's birth certificates.

Michelle were a little worried about what the kids would think when they found out their real last names were Shearer, but that was in the future. He was honored to be serving his country in this way.

Jerry and George, at their location in the open air bar, could see the entire street running past the inlaid wood shop. Being stationary was a great way to see others moving. Staying stationary but not looking like you are just loitering is a huge part of spy craft. 99.99% of surveilling turned up nothing and it was easy to overlook things that looked, well ordinary. Jerry was thinking that to himself when he saw something that caught his eye. It was a little Italian boy about 10 years old.

There was nothing strange in and of its self with the boy; it was more that Jerry had recognized he had been walking with a different couple earlier. Now, the boy could have simply been walking with some relatives while his mother and father were shopping somewhere else, but then Jerry recognized the couple with the boy was in the restaurant earlier. Strange, they were wearing different outfits and sitting at two different tables. Now that Jerry thought about it more, he was sure that the last couple he had seen with the boy earlier was also from the restaurant. Jerry asked George to watch them while Jerry looked the other way and pulled out his phone.

Jerry was already dialing his cellphone to call Frank, when George agreed with Jerry that the couple was in the restaurant earlier. Frank told Jerry he would see what his options were and get back to him. Jerry told Frank that the couple in question, plus the boy, was headed towards the store now.

Frank quickly asked the shop keeper, if they could please exit out through the shop area in the back. The old man at first said no, then he saw Frank reach for his gun and remove it from his holster. The old man said, "Sure, sure, it is right through here. The door is about 20 meters back."

Frank said to the old man, "Don't act suspicious, there will be a family; a man, a woman and a boy, coming in here. Don't look upset, don't volunteer we were here. They should come in here soon and may ask if their friends came in or something. Say yes we were here and left about 5-10 minutes ago."

"I want nothing to do with this."

"Don't worry they don't want you or your shop, they want us."

Jerry left George at the bar, and casually walked across the street. Halfway down the block he saw a narrow walkway between some buildings that should lead to the next block over. He realized that Frank would try to go out the back way, but feared that the other couple from the restaurant would figure the same thing and cover the back of the building.

Just as Jerry was about to emerge on the other street, he overheard a lady on the phone saying, "What do you mean they aren't in there, they must have spotted you. If they come through this side, we will follow them. See if there is a back door to that place and make sure they don't double back towards you."

Jerry melted back into the side of the building and started texting Frank as quickly as he could. He told him how the team from the shop was coming through soon and that there was a team waiting on this side, also he added where he and George were right now. Or at least where he left George 60 seconds earlier.

Frank felt the vibration of his smart phone letting him know that he just received a text message. He pulled it out and read it quickly. The group was just short of the exit, but now held up as Frank read the text.

"Change of plans," as he was looking around the small shop.

He spotted what he was looking for, on the side wall, a door. It could just be a closet, but he suspected that it was a stairwell to the residence above where the owner probably lived.

Most of these buildings had a similar arrangement, even though there was a separate entrance on the street for the shop and the residence, there usually was an internal staircase for the owner to be able to come down and check on the workers without having to go outside.

Frank hurried the family toward the door. He made the universal symbol of putting his index finger to his lips to signal that they should be quiet. Frank tried the door and thankfully it was not locked and it did have a stairwell leading up behind it. They all entered the stairwell; Frank locked the door from this side. The group climbed the stairs as quietly as possible, but the old wood under their feet didn't cooperate.

After climbing the stairs they entered the old man's flat. Standing in the kitchen, Frank took out his cellphone and dialed 113, the national helpline.

Frank said, "I would like to report a kidnapping by terrorist in Sorrento. They took a 12 year old boy and are now inside the Bunolli Wood shop in Sorrento. There is a man and a woman, about 30 years old inside and two accomplices outside the shop entrance. I saw that they had guns when they took the boy. Please hurry."

He then hung up and dialed 112, the number for the Carabinieri police headquarters. These police were really a military unit that was used for higher security locations and situations. Frank repeated the story and hung up.

"There should be about 20 men with guns here in about 2-3 minutes."

He texted George and Jerry the new plan, wait for the police to come. He asked that they let him know once the first units were on the scene.

The couple with the child realized that they had missed the Ward family in the shop about 10 seconds after entering, it was not that large. They immediately called the other team members that should have had time to get to the back of this building. They confirmed that the Wards had not come their way so the first team either missed them or they were still in the building. The lady in the street out front recommended that the couple and child find their way through the shop and flush the Targets out the back of the building.

The couple in the shop asked the shop keeper if there was a back door. He resisted for a little while until, the woman showed him a gun and asked again where the door was. He pointed. After the team entered the back workshop via the storefront, the old man ran out of his store. He thought to himself, two sets of people with guns cannot be good.

The team in the workshop had to move slowly, the darkened workshop was a perfect place for an ambush. They told the boy to sit by the door, and yell out if anyone else comes or goes through that door. The team then split up to find the Targets. Both team members crouched low, with their heads below the counter and table top level.

There were many workbenches, saw stations and stacks of wood drying that made the workshop area more of a labyrinth at the below 30 inch level. The team advanced about three to five feet every 30 seconds, at this rate it would take a few minutes before they would discover the side door. Just about the same time it would take for the police to arrive.

It took the man about 3 minutes to come across the closed door. He tried the door knob, but it was locked. He needed to finish the sweep of his side of the wood shop, but knew that they would need to explore what was on the other side of the door. Within a minute he met up with the woman, who completed the search of her side of the wood shop. She quickly took out her phone and asked the look outs if they had seen the family. They hadn't. She told them they were going to check out a side door that was locked.

As the couple walked across the now cleared woodshop, they heard some tires screeching outside. This was never a good sign. Police often times didn't use the sirens, but they sometimes forgot that if they stopped to quickly the tires could screech or the brakes could squeal. The couple knew they needed to get out of there and fast. Obviously they couldn't go through the front door or back through the shop. The windows were all bared and locked, if they used their guns to open the lock, the police would swarm. No, they had to get through the side door and out another way. Hopefully the side door was not just a closet.

The couple called for the boy to join them quickly, he was really the son of the man out front. The term crime family starts with the young in this area. As the boy started towards the side door, the man grabbed a large piece of wood stock and started breaking off the door knob. Being an old door and lock set, it quickly broke and splintered at the same time; enough to shoulder it open the rest of the way.

The couple and boy started to climb the stairs just as they heard the front door of the woodshop come crashing in, then a bright flash and loud noise shattered what windows were left in the front area of the shop. They only had seconds now. The police had also entered via the storefront entrance at the same time and in great enough numbers that the small space was searched in less than 10 seconds. The splintered and still swinging side door caught the attention of the police. A few seconds later the point man sent another flash bang grenade into the stairwell, as high as he could toss it without entering himself.

The couple and the boy got to the top of the stairwell just as they heard a noise below them on the stairwell. There was a door on the top of the stairs and the man was just about to shoot the lock when the flash bang grenade went off. A searing white light blinded them all at the same time that a deep thumping bang went off and seemed to suck the air out of their lungs. By the time they realized what had happened, it was too late. The police were on top of them, literally with a knee on their spine and pulling the now prisoners hands back to be put in zip handcuffs.

The boy was assisted out of the area. According to the call they had received the boy was kidnapped. They had no reason to doubt the story, because the two out front were carrying guns as the caller had described. In about 10 minutes they would realize that the boy was the son of the man they captured outside and they would really be looking for the person that called in to get to the bottom of all this.

The police team needed to clear the rest of the building, which included the second floor, where the criminals were just captured. They knocked on the door and identified themselves as police, next they knocked down the door and quickly searched the entire floor, apparently the living quarters of the wood shop owner. The area was clear.

After arriving in the kitchen and placing the phone calls to the police, Frank went to the window and saw that it was only about 4 feet between buildings. They just needed to get to the roof and jump over. He quickly looked for access to the roof; many of these homes had terraces and grew an herb garden on the roof.

He found the narrow stairway at the end of a hall between the living room and a bedroom. They quickly climbed the stairs, turned the deadbolt lock handle and exited onto the roof. It was a warm evening, but was very cool in comparison to the woodshop and the owners flat.

Frank made sure to close the door to the roof, no reason to make the police believe anyone went this way. They would search the area because it was a good procedure, but if they didn't find any signs that anyone was ever here, the search would end as abruptly as it began.

He told them to all stay low and walk towards the edge on the side where he was pointing. He calculated that police on either side of the building would not be able to see them in the middle of roof unless they called in a helicopter. Frank told Luke to jump over and roll as he hit the other side with his feet, he added to not hit his head when he rolled, that would hurt. A small chuckle out of Luke and he was gone. Safely crouched on the other roof, he was ready to catch the kids as they jumped across.

James went first, he climbed up on the parapet of their building and jumped across, clearing the parapet of the other building and into his father's arms. Next was Elizabeth, after seeing her twin brother do it, also jumped across with no problem. They had just heard a loud bang go off and Frank knew the police would be there shortly.

Bianca followed the kids and Luke also caught her, stopping her forward motion so she didn't have to roll when she hit. Right on her heals Frank leapt across the 4 foot canyon between the buildings. He did hit and roll, just as Luke had done less than 30 seconds earlier. Right as Frank hit the roof; another loud bang went off, this one sounding much closer.

Frank ran toward this roofs access door, as he suspected it was locked and the door was pretty modern, it was made of metal, these people had probably been burglarized via this door in the past. Frank knew he only had moments for them to be out of site, so he gathered the family and told them they needed to get behind a small potting table on the roof. It had a solid back and some plants on it. He told

Luke to help him as they slid the table forward about 5 feet and faced it toward the roof they just jumped from.

Frank was hoping that when the police searched the roof and looked over here that they wouldn't see anything out of the ordinary, from their angle it should look like a table, it would be hard to tell it was really 5 foot from the wall and that 5 people were cramped in the space behind the table.

Right on cue, the door to the woodshop roof opened and 4 men searched the rooftop and looked around for any signs of other people. Just as Frank had hoped, the search lasted only moments, the men returned back down the stairs the way they had come within 30 seconds.

Frank stood and quickly went to the edge of this rooftop, but on the opposite side from the woodshop building. The buildings were literally built on one another with no gap between, but with a 4 foot wall, topped with broken glass bottles. Frank asked Luke to help him carry the bench over to the wall after they quickly cleared the pots from the top. Under the bench Frank found a small canvas tarp and a garden trowel. He then climbed up on the bench top and using the garden trowel, smashed some of the tall glass shards off of the top of the wall.

He knelt down on top of the bench with one knee. He told Luke to climb up on the bench then on to Frank's knee, then to stand on the flattest part of the wall top and jump over the wall. As long as someone didn't slip, the glass with the tarp over it would not hurt them through their shoes.

Next over the wall were James, Elizabeth, and then Bianca. Frank had no foot hold so he just put his hand down on the safest area of the tarp covered wall and threw his legs up and over the wall, similar to a pommel horse vault.

Again Frank ran over to where the door was and this time was met with a locked but fragile old looking door. Sure enough, he had to only pull down on the door handle a few times until the latch cleared the old wooden frame.

They now needed to get out of the house without raising an alarm, it was 10 pm, and someone was sure to be in the house at this time.

He whispered to the group, "We need to be very quiet and get out of here fast. We don't want to wake anyone or the police will be on us and that may not be good right now."

The Wards didn't know why they were running from the police, they had gotten caught up in all the excitement of the chase and were running on pure adrenaline for the last few minutes, but now they had time to think about it; why were they running from the police? Frank saw the look of question in Luke and Bianca's eyes.

"I will explain when we get back to the hotel."

The group quietly, but quickly walked down the stairs, which didn't make a sound because the steps and the flooring in the flat were all tiled and very solid. They simply unlocked the door and went down the stairs to the street level.

They exited and walked towards their hotel, the opposite way of the parked police cars. By looking natural, no one would suspect them of anything, and no one did.

Frank texted Jerry to see where they were. Jerry called Frank's phone. He told Frank that the police got the two couples and the boy. He and George were about a block in front of them toward the hotel.

Frank confirmed that they were on a direct route back to the hotel, but that they would be getting their bags and leaving immediately. He asked Jerry and George to each get a car.

Jerry said, "It is late; we can't get a rental car at this time."

"I wasn't talking about a rental; we need to go off the grid, no records."

"When you say off the grid, you also mean no checking in with Headquarters?"

"Not via phone, we will talk back at the hotel in 15 minutes, the Wards room. Please explain it to George so that he doesn't call in either. See you in 15."

Frank punched the end button on his phone.

Chapter 15   The Drop

The assassins made bail by midnight and where none the worse for wear. All things considered, the most they had on them was having concealed weapons and breaking and entering. They really didn't kidnap anyone; the boy was the one man's son. They also had valid sports licenses for their guns and claimed that they were only transporting them as they were allowed to do.

Even the breaking and entering was a stretch considering that they didn't forcefully threaten the shop owner to show them the door. Their statement to the police was that they asked the owner if there was a bathroom that the boy could use and he pointed to the back door entrance into the shop. They were looking for the bathroom when the doors were broken in and they ran in fear, breaking down the side door and running up the staircase to escape whoever had broken in the front door.

When the men had been released from jail, they waited for the women across the street from the police station. Once the ladies were released, they all walked to a hotel bar, a few blocks away, to discuss their options.

"We need to find these people and eliminate them, or we won't get paid," said one of the men.

"Yes, let's call our contact, find out where they are and take them down right now. It is late and the children should be asleep by now," said the other man.

One of the women said, "I still think it is wrong to "do" the children, but we should finish what we started and get paid."

In the Venice jail, Silvano was sleeping quietly in his cell. He didn't really hear the click of the electronic release of his cell's door lock. He also didn't hear the door opening or see the man standing over him with a pillow. The last thing Silvano saw was the darkness of a pillow over his face with hundreds of shooting stars as the pressure was increased and the air in his lungs was used up. Right before he lost conscience, he saw bright pink colors flash in his eyes. Moments later his heart stopped beating, thus the blood stopped pumping and his brain stopped working.

If Silvano would have seen the man with the pillow, he may have been surprised to know it was a guard, or maybe he wouldn't have been surprised. The guard, took the pillow and put it back in the empty bunk on the other side of the cell, walked out and closed the door quietly, the click of the lock reengaging could hardly be heard.

The guard then went back to his station and placed a phone call to Edwin Grey, "It is done; the bird will no longer be able to sing."

Edwin Grey simply replied, "Your envelope will be a little fatter this month," and then he hung up. Edwin thought to himself, that fool Silvano, he thought that he was going to drag me down with him, that wasn't going to happen. We were business partners, and were not ever going to be cell mates.

Moments later the phone rang again. Edwin Grey thought to himself, that guard probably was calling for more money. Edwin answered, "Yes."

One of the assassins said, "This is Dominic, they got away. They called the police on us; they used flash/bang grenades and captured us within seconds. They couldn't really hold us for long, because we really hadn't done anything yet."

Edwin wasn't expecting this; these two teams had done work for him before and had never failed. Edwin said out of anger, "You failed, I am canceling the contract." Edwin thought that now Silvano was taken care of, the Wards didn't really need to die, but he was now more worried about Frank and the other CIA officers. They may investigate why two professional hit teams were hunting them down. Edwin couldn't leave that up to chance and decided that they all needed to die.

Dominic didn't expect to hear this, he had never been removed from a contract, nor had he ever failed before. He said, "Sir, please give us another chance. To show our gratitude for the past jobs and future ones, we will do this one for half price, simply tell us where they are and we will proceed."

As Dominic was begging for the job back, Edwin pulled up his laptop and activated the location beacons in the family's cell phones. It looked like they were in their hotel, all in the same location, most likely sleeping. He pulled up the locations for Frank, Jerry and George and they were also in the hotel.

Edwin said, "Alright, we will try one more time. They are all at their hotel, I gave you the information earlier today, they are not moving, and so I am guessing they are all asleep."

Dominic got off the phone with Edwin Grey and told the other assassins they were still employed, albeit at half price. They had heard the offer, but now would have Dominic share what was on the other side of the conversation. Dominic said, "At first, when I told him we failed and were caught by the police, he fired us."

The other man said, "He can't cancel the contract, it didn't have a time limit."

Dominic replied, "Yes, you are right, and you are wrong. I don't think he should go back on a contract, but he has used us before and I want him to use us in the future. My idea is to do this and get it over soon, collect our money and lay low for a while." The others agreed it was a good plan.

Dominic said, "Let's go to the hotel and finish what we started."

Once back at their car, they opened the trunk, picked up the false bottom that covers the spare tire to reveal an aluminum case. Dominic lifted the case out of the spare tire well and opened it revealing 4 Beretta F92FS pistols. These guns were manufactured in Italy, had 15 shot clips, and the new green laser sights attached. The laser sights attached below the barrel in front of the trigger guard, which left the regular sights usable as well. The laser sights were perfect for a darker environment, like the hotel room. A flashlight could be used to find their way around the room as the lasers pinpointed their targets easily.

A suppressor or silencer was also included for each gun. The Beretta 92FS requires a threaded muzzle silencer, so the guns barrels were threaded and fitted with the suppressors when first purchased. The silencers would lower the sound by over 40dB, where each 3dB reduction is half the volume. The actual sound of the shot was only as loud as the slide on the gun and the case being ejected. This would come in handy for the hotel room; no one would hear a thing even if they were walking by the door of the room.

The guns would not fit in the ladies purses or the men's waistbands with the silencers attached, so they would screw them on right before entering the rooms. The plan would be to grab a small piece of luggage from the hotel room to put the hot barreled guns into after they were used.

Right now it was about three in the morning and there wasn't too much motion on the streets. If they went into the hotel at that hour, they may raise suspicions, so they decided to wait until 5 am. The morning crew for the hotel was arriving at that time; the breakfast area would be open around 6 so they had a lot to do before then. They knew that the elevator required a room key to operate so they would climb the stairs up to the 3rd floor. Once they entered the hotel lobby, they walked straight to the stairs. The man behind the registration desk simply said, "Buongiorno." The group waved back to the man. One thing that Dominic had learned years earlier was that if you acted like you belonged in a place, others would believe that you did belong there as well.

The four assassins climbed the stairs to the 3rd floor. The Wards were in room 321, the CIA officers were in rooms 322 and 324 respectfully. They needed to hit room 322, across from the Wards first, that is where the officers would be watching.

They decided to separate into two couples and have one couple go past the room door. Dominic had a master key for the electronic locks, not as rare a thing as many had thought. He had taken one off of a maid service cart when he had checked out the hotel two days earlier. He knew that once the key released the lock it usually beeped and the electronic click as the lock unlocked would alert the people inside, they would have to act quickly.

The other man had a pry bar in case the room had a deadbolt or chain lock from the inside. Obviously this would make a lot of noise, but Dominic doubted that the officers would use either lock.

Dominic looked at his team, they all caught eyes and gave a nod, they were ready. He slipped the key in the lock and pulled it out, the light turned green and beeped twice as the internal lock catch clicked back. The team went in quickly but quietly, everyone was at a crouched position, if one of the CIA guys was waiting for them, unless he had night vision glasses on, would likely shoot over their heads where their chests are supposed to be.

Dominic was the first in the room; he went past the bathroom to the main room. The woman paired with Dominic checked out the bathroom while Dominic searched the main room. Dominic didn't like what he saw with his flash light, a room with beds that were made and not slept in. The bathroom had also turned up empty. The two assassins in the hallway now entered the room and closed the door quietly behind them.

"They may all be in the Wards room, it was a suite and they may have all stayed together for safety. This may make it a little more dangerous than what we planned, there is a better chance that they used an additional deadbolt or chain lock, which would slow us down and make noise.

We will check out the hallway to make sure no one is out there, walk across the hallway, open the door and all of us will go in. If it moves take it out. Let's divide the room into left and right. Ladies left side, men right side." Dominic had a very serious demeanor; he was all business, now. His military training kicked in and he was on autopilot.

One of the ladies joked, "Easy to remember because the men always think they are right."

No one really said anything after that comment, they had a job to do and it would all be done within the next few moments. The group exited the room, verified no one was in the hallway and unlocked the door. As Dominic turned the door handle the other man was ready with the pry bar, if needed. It wasn't, the door opened in quickly. The four team members at a quick walk proceeded into the suite. Again the room was dark and the beds were not slept in.

After verifying the suite was indeed empty they turned the lights on. The room was clean; no one had slept there recently. The only item in the place was a UPS Express box. Dominic looked at the box and saw it was addressed to a place in Rome. He opened the box and found cell phones.

He swore out loud and shook his head. The game had just gotten more complicated. Their prey was now on the move and Dominic didn't have a clue where they were or where they would be. He needed to contact Edwin Grey to see what the plans were going forward. Now, they needed to get out of the room before the morning maid service came down the hallway.

Chapter 16   Off the Grid

After ending the phone conversation with Jerry, Frank explained to the Wards that they were going back to the hotel, packing their bags and leaving within 15 minutes. Bianca, who would normally argue that there was no way to pack the bags in such a short time, didn't even flinch, she said, "No problem, Luke you pack our stuff and I will pack the kid's stuff."

The group was walking at a fast pace but was not running, they didn't want to attract any unnecessary attention. They got back to the hotel and after Frank cleared their room, the Wards packed as Frank went to gather his bags.

About 15 minutes later, Frank knocked on the Ward's door. James asked for the secret password, which Frank replied, "Open the door now or stand back."

James said, "Close enough," as he opened the door to a serious looking Frank.

Frank had two duffle bags in his hands along with a UPS express box. The one duffle bag Luke recognized from the boat, it held guns and flak jackets. The other one must have been Frank's clothing. Frank put the bags on the floor and went over to the desk, sat down, and started filling out a UPS shipping slip. Within 60 seconds there was another rap at the door and Frank made sure it was Jerry and George before opening it. They also each had a duffel bag in their hands.

Frank said, "Now that we are all here together and ready to go I wanted to let you know the plan. Right now, I am pretty sure that we have been compromised from within the CIA."

He let that thought settle in for a moment, then continued, "Silvano's guys have been a step ahead of us a few times, but just now, those two teams were not local thugs, they were professional assassins, they were meant to take us all out, including Jerry and George if they got in the way, otherwise you send one person, not four, let alone a kid for cover."

As he was speaking, Frank continued to work with the UPS express box, peeling off the strip and pressing the end of the box flap together to actually form a box out of the flat cardboard. He then slipped the shipping slip into a plastic pouch and attached it to the front.

"Please turn off all of your phones and put them in here; yes, Jerry and George you too."

He held out the box and they all dropped their phones into it. He then sealed the box and left it on the desk.

"The CIA has been tracking us through the phones. They will think we are all sitting in this room tonight. When the maids come tomorrow they will take the box down and it will get sent back to headquarters. By then we will be hundreds of miles away."

The group headed down towards the cars. Jerry and George each grabbed one of the Ward's bags, so Luke only had to carry two and Bianca could watch the kids and help them with their carryon bags that contained their iPods, books and a snack for later.

At the cars, they divided up, the Wards and Frank would be driving in a Renault Wagon and Jerry and George would be driving in a Fiat. Jerry and George acquired the cars by walking through the streets and trying to open every car they came to. If the car door was unlocked, they would quickly get in the driver's seat and see if there were keys in it.

Amazingly, they were able to find cars that were not locked and had the keys in the sun visor, ash tray or center arm rest storage compartment. They drove the cars a few blocks away, until they found a similar car, parked, then switched license plates with the other car.

It was late, the cars shouldn't be reported missing until the morning and by then the group would be 6 hours away from Sorrento. Even then, the cars now had different plates. Most people would not notice if their plates were changed for quite some time.

The group headed out of town as fast as possible without attracting attention. They went the same way they had come, north and east to get off of the peninsula that Sorrento and the Amalfi coast were located on.

They would travel in the northeasterly direction until they hit the E45 and take that east until they hit the major Autostrada, A3 which they would head south on. Salerno was located at this intersection and the group stopped to refuel and pick up some supplies, simple necessities like bottled water, prepackaged snacks, some bread, meats and cheeses. They were able to get all of these items at a petrol stop along the Autostrada.

The caravan continued south for hours, refueled then continued on. Bianca and the kids slept well in the back seat, while Luke and

Frank remained awake in the front, each man driving for a tank of gas and switching.

Jerry and George also rotated drivers for each tank driven. Being ex-military men, Frank, George and Jerry were asleep within minutes when the opportunity made itself available. They had deep instincts from their prior training to catch sleep when it was available; one never knew when they would be able to sleep again, so it was best to always be rested when one was in the field. Luke, not having the same training, found it extremely difficult to sleep when he was the passenger, he was wound up from all the excitement and he couldn't think of sleeping through anything that may present itself.

When Luke started driving, he found he was more tired than when he was the passenger, probably because his mind was concentrating on driving and didn't have as much time devoted to thinking about their predicament of multiple people trying to kill him and his family.

They drove until they came to the city of Cosenza. It was now morning and the Sun was up. Frank asked Luke to pull the car over in the parking lot of a modern strip mall, which was a block or so from the University of Calabria. These areas were always active, regardless of time of day. What had really caught Frank's attention was the bakery he saw less than 20 meters away. He said he would be right back; he was getting some doughnuts, croissants, and muffins for everyone.

Jerry climbed into the Ward's vehicle; George headed across the parking lot with Frank, but veered off to the coffee shop next to the bakery. George ordered 5 double espressos and 2 milks to go. It took a few minutes to make the espressos, by the time George had paid and started back towards the car, Frank had returned with the bakery items.

Everyone was hungry and dug in quickly. Jerry had taken a croissant and made a sandwich, using some of the meat and cheese they had purchased the night before. He went back to his car. George dropped off three espressos and two milks, grabbed a doughnut and muffin and returned to the car with Jerry. Frank enjoyed a muffin with his espresso, while the kids quickly ate two chocolate frosted doughnuts and shared a blueberry muffin with their milk. Bianca and Luke had croissants and some cheese with their espressos.

The espresso and baked goods really hit the spot; everyone ate more than they normally would. Lack of sleep and a little nervousness added to one's appetite. Besides the bakery and espresso shop, Frank picked this parking lot because there was a TIM mobile phone store here as well. After finishing his food and espresso, Frank told the Wards that he was going to get some phones for communications.

Frank entered the TIM store and quickly asked the man about prepaid SIM card(data card that contains the users phone number, features, privileges and restrictions) plans and also asked which phones were the most inexpensive that they had in stock, he needed 4 of them. The man showed him a low cost Nokia model that would work for voice and text, but was not a SMART phone. Frank said they would be perfect.

The people behind the counter helped Frank insert the SIM cards and test that they worked, they also entered in each of the numbers in the phone directory under Phone A, B, C and D, Frank explained they were company phones and were not going to be used by the same people all the time, so it would be easier to give the phones a name instead of using a person's name.

He purchased the phones, SIM cards, and two vehicle chargers and was out the door in about 15 minutes. He left all the boxes and packing materials behind in the phone store, his phone already tucked in his inside jacket pocket.

Frank walked directly to Jerry and George's car. He handed over two phones and let them know he was Phone A, Jerry was Phone B, George was Phone C and one of the Ward's would be Phone D. He also told him that they had been in the parking lot long enough and needed to drive to a new location, may be a bigger shopping area, with many more cars and people to help blend in a little better. He returned to his car and handed a phone to Luke letting him know which Phones in the directory list were for which person. Frank also warned Luke to not call anyone other than one of them from the phone.

Cosenza was not exactly an American tourist destination, but Americans were not necessarily rare either. The city itself only had about 70,000 people, but when you counted the immediate area surrounding the city the numbers were over 250,000 people. Needless to say, the area could support some fine restaurants and stores and without too much difficulty, hide a family of Americans.

The two car caravan drove towards the city center and found a shopping centre. They parked the cars and got out to stretch. Frank gave out some Euro coins, he got earlier in the bakery, to everyone to use for the toilets. He suggested that they all head in to the shopping centre but only use the restrooms a few at a time, so as to not attract attention, secretly, it was so he could verify that no one was on their tail as well.

This was a modern mall, not unlike some back in Illinois, Bianca was thinking. The store fronts looked the same, but all the advertising was in Italian, which was slightly disorientating. Also, the color choices for clothing were much bolder than back in the States. At first Bianca thought they were so loud that they were clown like, and then she looked closer and saw that the materials were finely made and the colors, though contrasting, went together fashionably well.

Luke and James looked at an electronics store. It was amazing how much more the electronics cost in Italy as compared to the US. The pricing was about the same in Euros here as it was in US Dollars back in the States, which really made it 30% more here when one converted to US Dollars.

Frank had warned the Wards not to use a credit card or the ATM or anything that could be electronically traced back to them. Luke still had quite a bit of the cash on him because Frank had been picking up the tab at all of the restaurants.

The Wards window shopped for most of the morning. They ate at one of the pizza places in the mall, ordering a large ½ cheese and ½ cheese and sausage pizza. Of course, there was a gelato stand in the mall and they all had a couple of scoops in a cup.

Luke asked Frank, "Where are we going to sleep tonight, I would prefer someplace with a bed?"

Frank chuckled and said to Bianca, "I was hoping your extended family could help. Is there a place we could all stay?" As he was talking, he also pointed to himself and generically to Jerry and George who were maintaining the safety perimeter. He continued, "We can't go to a hotel, they require passports, then "they" would know where we were and send someone to see us."

Bianca, "You mean kill us?"

Frank just nodded his head up and down.

"One of my uncles has a mountain house, I am sure that no one uses it during the week much, they all work and it takes almost an hour drive from their home to get to the mountain house."

"Do you think you could find it?"

"I don't know, I think so, but I haven't been there for 15 years, not since the last time Luke and I were here. I would need to see a map, but couldn't I just call them and ask for directions?"

"No, I think the fewer people that know where we are the better; someone can't tell what they don't know."

"Oh, do you think that someone will try to find us via my relatives?" But Bianca knew the answer before the words left her mouth, of course they knew about her relatives, she was now concerned about their safety.

Frank, seeing the pain in her eyes said, "They will probably just interview your relatives, and judge if they know your whereabouts. That is why we shouldn't really contact them if we don't need to. I doubt that anyone would think to mention they have a mountain house and think that you would be holed up there, considering the last time you visited was 15 years earlier."

He thought there was at least one inside person at the CIA who assisted Silvano's thugs and now had sent two assassin teams after them. There was only one person that would not have to get clearance to hire the assassin teams, Edwin Grey. He also either had someone working for him on the inside or was getting the information from some unsuspecting or unwilling accomplices.

Frank knew from the CIA's intelligence that the counterfeiting business was worth billions and just a tiny slice of that to help with customs in the US or not to prosecute was worth millions more than a top level CIA in country director earns. This may be an example of having even very good people being corrupted by money. Edwin probably had Silvano on some solid charges and Silvano shared with him how rich he could become. How he could really afford to live in Tuscany after he retired. He couldn't afford that on what his country paid him, or at least not afford the style he had grown accustomed to.

Edwin actually had already purchased a large plot of land in the Chianti Hills with a vineyard on it. The property was really more of a farm; they didn't make any wine on the premises, but sold all of their harvest to local wineries every year. After Edwin retired, he would hire a wine maker and start making his own label. He would call the vineyard, Segreto Amare, Secret Love. Kind of a play on words for his secret CIA life, secrets of how he gained his wealth, but the real secret was how he had killed the love of his life many years earlier in Russia.

The CIA had taught him how to kill and make it look like an accident, but they didn't teach how to not fall in love with a double agent that was using you. He would never know if she had true feelings for him or if he was just part of her master plan.

Her name was Oksana Palamarchuk Skovoroda and she was a school teacher at the Anglo American School of Moscow in the early 80s. The school catered to children of US, UK and Canadian diplomats and was mostly instructed by teachers from those countries. However, there were a few classes taught by local teachers that were fluent in Russian and English, such as Physical Education, Swimming, Russian language classes and Russian Sociology and Culture. Oksana was one of 5 Russian language teachers on campus of about 140 teachers.

Most of the teachers stayed in dormitories on campus or in the immediate area, sticking with the other English speaking teachers, it was a close knit group, except for the Soviet Union born teachers, they commuted in to work from wherever they lived in Moscow. The Cold War was still on-going and most of the teachers would stop talking in the presence of the native Russians. Oksana was alright with that, she was here for a reason, she had a mission and she really didn't need to make friends.

Oksana started working at the school in the middle of the school year. One of the Russian language teachers had a car accident and required bed rest for a few months, so the school needed a replacement. The school needed to have any potential teachers totally vetted by the US, UK and Canadian secret services, after all these teachers would be in contact with diplomats' children. The school went through a local jobs manager run by the State. Everything was run by the State back in that time era, The Soviet Union was run to be efficient, only about 20% of high school graduates were allowed to go on to University. The students were told which field of study they excelled at and had to enter that field.

The KGB was always interested in language stars, they were needed for SIGINT, signal intelligence and also were drawn upon for field work. The better language students would likely know three or more languages, sometimes four or five. Like Oksana from the

Ukraine, many spoke a local dialect; she learned formal Russian in State run school and quickly learned a little English from bootleg American movies on VHS tapes. By the time she took the language proficiency test, she had 2 ½ languages under her belt. Once in university she quickly mastered English, becoming so proficient she could pass for an American with a slight accent. She also quickly became fluent in both Spanish and Italian.

Oksana was a decent athlete, nothing varsity level, just good at running and jumping and general track and field events. The KGB recruited her when she was just a Sophomore so she spent her summers doing paramilitary training, surveillance training and general field operative training for how to do a secret meeting, how to recruit agents, how to do a dead drop and other useful traits. The Cold War was still in full swing in the Eighties and the KGB assigned her to the Anglo American School of Moscow to see if they could get information from the Diplomats' children.

It was amazing what could be inferred from knowing that a child's Dad couldn't attend a school play because he was going to be out of town. Sometimes the children talked about how their Dad's were yelling at them or their Mom more. This helped the KGB know whether to try and see if they could seduce these men or turn them as an agent if they were angry because they were short on money or had some other issues.

Edwin Grey didn't have children, didn't want to have children and didn't necessarily like children, but he needed to go to the Anglo American School of Moscow, to pick up two children for his boss, Kevin Duley, at the American Consulate in Moscow. The security at the school was pretty tight and for good reason, no one would want one of these children kidnapped. Edwin pulled the car up to the parking lot for visitors, parked the car and headed toward the office.

He wasn't the children's father so he needed a signed, permission slip from Duley. He stopped at the school office to show the paperwork, before the children would be released to his care. When he was cleared the children would be brought to the office and released into his custody. As Edwin was sitting in a comfortable chair in the waiting room, he started looked on the table and found the latest editions of American news magazines.

Time had a Bull on the cover; the Dow was around 1500 and had been moving sideways for a decade or more. It was hard to believe at the time that the Dow would ever reach 2000. Edwin's thoughts were interrupted by a beautiful young woman walking into the waiting room area. Oksana was radiant, with deep brown hair and dark brown eyes, she was thin, yet had curves in the right locations.

About 30 seconds after Oksana walked in, the Duley children entered and said hi to Ms. Skovoroda. The children introduced Mr. Grey to Ms. Skovoroda.

"Please call me Oksana."

"I am Edwin, nice to meet you, what subject do you teach?"

"I am the children's Russian language teacher. Grey, I don't believe I have any of your children in my classes."

"No, I don't have any children, I work for Mr. Duley at the Consulate and he asked me to pick his children up."

"Oh, I hope everything is alright, is he ill?" Oksana had a pleasant way of feigning that she cared when really she was just trying to glean some information to pass on to her KGB boss.

Edwin knew better to relay any personal information to a stranger, so he would provide a little disinformation, "He is simply busy working on a special visa request for a US citizen that wants to visit parts of Russia and the Ukraine."

"I am born in the Ukraine; it is not very warm there now, not a place for a foreigner to visit."

"Oh, the couple would be traveling in the summer; it just takes months to get visas approved through your government so they really need to start the process now if they want to be able to make their travel arrangements."

Edwin, struck with the young woman's beauty asked, "Maybe we could discuss Ukraine over a coffee sometime?"

"I would like that," replied Oksana.

They would have that coffee and many others. They became a couple and Edwin was happy, until he found out that she was really a KGB spy. Some of her reports about him had been intercepted and he was brought in to answer questions by his CIA superiors. He realized that she was really using him and that he could only be rid of her one way, to assassinate her and make it look like an accident.

He went to her apartment late one night and found her car parked in the lot, outside her window. He slid under the car and using a large wire cutters, cut into the brake lines of her front passenger side brakes, not all the way through, just a little bit, so the brakes would work the first couple of times before the whole system failed.

Later the next day on her drive to school, Oksana was killed in a terrible car accident; she had run right through a controlled intersection against the red light and was run into by a bus. The bus driver also died, and 10 people, the ones standing on the bus at the time were injured, 2 of them seriously. At first Edwin was shocked to hear the news and even accused his boss at the CIA of having her killed. All of this was of course just for show, after all Edwin was the one who killed her, she was his first, but was not going to be his last assassination.

Frank had decided that Edwin Grey was definitely crooked and the one that ordered the hit on the Wards and himself. Frank could deal with Edwin himself, but couldn't figure out how he, personally could ferret out any other accomplices within the CIA that Edwin had been dealing with. Frank had to go through the proper channels with this one. It meant a call to the Counterintelligence Center Analysis Group (CIC/AG), which had the unique responsibility of being able to investigate the CIA and its directors, officers and agents, kind of like the Internal Affairs department for the FBI and local law enforcement.

Frank called the CIA US Headquarters and got a hold of the top deputy director of CIC/AG, William Bowles. He listened well, taking notes, even though the entire conversation was being recorded, as he had informed Frank he had to do.

Bowles of course was shocked by the allegations against Edwin Grey. He personally knew Edwin and that always made the job a little harder. He did acknowledge what Frank had laid out as the evidence, but told him he needed to verify as much as he could, as quickly as he could. He also realized that Frank, Jerry, George and the Wards were off the grid and were going to stay that way until they got the all clear from him.

Frank agreed to call him back the next day to see what they had found. Just before Frank was about to hang up the phone, he was walking past a display of TVs, when he saw the breaking news that Silvano Rosito had been found dead in his cell, apparently from a heart attack.

Frank told Bowles, "Silvano Rosito is dead; I think that Edwin had him killed while he was in jail.

Normally, the Wards would be safe, but I think that Edwin must know that we are on the run and he probably wants to finish what he started to make sure there are no loose ends, namely me. He was using two hit teams, they looked Italian, and you may want to start there. I am sure that the Italian police will cooperate with a request for information from the States."

Frank did not tell him where they were in Italy or for that matter if they were still in Italy, but with Edwin having the power to watch the train stations and airports, Bowles knew there was a good chance Frank and his group was still in Italy.

The Ward group had previously agreed to meet back in the food court area around 2:30pm. Frank relayed to the group about Silvano's well timed heart attack. Luke excitedly said, "Great, then no one should be trying to kill us anymore."

Frank responded, "To be honest with everyone here, I believe that there is a traitor in the CIA that had been feeding our whereabouts to Silvano in jail. I also think that person is responsible for Silvano's death. Finally, I believe that person arranged for the last attempt on our lives and hired the two teams to take all of us out, not just you and your family."

Jerry and George didn't really show a change of emotion on their faces. They already knew that Frank thought there was an unnamed inside person, but the news of Silvano's death kind of confirmed this theory and they started to suspect Edwin as well. They knew the situation was probably going to get a whole lot worse before it got better.

James asked, "Who do you think it is and why?"

"I think it is Edwin Grey," Frank let that settle in for a few seconds, then continued, "As you all know I suspected an inside mole or traitor early on because we didn't see anyone tailing us at times, but they knew how to locate us, that made me think about the tracking devices in the phone.

I was able to confirm this when I took my phone and put it close to the alarm clock radio in my hotel room. When the GSM phone is transmitting data, the transmissions are strong enough that any nearby speaker will pick up a buzzing sound. I heard the data buzz sound even when I turned the power off on the phone, the CIA was using the built in GPS tracking device and automatically sending the coordinates back via data on the phone."

Elizabeth said, "That is why you had us all give you our phones."

"Yes, and if someone looked at the location data, it would show us all in the hotel. That gave us a head start to get out of the area." Frank said this next part in almost a whisper, "The cars that Jerry and George got for us are borrowed."

James excitedly said, "You mean stolen?"

"Yes, you could call them that, but we needed to be off of the radar screen for a while. We changed the plates; it will take a while before the police put out a notice for the cars and plates. Hundreds of cars are stolen a month in Italy, so these should not stand out." Frank continued, "Now, we need to figure out how to get to the mountain home. Let's stop and get some supplies for our stay."

They left the mall and drove around for 45 minutes to makes sure they really were not being followed, they weren't. The next stop was at a large grocery store to get food and drinks, candles, some batteries and flash lights, Bianca had told Frank that the place was rural and used a gas generator for the electricity. Frank didn't want to count on the generator and would only use it if they had to, it may attract too much attention by neighbors, and the sound of a generator can carry pretty far up in the mountains.

At a hardware store they purchased bolt cutters, padlocks, 2 cycle mixing oil and a gas can. Before heading out to the county, the small caravan filled up on gas, including the 5 liter gas can, and bought a map of the area.

Bianca unfolded the map and found the town of Mirano Principato. She started looking at the map and noticed there were a lot more roads listed on it than she thought there would be in that area. She could see from the coloring of the map that the town was actually at a much higher elevation than Cosenza was, but the mountain house was higher yet, on top of the mountain.

She gently shook her head. Frank picked up on this and asked, "Can you find it?"

"I think so, I am not sure I can find it on this map, but I think that I could get there from the town. We should start by my uncle's business and house, and then I can get us there."

Luke added, "I think I can help, it has been 15 years but I know that we passed a hunt or gun club and a forest park campground or picnic area on the way. Also, the town's water supply came from springs up in the mountains and they passed some pipes and pump stations as they climbed the mountain."

Frank said, "Let's get to that town and start towards the mountains as soon as possible. You said it is about an hour trip once we get to Marano?"

"Yes, about an hour."

Dominic and the others exited the Hotel in the early morning to find the Sun was still shining, the temperatures were in the high 30s, Centigrade, but somehow he still felt a chill. He called Edwin once more, to see if he could help locate the targets. The call was short and to the point.

Edwin answered his private cell phone, "Yes."

Dominic said, "They were not at the hotel, they were all gone. The only thing in the rooms was a UPS box full of phones. The beds weren't slept in; my best guess is that they were gone before we got released from the police station."

"I see, let me check," as Edwin typed into his computer to look for the locator beacons, "the trackers show them still at the hotel, so they are off the grid now."

Dominic asked, "Where do you think they are?"

"I will call you back at this number in 5 minutes. I need to look a little deeper to see where they may have gone. Also, now that you will need to hunt for them a little, I will pay your original fee, you just need to get them within the next 48 hours. I will narrow down their location and get back to you."

Dominic could hear the stress in Edwin's voice; the man didn't know where the targets were. Dominic explained the situation to his crew, Lisa, Benjamin, and Linda. Benjamin groaned, "How are we supposed to find them?"

"Don't count Edwin out, he has more information about them than you can imagine."

"If you say so, I guess I have nothing better to do for the next two days."

Edwin Grey was worried; he now knew that Frank had figured out that someone in the CIA was providing information to the assassins. Frank probably also figured out that Edwin may be involved, not too many people have the pull to call in assassin teams, and the local mob guys would just use their own guys, like the other attempts before Silvano died.

The news about Silvano dying was on the news; Frank would easily connect the two. Frank, Jerry and George were well trained CIA field officers, they wouldn't make too many mistakes, but they still had some big disadvantages, they had a family to watch after and Edwin had massive intelligence gathering resources available to him.

Edwin pulled up Frank's records; he had no family, friends or associates listed in Italy. Frank was somewhat of a lone wolf since coming to Italy. He was all business, which is great in an employee, but bad when an adversary. Next he looked at George and Jerry's records, George had no contacts in Italy, and Jerry had a family here in Rome. Edwin found the week link, Jerry's family; they could be used as a bargaining chip later. Edwin read through the Ward's jacket. "Of course, Bianca Ward had family in Italy, that must be where they were headed," Edwin thought to himself.

Edwin called Dominic, "Bianca Ward has family in a small town called Marano Principato; a couple of uncles, Carlos and Salvatore Fragatelli. Pay a visit to the uncles. Find the Wards and the other three."

Dominic asked, "How sure are you that they are there?"

"We don't know for sure, but it makes sense, they haven't left the country, at least not through normal channels and this is the only place they could go where we couldn't track them. If they stay in a hotel, they need to use their passports. That gives me an idea, hold on."

Edwin typed in his laptop and pulled up the Italian police wire website, a private website used nationwide by the Italians to list stolen cars, bank robberies, and other crimes where the crimes may involve multiple local jurisdictions. Edwin narrowed down the list to cars stolen earlier today or last night in the Sorrento area. There were only 3 cars stolen.

"I looked up the stolen cars in your area and there were only 3, a brown Renault Wagon, a red Fiat sedan, and a Mercedes SL600. The Mercedes sounds too flashy and only seats 2 comfortably, so I would look for the Renault and the Fiat."

Dominic had a portable GPS unit and typed in Marano Principato, it looked to be over 300 KM and about 4 hours of driving time. The group decided to leave immediately, their targets were half a day ahead of them.

Chapter 17   Mountain House

It took about forty five minutes to drive to Marano from Cosenza and another 5 minutes to locate Bianca's Uncle's house and business. Her Uncle Carlos was a cabinet maker and used to make furniture by hand years ago, now his business is mainly selling and installing modern kitchen cabinets. They still custom build wardrobe closets. In many parts of Italy the homes never had built in closets. More than 50 years earlier most people didn't have enough clothes to fill a closet, they were kept in dressers or chests.

Bianca and Luke both agreed that they needed to stay on the main road that her Uncle Carlos lived on and head toward the mountain. After about 15 minutes they passed a hunt club, so far their memories of how to get to the mountain house were good, but they all knew the closer they got to the top of the mountain the trickier it would become.

About 10 minutes later they passed a campground/picnic area on the left. The road now was shaded by large trees. Bianca pointed out that they were chestnut trees and that when she was younger her and her family would go through the woods in the late summer picking up the chestnuts that had just fallen.

After about 50 minutes of traveling, they seemed to be cresting the mountain. This is where it would be hard to go off of memory and they may need to explore a few roads to find the right one. Luke pointed out that he remembered the mountain house being near a lookout point that overlooked the town of Murano and the valley below, so they decided to always take the road that was now on their left every time they came to a fork in the road. The asphalt road quickly disappeared, leaving a deeply rutted gravel road in its place.

Being in regular cars as opposed to 4 wheel drive vehicles, the drivers really had to pick their routes to avoid the largest ruts or they would have surely gotten hung up on one of the lips. There were a couple of times that the whole road dipped down a few feet, where water had quickly streamed across the road in flash flood fashion and cut the road away. The road also was quite steep at times and the cars were driving in Low 1 and Low 2 gears to not overstrain the engines or transmissions.

Bianca was starting to stress that they wouldn't find the mountain house, everything was starting to look the same. Just as she was about to lose hope, the car crested a small hill and she recognized the house on the left as her Uncle's. With elation she confirmed with Frank that this was the right place.

They had not passed any cars or people for the last 10 minutes and there was not another home within line of sight. Frank pulled up in front of the wrought iron gate and placed the car in park. He then retrieved the bolt cutter from his trunk and walked up to the gate and cut off the lock. He took the broken lock back with him to the car.

He knew that if someone came by and saw a broken lock on the gate or ground that they may call the police to investigate. He then pulled his car inside the fenced in area, as did the other car. After they were all in, he closed the gate and put a new lock on the gate. He had noticed that almost every home they passed on the way had their gates locked; he thought it wise to mimic them.

Now that they were all inside the compound, Frank took the bolt cutters to the lock on the back door. There was a wrought iron security grill door, with a regular door behind it. The first door had a padlock, similar to the gate. That sniped off in seconds similar to its twin on the gate. The inner door had a deadbolt as well as a door knob lock.

The wooden door was beautiful; hand crafted not your standard run of the mill door from a big box hardware store. Frank knew that the wooden door or the wooden door frame would give if he shouldered it hard enough, probably both would give a little. He hit the door hard with his shoulder; it made a slight cracking sound after the initial thud. He hit it again and almost fell inside with the left over force of the door giving way.

Examining the door and frame, neither had been totally broken, instead they both bent a little and cracked a little, but to get the door closed again the double deadbolt would have to be removed. A quick search of the few cabinets yielded a screw driver that was used to completely remove the deadbolt. The door would now close after being slightly realigned.

The next job would be to scout out the property and the surrounding area. If someone were to find them, how would they attack, was there a good place to make a stand, or a good escape route not visible from the road.

George and Jerry volunteered to do the scouting, while Frank and Luke unloaded the vehicles. The Ward's family luggage is a few trips alone for Luke. Frank got his team's bags, including the weapons bag. He also removed the gas and oil cans and puts them by an outbuilding.

After cutting the lock on this building, he found the generator. He looked at the gas cap on the generator and sees it is a 50:1 ratio for the oil and mixes the gas and oil accordingly. He won't start the generator until George and Jerry get back and report how far the closest houses are, and if they are occupied.

There were enough large jutting rocks and trees in the area to afford good cover for the men on reconnaissance and they should not be spotted easily, but then again, a stranger in these parts would really stick out, this was a very rural place.

15 minutes later, George and Jerry return and report to Frank that the next nearest house was about ½ click and the next closest was 1 ½ clicks, it should be safe to run the generator. There also was a 10-15 mph wind that was changing directions that would help muffle and distort any sounds from those distances.

The generator was a residential model and wasn't any louder than a lawn mower. It started up on the second pull. When the generator started, the lights in the mountain house came on, even though it wasn't dark yet. They probably never turned them off, because they had only used the generator when they needed electricity. Frank also noticed an extension cord that was not plugged into the power strip of the generator. He plugged it in and heard water flowing. The cord had been for a well water pump.

The house had a water tank that once full, started overflowing using a drain spout on the outside of the house. Frank unplugged the well pump and turned the generator off. No reason to waste the gas during daylight hours.

Benjamin was driving, with Dominic and the others taking a nap. Benjamin nudged Dominic, sitting in the front passenger seat to wake him, as they entered Cosenza. Benjamin said, "I am hungry."

Dominic said, "That sounds like a good idea. Where are we?"

"Cosenza, it is the biggest city around here, Marano is only about 30 minutes or so from here," replied Benjamin.

"OK, find a petrol station to fill up, then we will eat"

Dominic had used his smartphone back in Cosenza to look up Carlos Fragatelli's address. They would be paying a visit to Carlos soon. The roads climbed gracefully into the mountainside community and within 30 minutes they were outside of Carlos's house. Do-

minic said that he and Lisa would go and ask about the Wards, saying that they had spent some time with them in Venice and told them
to come and visit in Marano if they could make it.

Carlos's wife said that Bianca hadn't showed up and that they
were worried about them, they hadn't heard anything. The lady was
convincing, but Dominic couldn't really take this as the dead end it
probably was. Dominic pushed the lady back into her own house.
The lady was really too startled to fight it. Lisa followed them in
through the door.

Seconds later she and Dominic were holding their guns out in
front of them. The lady asked what this was all about. As the wom-
en started to cry, a young man came running in to see what was
wrong with his mother. The young man stopped quickly when he
saw the couple brandishing their weapons. He asked, "What do you
want?"

"We are looking for Bianca Ward and her family, have they
come here?"

Carmine, the young man said, "No, they haven't made it here,
they were supposed to come today, earlier, we went to meet them at
the train station, but they weren't on the train."

"Do you know any other place they could be, what about her
uncle Salvatore?"

"No uncle Sal went with us to the station, they aren't there."

"I don't want to hurt you or your Mother, but I need to know if
you can think of any other place they could be right now?"

The young man confused the polite talk for an unwillingness to
do harm. He said, "Why should I help you, you have guns, you
don't seem like friends."

At that moment Dominic fired the gun toward Carmine's Mother, just missing her by a foot to the left, shattering the relative quiet-
ness of the room as well as a vase that was sitting on a stand.

Dominic then said calmly, "Think hard, the next one may hit
your Mother."

He thought hard, "We have a mountain house that Bianca and
Luke went to with us the last time they were here. But I doubt they
could find it, there aren't really any addresses up there and it has
been 15 years."

Dominic said to Lisa, "Tie her up, he is coming with us."

Dominic said to the Mother, "If you tell anyone where we are
before tomorrow, we will kill your son."

He put Carmine in the back seat between Lisa and Benjamin and started on their way to the mountain house. The young man gave good directions, having been to his mountain home hundreds of times. He was worried for his cousin Bianca and for himself for that matter. When they were less than ¼ mile away from the mountain home Dominic pulled the car over. They tied and gagged Carmine in the car and left the windows open; hopefully he wouldn't die from the heat, they might have to use him in the future.

Dominic clicked the key fob to open the trunk. Inside, were two duffle bags, each containing; a rifle, binoculars, range finder, hand-gun and ammunition. Once the teams loaded up, they split up, two on either side of the road, one riffle in each team. Dominic knew that the CIA field Officers were most likely ex-military, as was he, just from a different country.

The CIA officers would set up a perimeter and watch for intrud-ers, namely them. Right now, Dominic had the advantage. He knew that Frank and his crew had to be close to the house and that would allow him to locate and eliminate them faster.

Dominic figured that they could take two or three of the men out using a riffle, and then they would rush in and set fire to the house, which would flush them all out into the open. Dominic and Lisa were positioning themselves on slightly higher ground across the street from the mountain house.

He and Benjamin had agreed ahead of time, that Dominic would take out anyone to the right side of the compound and Benjamin would terminate anyone to the left or back side.

They had also agreed that Dominic would take the first shot, but that if Benjamin had a good shot and Dominic hadn't taken one with-in 15 minutes, he had the green light. Both teams set up about 200 meters, about two football fields, away from their target areas. The women were the lookouts, when the men were sniping, they needed to concentrate on the job at hand and not worry about being shot.

The men methodically assembled their riffles and scopes. They then looked through their glare resistant binoculars to get a lay of the land.

Dominic was happy to see two men positioned on opposite cor-ners of the property; they were stationary and obviously hadn't spot-ted him or Benjamin. He took out his range finder, read the distance, and clicked it into his scope. He was using a M40 sniper rifle with 6.5 x 47 Lapua rounds. This weapon ammo combination allows a sniper to work without a spotter because the slight recoil wouldn't make the shooter lose site of the target after firing, but still had an effective range of over 1000 meters. The M40 sniper rifle was originally designed for the US Marines and also featured a muzzle break or flash suppressor. It pays to have contracts with the CIA; they have access to all the fun toys.

Dominic slowly set his gun in position, with the front propped up on the duffle bag. At this distance he would be near impossible to spot with the naked eye, but almost any motion could reveal your location.

He liked this particular gun for another reason, it had an ammo clip. Most sniper rifles were single shot bolt action guns, requiring the shooter to have ammo within easy reach and manually load every cartridge by hand. The occasional sniper liked the convenience of simply pulling back the bolt and slamming home a new round without having to manually load each round individually. The way it was, he had enough on his mind.

Dominic now pulled the bolt back and loaded the first round into the weapon. After a few seconds, he readjusted his body on the rocky surface to avoid one rock edge that was starting to dig into his side. The adjustment completed, he did a dry practice run on firing the weapon, reaching up and pretending to pull the bolt back and push it forward, then returning his hand to the firing position.

He figured he could fire three shots within 6 seconds, not bad, about the same time used by Oswald to kill Kennedy 46 years earlier; some things don't change much with time. Dominic glanced at Lisa to verify that she was looking around instead of at him; she was, so he went back to the scope. His 15 minutes of time was about to elapse, but Dominic never allowed himself to feel rushed one he entered his zone.

He looked in the scope again. He saw some movement this time. The men on patrol were shifting positions, he couldn't see the man on the left now, he was in Dominic's blind spot created by the mountain house. Dominic was about to take the shot, when the man he was spotting quickly jumped behind a stone wall. A split second later, a shot could be heard from where Benjamin would be, he must have taken out the other sentry, Dominic thought to himself. But, what had caused his mark to jump to safety right before the shot, could Benjamin have been spotted?

Dominic didn't have too long to think about it before another shot rang out less than 10 feet from him. He looked up in time to see Lisa falling toward the ground. Dominic was now the hunted and being on the ground was a huge disadvantage. He was lying on the ground and could not easily move. Even worse, the only gun within easy reach was the sniper rifle, which was not very effective for close range shooting. Those were his last thoughts, as two rounds hit him center mass. Already being on the ground, Dominic didn't have far to fall, he simply slumped over backward, the weapon still in his death grasp.

Frank ran up quickly to disarm Dominic, and then did the same to Lisa. He felt for Lisa's pulse, she was dead, as was Dominic. He then radioed that he had taken out the team across the street, and that there were no prisoners.

Jerry had spotted Benjamin and shot him before the sniper was set up. Jerry had seen a reflection on the hillside, it ended up being the sun shining off of the woman's ear ring. He and George were advancing with caution to the sniper's location. As they crested the hill where the sniper lay on the ground, they saw a person running towards the street, about a hundred yards away. George radioed Frank to let him know they were in pursuit.

Frank took up the binoculars that Dominic had been using and saw the women running toward the road. Frank could also see a ve-hicle in the distance. The woman had a hand gun and was firing the weapon back toward Jerry and George. Without hesitating, Frank dropped to the ground and brought the M40 to bear on the woman now running down the street. The range was over 400 yards, well within Frank's expertise with this weapon. After clicking in the range, he verified there was a round chambered and set up for the shot.

She was running away from him so it was a much easier shot, he didn't need to lead further than what he could see through the scope. He calmed his inner self, exhaled; not taking another breadth, then oh so gently squeezed the trigger. About two seconds later the woman stopped running and fell to the ground.

Jerry and George reached her about 45 seconds after she hit the ground. They didn't really need to search for a pulse; she was clear-ly no longer alive. They retrieved her weapon, and then started to-ward the vehicle parked down the road.

They had spotted the car as they came up on the woman's body. There was some movement within the car and they quickly devised a plan to split up and converge on the car from two different angles, George would cover Jerry as he would actually go to the car to investigate. As Jerry got closer to the vehicle, it became clear that the only visible occupant was gagged and was frantically trying to free himself from his bindings. Jerry still proceeded with caution, what if this was a trap and someone was waiting inside the car, but that was doubtful, the car hardly looked big enough to carry the two teams plus this one person.

Jerry came up on the car rapidly, looked through the windows and confirmed that only the one young man was in the vehicle. He removed Carmine's gag and helped him out of the hot car. Carmine spoke rapidly in Italian, asking who the people that tied him up were and if Bianca was safe. George came to the car as Jerry was untying Carmine's hands. George asked, "How do you know Bianca?"

Carmine responded, "My name is Carmine, she is my cousin, these people came to our house and threatened to kill my mother and me unless we helped them. The mountain house was the only place we went with Bianca the last time they were here. If I really thought that she was here, I wouldn't have told them." Carmine shook his head and put his hands up to his face with shame.

Jerry said, "Carmine, if you wouldn't have helped them they would have killed you. If we wouldn't of been here, they may have killed you anyway, fewer witnesses."

Frank checked through Dominic's and Lisa's pockets. They each had a cellphone, he took those and put them in his own pocket. Dominic had a wallet with 200 Euros a Visa and a drivers license in the name of Dominic Benedine, residing in Rome. Frank took the 200 Euros and threw the wallet back down on Dominic's chest. Frank then proceeded in partially disassembling the gun and tucking it back into the duffle bag. He checked the contents of the bag and found more ammunition and a cleaning kit. He made a note to himself to clean the gun later, it may come in useful.

Jerry radioed to Frank that they had found Bianca's cousin Carmine in the vehicle and that they were going to bring him and the car up to the house. Frank said OK and asked that George search the other two and brings back any weapons or anything else that could be useful like phones or money. Jerry drove the car to the gate in front of the house; Frank had made his way across the street and unlocked the gate so that the car could be brought inside. After parking, Carmine jumped out of the car and headed toward the house, calling out Bianca's name as he went. Hearing her name, Bianca came out of the house. She was surprised, but happy to see her cousin Carmine. They embraced and did the double cheek kiss thing.

The kids and Luke came out of the house as well. Luke went up to Carmine and looked him up and down, "You look much older than the last time we saw you." Bianca translated for Carmine.

Carmine looked Luke up and down, "You look a little older also, not as much hair, but almost the same as 15 years earlier." Bianca translated back to Luke.

Then Luke and Carmine did a big guy hug with the double check kiss and patted each other on the back. Carmine's face broke into a huge smile as he realized that Bianca's children were right there, he had only seen pictures before. They were so tall.

Elizabeth said, "Buon giorno."

Carmine said, "Ciao, bella."

Elizabeth laughed. She wanted to learn Italian and only knew a few phrases, but she understood that Carmine had said hi beautiful. Both Elizabeth and James gave hugs and kisses to their second cousin. After saying all the hellos, the group headed into the house to make their next plans.

Carmine wasn't happy when he saw the damaged door and locks. Bianca saw his worried look and reassured him, "We will pay you for the damages, we cut the locks on the gate and the storage building, but put new locks on them, we will give you the keys. We really had nowhere else to go and as it turns out, this was not a good place to go. We also put you and your family in danger unnecessarily, sorry."

Carmine responded, "No problem, I am glad that you and your family are safe. Where will you go now?" After Bianca translated, she thought to herself, "Yes, where will we go?"

Frank was already working on that. He gathered everyone around the large family dining table in the kitchen area. He explained that he was sure that Edwin Grey was not going to give up and that he along with the proper CIA authorities needed to capture Edwin and find out if he had more double agents or moles in the organization.

Frank said he was going to call William Bowles again and bring him up to speed, hopefully by now Bowles' people had found out more about Edwin that could help bring him in. Frank's proposal was to go to Rome, confront and capture Edwin. Enough people had died, and so far, not any of the good guys; he wanted to keep it that way.

Frank walked into one of the bedrooms and closed the door. As promised, Frank called Deputy Director, CIC/AG, William Bowles. Frank laid out how they had gone off grid, went to Bianca's relatives' mountain house, how the four assassins found them, were eliminated and that Frank wanted to be involved with taking down Edwin Grey, before he ran.

Bowles said, "Frank, we found more evidence of Edwin's involvement with Silvano and his eventual murder in jail. We were able to follow the money train; down to the 5000 Euros he paid the guard at the jail to kill Silvano. Edwin is dirty and we will take him down."

Frank passionately said, "He will see you coming and run, I need to confront him, but I need your help…" Frank went on to provide a plan he thought would snare Edwin and restore the safety of his fellow CIA officers and the Wards.

Frank finished the phone call and walked back into the kitchen. He addressed the eager crowd around the table, now sharing the food they had purchased earlier in Cosenza.

"I will be meeting with Edwin, I will tell him that I am tired of running, I am tired of working for peanuts and want to be a partner in his operation. He won't really want a partner, but will say he does to get me close enough to kill me. That is where you guys come in, pointing to Jerry and George, you will be covering my back using the M40s donated by the guys outside."

Luke said, "You are going to be bait, that sounds kind of risky, I assume that Edwin Grey has much the same training that you have had. For him to be in his position, he must be a little crafty, like a fox."

"True, he is like a fox, but like a fox in a hunt, we will keep him off balance and corner him. It will be up to him whether he lives or dies, I know that these guys won't let anything happen to me." Frank pointed again to Jerry and George.

Frank said, "Luke I would like for you to be a look out for George and Jerry, we will get some new radio headsets from the CIA guys that come over from Langley. I requested you to help, because I trust you, I don't know if Edwin had gotten to any others in the department, but I know you are motivated to help."

"Of course I will help, but we need to find a safe place for Bianca and the twins to hide while this is going down."

"I have an idea for where to put them, and they will be safe, but I won't share their location until we get to Rome."

Chapter 18   Rome

Edwin knew that something had gone wrong, Dominic hadn't checked in with him as per there agreed upon schedule.   Edwin could only assume Frank and the others would either leave Italy or come for him, either one of the prospects wasn't good.   There was still a chance that he could stabilize the situation if he could find them and eliminate them.   As he was thinking this his cell phone rang, from the caller ID, he could see it was Dominic. Edwin answered, "Yes."

Frank said, "Edwin, good to hear your voice," letting that sink in for a moment, he continued, "We both know that this needs to come to a head.   You are getting rich selling bags while you sent some goons to put the bag on me. I want in."

Edwin thought to himself, could it be this easy, would Frank just present himself as a partner letting Edwin take him out, it smelled like a trap.   Edwin knew he had an ace in the hole and responded, "Frank, I could use a man with your skills, but what about the Wards, Jerry and George?"

"The Wards will go home and be happy to be home, this has been a bad trip for them, and they don't know anything about your involvement.   Jerry and George are not at partner level, but would like to work on our team as well."

"I see, when you said they weren't at partner level, it sounded like you thought that you were?"

"I figure that you could part with 30% of the net profits. I have contacts back in the US as well as here in Italy and also in most of the other European countries, plus what I know about you could cost you 100%, 30% is a bargain, no?"

Edwin thought that either Frank was a good actor or he really did want in. Edwin said, "20%."

"Edwin, 30% is the price, and a fair one, what do you say?"

"Done, 30% it is. You can start right away, let's meet tomorrow night, we have a shipment coming in via train and need to divide it and ship some out to the US in a container the day after from Naples. I will explain how it all works at our meeting."

After hanging up the phone with Frank, Edwin thought to himself, I don't really trust Frank, after all, I just had a contract out on him and he obviously took out Dominic and his crew, he is a very dangerous man. Edwin then chuckled to himself, he knew that he was in control of the situation and that in the end it was Frank that would get 0%, because he would be dead.

After hanging up with Edwin Frank used one of his prepaid phones to talk with William Bowles at CIC/AG, "Did you hear it all?"

Bowles sadly responded, "Yes, he admitted on the phone that he was getting a shipment in. That information will help us back track and see where it is coming from, we also need to see who in the U.S. is helping him bring the goods in and distributing it. You also know that he wants to eliminate you? I don't think he bought your story. You will be walking into a trap; I think that it might be best if you just let us go get him. He practically confessed on the phone."

"He could just claim that I was trying to trap him and that he was simply playing along to get a rouge officer under arrest. I agree with you, he wants me dead. I think that we need to get the jail guard to turn on him so that there can't be a doubt. Even saying that, I don't think that Edwin is the "go to trial, go to jail kind of guy," I think that he would not go down quietly, taking out a few people with him."

"You are right about that one. Our team should be landing any minute; tonight you can be in Rome and meet them to get the gear you requested. I sent two men to help you apprehend Edwin; you have a green light to eliminate Edwin if your life or other lives are in danger because of him.

He knows a lot of secrets of the CIA, NSA and some other secret agencies that you don't have the clearance to know the initials of. He is illegally importing counterfeit goods into the U.S., worked with a known crime boss in Italy and used CIA agent assassins to try and kill you and the Wards. Edwin will not go quietly, but and this is the only reason I am letting you meet with him, if possible, we would like to take him alive. We need to make sure we don't have other moles or minions in the company."

"I thought the same thing, that is why I called you to start with or else Edwin would have already had a bad car accident and we wouldn't be having this conversation. He drew first blood."

"OK Rambo, that is enough talk like that, this call is being recorded as I am sure you were aware of, so let's stay on task."

"Sir, yes sir, understood."

The line went silent. Frank gathered Jerry and George. He said, "I just spoke with William Bowles at CIC/AG about our situation. He is fully briefed and on board with our plan. He has sent two guys to assist us with this operation; he also sent some communications equipment as well as some monitoring equipment that I will go over once we get it. We need to move fast and get up to Rome by tomorrow. The Wards are coming with us; I have a place I think is safe for them. Luke can come and help us with the monitoring equipment."

Edwin needed to move fast. He didn't really trust Frank so he was going to play his ace in the hole, Jerry's family. They would make a great insurance plan. Edwin called Michelle Banks and let her know that he had something for her from Jerry. He told her that Jerry wasn't available to bring it home himself. Michelle asked what it was, but Edwin simply said he didn't open the small box, it was wrapped; he did mention it was the size of a ring box from a jewelry store.

Michelle thought to herself, Jerry probably was worried about the additional burden he was putting on her by being gone so many days and not being able to check in. She also wondered if somehow Jerry had found out that she was pregnant with their first boy; no, he couldn't know, she just found out yesterday and even though she knew he worked for the Government, he couldn't know the news.

All the same she was very curious about the gift. She told Edwin that she would be home for the next hour before she had to run the kids to a summer art school they were taking for fun. Edwin agreed to bring it by her home in the next 30 minutes.

Edwin made a call to his special assassin backup team, a secret team that no one within the CIA knew about. They were off the record, not on the books, a black ops team. All of the regional section heads had their own black ops teams that they compensated with a slush fund; their superiors wouldn't want to know how it was spent or on what, they just wanted results.

Edwin asked John Doe to bring a van and some chemicals to subdue one adult woman and two children. John Doe would also bring John Smith and enough weapons and ammunition to wage a guerilla assault. He gave John Doe Michelle Bank's address and told him to meet there in 20 minutes.

Edwin shared his plan of going up to the house by himself, Michelle would invite him in. He would give her the package as the two man team came up to the front door that would be unlocked and/or open. The men would burst in, Edwin would grab Michelle and the two men would gather the children. They would then use the drug Rohypnol more commonly known as "Roofies" or the date rape drug on the Banks family.

With this drug, within minutes, the victim feel no inhabitations and will do as asked, the family would walk out to the van, and would not have to be carried, which could attract attention. The drug also rendered the user with memory loss of events. They were kind of walking zombies until the drug put them into a deep sleep. That was the plan, but seldom do plans go off the way one wishes in the field, they sometimes require compromise and being creative while real life unfolds.

Frank decided to break up the Wards between the two cars for the long drive to Rome. Bianca and James went with Jerry and George. Frank started out driving with Luke in the front seat and Elizabeth in the back seat for their six hour drive.

Bianca asked George, "Do you have any family in Italy?"

"No, I don't, I really don't have much family alive right now. My Mother died a little over 2 years ago, my Father is an alcoholic that left me and my Mom 20 years ago and I don't even know where he is right now. I don't have any brothers or sisters, so no, I don't have any family here. Jerry does though."

Jerry chimed in, "I have a wife, Michelle, and two girls, Emily, 6 and Susan is 4. We have been trying for another one the last couple of years with no luck, I would really like to have a boy, not that the girls aren't my little princesses, they are, but sometimes I think about how it would be great to play catch with a son."

Bianca said, "Two girls, God bless you, I can hardly deal with one right now. The twins were a hand full when they were babies, it was impossible to pick them both up at the same time by yourself, so one would cry when the other got picked up. We tried to have two people there at all times for the first couple of months.

It was great starting with the toddler age; they had built in best friends and were never lonely or bored. As they became 9 year olds the boy, girl thing started getting in the way, Elizabeth is more of a girly girl than a tom boy so she wanted to play with dolls while James wanted to play with video games and Lego. Today, they both play sports; Elizabeth does soccer and dance and James plays baseball and golf."

Jerry said, "Yes, my girls like soccer, here they call it football. Every kid plays it, it is a national obsession. That reminds me, I should check in with Michelle to see how she is doing; she had been sick on and off for this last week, throwing up and just not feeling like herself. Also, today the kids are starting an art class for fun; she probably is running around right now trying to get the kids ready for it. She thought while in Rome..."

Jerry called his wife using the disposable phone that he had been given by Frank when they had first arrived in Cosenza. The phone rang a few times, she must be busy doing something, and then she picked up.

Michelle said, "Hello?"

Jerry answered, "It's me, I only have a second, just wanted to see how you were feeling and how everything was going."

Michelle giggled, "Edwin is here with the present you got me, and I haven't opened it yet, hang on."

Jerry took only a split second to realize that Edwin was Edwin Grey and he didn't have a real present for his wife. Jerry screamed into the phone, "Run, Edwin is bad." But, he was too late; he heard a scuffle and his wife screamed in the back ground. This was torture, he yelled, "Michelle, Michelle are you all right?"

Then he heard one of his girls scream, this was almost too much for him to take, he wasn't focused on driving anymore and drifted from the left hand lane and started onto the shoulder, when George grabbed the steering wheel and brought the car under control as Jerry let his foot off of the gas pedal and finally put it on the brake. They were in the lead car so Frank pulled in behind the now stopped car on the shoulder in front of them.

Jerry listened intently; the phone was still off of the hook. He heard men's voices, but couldn't make out what they were saying until Edwin came on the line, "Jerry, this is Edwin, Michelle is OK, and your kids are OK, for now." Edwin let that wash over Jerry for a few seconds.

Jerry barked, "What are you doing? They are innocent."

Edwin responded calmly, "Jerry, I honestly don't know if you are on board with me or if you and Frank and George are plotting to get me. I needed a little insurance policy to make sure you behave as planned. Is Frank there?

As Edwin was asking this question, Jerry heard a rap at his car window, it was Frank. Jerry opened the window and told Frank that Edwin had his wife and kids and was asking for him on the phone. Frank took the phone, opened the back door and sat in Jerry's car. After closing the door and Jerry closing the window, Frank spoke into the phone, "Edwin, what is this I hear about Jerry's family?"

Edwin laughed, "Frank, you don't think I got to this position because I am good at paper work do you? I got here by first being in the field, being one of the best in the field. Jerry's family is simply a way to make sure that you really do what you say that you will do; and I will be the only link to them so you won't be as quick to try and kill me."

"Go on. What do you want?"

"Our meeting has changed; you now need to meet me in Naples around 6 pm. Obviously, I am not bringing the family with me; they will be safe as long as I am. If I don't contact my people at the prearranged times, they won't hesitate to kill the woman and the two kids. Do we understand each other?"

"Yeah sure, I get it. Where are we to meet?"

"As you know Naples is a port city, we will meet at shipping container area 25, the guard at the gates to the complex will have your name. Bring Jerry and George, so I know there isn't a gun pointed at my head. Don't try anything too heroic or the family will die, not a threat, just a promise." The phone went dead.

Frank said, "Change of plans, we are meeting him in Naples. I don't like the situation. He is smart and I don't trust that this isn't a trap. If he simply wanted to kill us he could have just sent some assassins to meet us in Rome. I think he wants to just put us off balance and stay in charge of the situation. I will call William right now to see if we can get our support guys down to Naples right now, or they won't be of any use to us."

Jerry said, "Before a few days ago, I never thought that Edwin was dirty, I can't believe that he took my family, now I want to kill him."

Frank responded, "We can't do that, at least not yet. He has people watching your family, if he doesn't communicate with them at certain times he has instructed them to ......"

Jerry finished the sentence, "Kill them. That is why we need to figure out a plan where I get my family back and Edwin dies." Frank and George just both silently nodded.

Bianca was beside herself. She was thinking about what Luke would do if she and the kids were being held captive and he had to put himself in grave danger to protect them. Maybe being a spy family wasn't all it was cracked up to be. Up until now, her family hadn't had much of a choice, very bad people had tried to kill them, and there was no choice but to continue on and try to end the madness. But, now she started reflecting back on how close they had all come to being killed, including the kids.

Bianca could see the pain on Jerry's face. He may have been a mighty warrior, but he was still a husband and father and his family was in danger.

Frank told Jerry and George, "I will go call William Bowles, let's start towards Naples, the sooner we get there the faster we can have a plan. I will ask William to forward me some overhead photos of the container yard and any other intelligence that they can gather. Once we get to Naples, we will stop to eat and make our plan. We will also know if we have any help or need to do this one by ourselves."

The men agreed and Jerry watched Frank walk back to his car. Jerry knew that Frank wanted to be able to talk to Bowles without Jerry being present. Jerry was worried that he would instruct Frank to take Edwin down regardless of his family's safety; the US government didn't negotiate with terrorists or criminals. He would have to cross that bridge when he came to it. Right now they were on their way to Naples.

Frank got back into his car and relayed the events to Luke. Luke asked Frank, "Do you have a plan?"

"Not yet. I am going to call Bowles now and see what help he can offer."

Frank called him, it was about 3 in the morning so understandably he sounded a little groggy, but the fog cleared instantly when Frank laid out what had just transpired. Bowles told Frank to stay on the line, while he used another phone to see where his two men were. Their plane was about to land, and he would get them down to Naples as soon as possible. It was about a two and one half hour trip via car.

Bowles told Frank, "I will get you aerials of the place and other info, like who owns that area, what is in most of the containers in that lot, etc. With Jerry's family being held captive, we will also try to play this one a little closer to the rules.

We don't know who to trust that is already in country.

One of my guys will travel to Naples with a cellular phone interceptor, it can listen and record the cell phone conversations and provide us with the number he is calling. Once we get the number he is calling, then we can get cooperation from the cellular service provider to find his accomplice's location.

My other guy will stay in Rome and get Jerry's family back safely."

Frank said, "That is a decent plan, I wish we had more than one guy to help free Jerry's family, but it is all we have right now.

On our end we have Luke to use with your man to cover our back and get the cell number to help with the location. Luke is also a decent shot, even though he hasn't been properly trained, he has held up better under fire better than others I have seen who were trained."

Bowles said, "As we have been talking, I looked over the files of both men I have sent, I believe that Mark Black will be the one I leave in Rome and Jack Green will be going down to Naples. What do you have for supplies?" Bowles knew that this was not an encrypted line so he was asking slyly for Frank's weapon and ammunition supply.

Frank responded, "2 M40s and enough to do the job." So much for discretion, Bowles thought to himself.

Bowles said, "Great, then Mr. Black will have all that he needs." It was not an easy task to have armed people or that kind of firepower legally in a foreign country since 9/11, it could be done, but now there was no time to get the proper approvals.

Mr. Black and Mr. Green weren't traveling to Italy via regular commercial airlines, at least not the people kind. They were arriving in a FEDEX transport jet. The commercial jets didn't have to go to the regular gates and it was much easier dealing with a customs and immigrations agent away from the general public. The two traveled with some diplomatic suitcases, which meant that the customs officer was not allowed to open or search their contents. The commercial end of the airport still had radiation and chemical weapons detectors, so the officer wasn't worried about weapons of mass destruction.

He asked, "What is in the cases?"

Mr. Green responded, "We don't know, they don't tell us, but we are computer guys, so they may be some high tech computer stuff."

As the customs officer was stamping their passports, he said, "Yes, computers." He handed them back and said with a forced smile, "Welcome to Italy Mr. Black and Mr. Green."

Mr. Black and Mr. Green went to the Hertz rental car agency and each picked up a Ford Focus. Not exactly the spy type car that most imagine, but that is why it works. No one thinks twice about seeing the Ford Focus in this setting. They drove about 10 minutes outside of the airport to a petrol station. Leonardo Di Vinci Airport was more in the countryside than close to Rome. The men divided the weapons and cellular monitors into separate nondescript, black duffle bags that were also inside the diplomatic shipping cases. They retrieved and loaded their pistols.

They removed their light jackets and put on shoulder holsters. The light jackets were a little out of place, considering it was in the mid to upper 80s outside, but it couldn't be helped. They also each strapped on a small ankle holster and .22 cal gun. These were needed in close combat situations, it was always better to bring a gun to a knife fight than the other way around.

They verified that the specially encrypted phones they brought with them worked and that the blue tooth headsets also worked. Jack Green used the communications equipment, testing each ear piece and making sure that the master radio link could also work with the encrypted cell phones. This gave them both near and far communications using the civilian cellular systems.

One item new to both of them was new bullet proof vests, more like a bullet proof T shirt, made out of new materials, Carbon nanotubes, CNTs, that are six layers thick woven into the shirt material. This new material basically expands, absorbs the energy, prevents penetration, then rebounds or bounces back the bullet.

Once all the equipment was divided and checked out, they shook hands and wished each other well.

Mr. Green got in his car and started toward Naples, while Mr. Black headed into Rome. He would check into a centrally located hotel and wait for Mr. Green to tell him where Jerry Banks' family is located.

Mark Black had a hard task ahead of him. He didn't currently know where the family was being held, how many people were there and armed, nor how accurate the location he would be given was. Usually, with a good fix on the phone, they could get to within 50 feet. This was fine in a residential area with single family homes, but in Rome there were plenty of areas where there were apartments and flats.

The coordinates usually didn't provide altitude, so the element of surprise could not be counted on. His plan was to get the location and recon the building from a safe distance through binoculars and/or under the guise of a telephoto lens on a camera.

This normally would be a 2-3 man team minimum job; one to be a spotter/sniper and two to penetrate the holding area. Mark Black knew why he was selected for this job over Mr. Green. Mark had been involved in a hostage operation about 2 years earlier in Iraq.

The US Special Forces unit had captured an unfriendly while searching for a US soldier that had been abducted after being wounded in a firefight and couldn't walk. The Iraqi was all of 17 years old and scared to death of being killed and buried with a dead pig; a rumor started by Al-Qaida.

He told the Special Forces men what they wanted to hear; there was a hurt American about 2 blocks from here, but he was almost dead. He told them that Al Qaida was going to make a video of the US soldier and execute him before he could die of his wounds.

The Special Forces leader radioed the information in to Command. They didn't have anyone else in the immediate area and the 6 of them were all that was going to be available for the next 30 minutes. This would have been a risky endeavor using a proper sized team with good Intel. For example, on how many boogies were in the building, the floor plan of the building, including how many entrances and exits there were.

In Iraq, the Special Forces learned early on that it was faster to make your own door than to go through one that was already there. It could be booby trapped, have a man waiting for someone to enter, or could be alarmed. One common way to booby trap it was to put a grenade in a glass jar, pull the pin and balance the jar on a shelf on the back of the door. When the door was opened or broken down the jar would fall and break open, that was the alarm part, as well as the grenade going off about 4 seconds later, the delay just long enough to have a few young troops in harm's way.

The plan was for Mark to be the first to enter after the wall was breached. Without proper intelligence, hopefully the hostage wasn't tied up next to that wall, or in that room, it was going to be very noisy and very dangerous for the people on the other side of the wall.

The first Special Forces guy pulled out a prepackaged satchel charge which consisted of about 6 pounds of C4 plastic explosive. He took out one and one half feet of detonation cord and stuck it into the C4. He then placed a 4 foot stick with one end stabbed into the ground and the other leaning against the satchel and the wall at about shoulder height.

He then placed a detonation device on the detonation cord. Everyone else was already about 20-30 feet sideways down the wall. The shaped charge was going to go mainly forward and backward. The explosives guy reeled out about 40 foot of electric wires, attached them to a detonator, gave the signal so the initial blast wasn't a shock to the men and pressed the recessed button. Without delay the C4 did its job, opening up a 4 foot wide by 8 foot high hole in the external wall of the building.

As was the plan, Mark entered first. He was pretty sure that anyone in the room at the time of the explosion would either be dead or in no shape to fight. He was right; he passed two bodies as he ran to the hallway. When he got to the next room, he tossed in a flash bang grenade, which again would incapacitate anyone not anticipating it. He rushed into the room, it was empty. He heard a couple of other flash bangs go off behind him in rooms across the hall, but he hadn't heard much else until the gun fire started.

It was coming from the end of the hall and most likely where the hostage was being kept. Two of the Special Forces men had stayed at the breach to protect their flanks, two were engaged with the gun fight and two, including Mark were searching the last couple of rooms. When the room search didn't yield anything, Mark put two bursts of gunfire chest high through the open doorway at the end of the hall. He hit one guy square on and he fell straight down. The other one, seeing the numbers in the hallway increasing, decided to close the door. He was going back to kill the hostage, or at least that is what Mark thought.

Just as the last burst from Mark's gun cleared, he started running toward the door. As the door closed toward Mark, he burst through with his shoulder. The door splintered, leaving Mark's momentum to carry him into the room and roll onto the floor. As Mark was hitting the floor, bullets tore at the flooring around him. He managed to get his feet under him and locked eyes with the guy that was just at the door. One burst from Mark's weapon and the door man was no longer standing.

There were two other men in the room besides the hostage. Mark had sized up the men and their location in the half second it took for him to decided he need to change weapons to increase his accuracy because they were close to the hostage. He dropped his M16 and pulled his Glock from his leg holster. Mark didn't wait the extra second it would take to control his breathing as he would with a longer shot, but instead squeezed off two shots per man at center mass, both crumpled to the ground without getting off another shot.

The hostage was in that room, he lived to thank Mark, but died in the evacuation helicopter on the ride back to base. Mark had taken down three armed men, without losing the hostage within the span of about 5 seconds.

Chapter 19   Naples

James asked Frank, "Why would Edwin, your boss, decide to be a bad guy? It sounds like he had a cool job."

Frank replied, "James that is an excellent question. It is hard for me to imagine a person that has done so much for his country, in ways we will never know, deciding to do illegal things. His betrayal goes deeper than money. He knew that funding from the sales of the counterfeit purses, watches and other items was being funneled to terrorist organizations. That goes against the core of our duties as officers of the CIA and is un-American in general."

Luke said, "James, Frank is right that it is hard to reason why a person that has done good could do so much bad, but most people like Edwin are not rational thinkers. In the end, most bad or evil doesn't succeed, and that is simply because there are more good people than evil people, so good tends to win out over evil. That is not to say that evil doesn't do a lot of damage in the mean time, until it all balances out."

James said, "I guess I understand, but it sure seems like a waste of a good thing, I mean we are going to catch him and he will go to jail for a long time. Won't he?"

Frank paused for a few seconds, wondering to himself if Edwin was going to be caught or would more than likely end up dead, then said, "Yes, it is a waste of all of our time and energy, but he will pay for his actions....one way or another."

The drive down from the Mountain home was beautiful, one could see for 20 plus miles. The hills and valleys alike were lush and green except for the dots of small towns that were peppered about. There was not much to be said on the drive. Frank had outlined the plan to Luke, taking into consideration that James was listening intently.

James thought it was like James Bond, that they could listen into a cellular phone call and track the location of the other person on the call. He really also feared for Jerry's family. James thought to himself, how unfair it was that Jerry's family was brought into this mess, kind of like the Ward family was. Neither family got what it deserved.

The two car caravan stopped near Pompeii for lunch. Pompeii brought back some bad memories; the Ward family had been am-

bushed there within the last week. James and Elizabeth hardly escaped; really their father had saved their lives that day.

After a quick lunch of Italian, Panini sandwiches, the cars again
started toward Naples where they were going to meet Jack Green at a
hotel.

Jack had arrived in Naples earlier and rented two rooms and one
suite. The CIA officers would double up and the Wards had a larger
suite to accommodate the four of them. Frank held a meeting with
Jack, Jerry, George and Luke in the CIA Officer's room. They went
over the communications equipment that Luke was going to help
Jack use. They also went over weapons they were going to carry and
discussed the aerial view maps that William Bowles had emailed to
them.

The overhead pictures were about 10 times better resolution
than what one could see on Google Earth and they were a lot more
recent, about 2 hours old. There would be a satellite in position by
this afternoon to cover the meeting live. The satellite would be able
to provide real-time images, infrared and heat signatures to Bowles
people back in Maryland. They would analyze and provide intelligence to Jack and Luke via the encrypted cell phone link that Jack
had set up earlier.

The hope was that Edwin wouldn't expect the CIA's tie in with
this meeting.

There are ways to hide body heat, if one wants to, but a good
analyst can spot the anomaly almost as fast as a regular heat signature. A sniper may cloak their body heat by using what is known as
a cold blanket, which will usually be setup to be at air temperature,
the only thing is, in a shipping container yard the containers will re-
tain a certain amount of heat from the daylight hours and release it
during the dark hours; their surface temperature is seldom at the air
temperature. When viewed from above, it would look like a cool
spot on a warm surface.

After looking at the surveillance images, Jack suggested going
right now and setting up the phone monitoring device on the mova-
ble crane support.

One of Bowles analyst noticed that the container crane was
manufactured in the U.S. and a call was placed for their cooperation.
The plan would have Jack go with one of their local maintenance
companies for an emergency inspection. The cover story was that
they needing to inspect the crane immediately because of another

similar structural crane that failed due to some counterfeit bolts being used from local builders. The inspection wouldn't take long and a vibration device (the cellphone monitor) would be fitted to monitor it over a 24 hour period to ensure all was well, this wouldn't require the bolts being replaced if everything checked out fine.

Jack left within 10 minutes.

Frank looked at the surveillance images and gently shook his head. Luke asked, "What is wrong?"

"Like I said earlier, Edwin is not stupid. He picked this location for multiple reasons, least of all; there is no natural location where a sniper could be located. Look here, this is area 25, it is walled off by containers that are at least 2 containers high, about 20 feet and they run parallel to the water's edge. When we are in the roadway between them we are cut off from all structures inland and from the sea. It is a virtual valley that we can't see into.

We will still put you and Jack across the street on top of this building that has a good view of the entrance to the shipyard. Together with our communications link, this vantage will at least allow you to take out Edwin, if he double crosses us. It should also allow you a vantage point over anyone that Edwin could place in the area, they would have the same issues we are having with not being able to protect him during the meeting itself."

Luke responded, "I see, so you will be vulnerable during the meeting?

"Yes, but so will Edwin and that's about as fair as this game will get. I will also ask that he call Jerry's wife while we are there so that we know that she and the kids are safe. He should do that and then we can begin the trace. Edwin should not think that we have that many allies right now. He thinks we are cut off and on the run, ready to make a deal. This too, will work to our advantage. It will help us get Jerry's family back safe and sound."

John Doe was telling Michele and the kids to be quiet and behave or they would be gagged and tied up the whole time. They were being held in a small one bedroom apartment; there was a main room that contained a TV, couch, 2 chairs, table, a small kitchen area, and very small bathroom. The whole apartment couldn't have been more than 400 square feet.

Michele asked, "Who are you, why are you doing this to us?"

John Doe said, "I am John Doe, he is John Doe, we don't exist, at least not with those names, just think of us as very overpaid baby-sitters. As long as your husband does what is asked of him, you will all be freed within hours."

Michele asked, "What if he doesn't cooperate?"

John Doe didn't say a word he just looked her in the eyes, and then glanced at the kids and back at her, shaking his head. Michele cried quietly to herself, not wanting to alarm the kids. She knew that these men were evil and would kill them all if they were told to.

John Doe said, "Watch TV, we have food and water in the refrigerator."

Michele noticed that his English was exceptional. He didn't look American but spoke like one.

After about 10 minutes of TV watching the girls had to use the bathroom. They were scared and wanted their mother to come. John Doe agreed that she could, but that he would be right outside the door. John Doe said, "Don't lock the door, don't open the window in the bathroom, and don't try anything that would make me come in there."

Michele quickly noticed there was not enough room for three people to stand on the floor in the bathroom, so she stepped into the old fashioned cast iron soaking tub to give her daughters more room. They all took turns and the girls thought it was funny to have to go in the tub; they all had a good chuckle. But, as soon as they opened the bathroom door and saw John Doe standing there with a large automatic gun strapped around his neck, they quickly stopped laughing and came back to reality. These were bad men, very bad men, and they all feared for their lives.

Jack Green came back to the hotel and let Frank know that the cellular interceptor was in place on the crane.

Frank asked, "Any problems at the shipping yard?"

Jack answered, "No, they were glad that the American crane company was being pro active about looking for a problem. The shipyard manager wanted to go for a drink with us, I think it was customary for him to get a free lunch or something, but before going into the shipyard I told our man to make it as brief as possible, I didn't share why and he didn't ask."

Frank said, "Good. Did you recon the area at all?"

Jack said, "Yes, let's look at the overheads again." They pulled out the latest overhead photos that William Bowles had emailed to them.

Jack continued, "Here, here and here, I saw armed security guards walking around. There was only one way in and out as we can see, but what I missed on the photo was this little guard shack by the entry way, it was so small that it looked like just part of the fence. It couldn't have been more than 10 square feet big, just large enough to have a chair in it."

Frank asked, "Where there many other people in the area, is a ship being off loaded or anything else you would note?"

Jack responded, "No, there was no ship in the port. I didn't really see much action there at all, just mainly the guards walking around."

Frank said, "Good job Jack, we should be in a better position for the meeting."

Jack said, "I will get Luke and we will leave in 5 minutes to set up across the street. You probably want to follow within 20 minutes, don't forget that there is a lot of traffic this time of day."

Frank said, "Thanks, I will keep that in mind. Jerry, George and I will be wearing the new ear pieces that fit entirely in the ear canal. When we get to the gate I want you to talk to me and verify the receiver and microphone is working. If I don't hear anything while we are at the gate, I will put my arm out the window, resting my elbow on the window sill. If I hear you, I will say out loud, you can really smell the dead fish down here by the water.

Let me know once you have the trace information and get an ETA for Mr. Black, so I know when we can get out of there."

"Will do, it shouldn't take long once he places the call. If he is calling a landline we will know instantly, if it is a cell, it will take a few minutes."

Edwin called John Doe and said, "I am sure that Frank and Jerry will want to talk to Michele and the kids right around 6:00 pm, make sure you tell them not to say anything other than that they are being treated well and that everyone is fine. I trust you found the envelope in the kitchen drawer as I promised."

"Understood and yes I found the envelope, thank you."

"If you don't hear from me again, after the meeting, by 6:30 pm, something is wrong, eliminate them, clean the apartment and leave.

If you don't hear from me in the next day or so, it has been good dealing with you."

"That's what you pay us the big money for, talk with you after your meeting. As always, it has been good dealing with you as well."

Edwin didn't like using Jerry's family as collateral, but he was really pressed into a corner, he didn't know if Frank and the guys really wanted in on this very lucrative business or if they were playing him. Edwin thought to himself how it would all be over in the next few hours and that he would know one way or the other.

Right now he was starting to feel those pangs of anguish that he always felt before a big operation. This was very similar to how a singer feels before taking the stage, the main exception being, if a singer doesn't perform well they may get booed off of the stage, if Edwin's operation didn't go right, many people would die, maybe even himself.

Frank's team made it across town with plenty of time to spare. They decided to go to a little outdoor street café and have San Pellegrino sparkling water and a small snack. Depending on how the meeting with Edwin went, they might not have a chance to eat again for a while. The plate of assorted meats and cheeses along with a basket of thinly sliced bread made for a satisfying mini meal. The three Americans did look a little out of place, considering this was not a tourist area, but they could have been importers coming to check on shipments.

What would have been really out of place, had what they were carrying been visible, were the many guns and ammo clips hidden just under their loose fitting jackets. The thinnest bullet proof vests in the world were under their shirts. The men, being in such good shape, gave the appearance of being only a few extra pounds heavier than usual, a testament to how new technology had improved their safety as well as their killing capabilities.

It was time; Frank, Jerry and George got back into their car and drove the few short blocks to the shipping container yard. As they approached the guard shack Frank heard Jack in his ear, "I can see you at the shack now. Can you hear me?"

Frank said to Jerry who was driving, "You can tell we are getting closer to the water, the smell of dead fish is in the air."

The guard heard Frank and said, "Yes, but you will get used to it soon and not even notice it. I come here every day and within minutes don't notice it."

Frank nodded his head in agreement. Jerry asked the guard, "Where is area 25, we are meeting a person there to check on a shipment?"

The guard shook his head up and down saying, "Yes, I was told you were coming, we don't get many visitors, let alone at 6 pm. It is down this way and then to your left, the numbers are painted on the roadway, you can't miss it." He again pointed down to his left, the only real way to go without driving into the water.

As they turned the corner, they saw a parked Mercedes Benz about 200 yards from them. Jerry eased the car within 20 feet of the black sedan with its matching black tinted windows. As they approached, the door on the Benz opened and a familiar figure got out, Edwin Grey. He was dressed casually compared to his usual sport coat look, now only in a lightweight pair of grey trousers and an airy red Tommy Bahamas like silk shirt. Edwin appeared to be alone. As the overhead images promised, there was not a good line of sight to anywhere outside of the shipyard.

Back in Langley, they were also watching the meeting. There were 4 analysts looking at the real-time satellite images, in turn looking at the infrared, heat mapping and the super top secret backscatter X-Ray images, which let the user penetrate solid materials. The CIA operations room main screen showed the visible spectrum video in the center with the other images arranged around it. The audio from the analysts as well as Jack in the field, along with Frank's live feed were all available for monitoring in the Op room. William Bowles, his two deputies, and their assistants were all in the room.

Bowles asked for a status report from his analysts. They reported that there were no accomplices in the area. They also noted that they could see Officer Jack Green and Luke Ward in the building across the street from the shipyard.

Bowles told Jack, "Jack, we don't see anyone in your area using the satellite, what are your eyes on the ground report?"

"The place is quiet, when I was out here earlier, the shipyard manager said that the place usually was empty by 4 or so. They started at 6:30 in the morning and with the economy being slow, they don't really work two shifts anymore."

"Jack, please pass on to Frank that the area appears clear."

"Will do."

Jack clicked his microphone button on his headset to communicate to Frank and said, "Frank, it looks like all clear, both visual and by bird."

Frank took a little cleansing breath after hearing there wasn't anyone with their sights on him. Frank said to Edwin as they came together and shook hands, "So this is how you look outside of the office."

"Yeah, it is good seeing you as well Frank." Edwin then looked at Jerry and George and nodded.

Jerry said, "Edwin, now that the niceties are over, I want my family back."

"Jerry, I am sorry I needed to hold them until I could judge for myself that this wasn't a takedown and that you guys are really interested in the operation."

"Where are my family, I want to see them?"

Edwin waved his hands around, palm side up, and said, "Obviously, they are not here, they are safe, I can't let you see them, but you may talk to them."

In Frank's ear Jack whispered, "I heard that, the cell phone interceptor is working and I will let you know when we get the location." Frank had been doing this long enough to not show that anyone was talking in his ear. A sure sign of a person with a hidden radio receiver was a simple nod of the head when one agrees with a statement or order. Again, Frank was a real pro, he didn't flinch, move his head or say a thing.

Edwin took his cell phone out of his pocket, pressed in the screen saver lock code and dialed John Doe in Rome. After a few words to verify Edwin's identity, he handed the phone to Jerry.

Jerry grabbed the phone and placed it up to his ear, a moment passed then he said, "Hello, Michelle?"

"Oh Jerry, it is so good to hear your voice, the kids and I are fine. What is going on, why did Edwin lock us up with these two guys?" She got some crucial information out to Jerry, now he needed to relay it to Jack and Jack in turn to Mark. The phone clicked dead. Jerry's face looked like a sad puppy, but then changed to an angry Pitt Bull.

Jerry said out loud to Edwin, "Your two goons with Michelle and the kids better not hurt them."

"Jerry, I promise you, that no harm will come to them, as long as I keep checking in with them. But, they are professionals and will carry out my orders to the letter; so don't get any big ideas about trying to beat out your anger on me."

Jerry gritted his teeth and responded, "I understand, I don't like it, but I understand, let's get on with this."

Within seconds, using the cell phone interceptor, Jack got the dialed digits to the cell phone that Edwin called. Jack relayed it in to William Bowles analyst who contacted TIM (Telecom Italia Mobile) to get a location. Within 2 minutes, TIM had pinpointed the phone to a street address. William Bowles had an analyst look at aerial satellite images of the building in question, they also used Google Earth to get a street side view.

Bowles team called Mark Black and had him start toward the address; it would take him about 20 minutes to get there at this time of day, Rome was a very metropolitan city and the streets were still busy.

Bowles then asked another analyst to use the satellite background scatter X-RAY on the building in question to find the two men, a woman and two children. Within 2 minutes they identified the exact apartment and provided the details directly to officer Black.

Mark knew that this was not going to be easy; he would need to open the door, throw a flash/bang grenade and take out two bad guys without allowing the captives to be hurt or killed. He was a little concerned because the door could be booby trapped, but he had no way around it.

He was provided the three room's dimensions and realized that Jerry's wife and kids would also be disorientated by the flash/bang and might be in the direct path of the door and the bad guys, not a good predicament to be in.

Bowles provided Jack with the address and apartment number. He also told him that Mark was in route and about 19 minutes away. Jack relayed the timeline to Frank via the earpiece.

Edwin said, "Frank, you are one of the best field officers we have, you must have enough contacts from previous assignments to help grow this business. I already have Italy under control, but I know you were in Spain and Germany for some time, and we could expand our business there."

"I think we could expand in those two locations, it may help if I get transferred back to Germany, so that I could spend more time on the ground there to get everything going."

"Agreed."

Jerry spoke up, "Edwin, when are you going to let my family go?"

The group thought that Jerry should try to negotiate for his family, if he didn't Edwin would become suspicious. Also, they knew it would take Mark a while to get to the location so they wanted to tie Edwin up for at least 10 minutes and see if they could get any more information on when he had to call his goons again.

Edwin said, "Jerry, again I apologize for taking your family hostage, it was the only insurance I had on all of you. They will be fine as long as I call every half hour."

Jack heard the comment and looked at his watch; they had about 24 minutes until they would be running up against the time limit. Jack relayed to the team in Langley, Mark and Frank the time line. Mark indicated that he was making good time and should be able to make it ahead of his original schedule. Just as he was saying that, the traffic stopped in front of him.

It was a good thing that GPS units can recalculate quickly. He took a left turn when he spotted the tail lights and now was headed down a new, not busy, road. The unit recalculated and said that the new time until arrival was still close to 20 minutes. Mark was going to test the limits, the best he could, but once he got closer to downtown Rome, the slower it would become.

Jerry pressed, "Again, when will I get my family back?"

"You will get them back in a day, as long as I am safe and your new life of crime is underway."

"What do you mean, 'my new life of crime is underway?'"

As Edwin reached into his pocket, Frank, Jerry and George started reaching for their guns.

Edwin said, "Guys, calm down, I am getting an address out." Edwin pulled out one of his business cards that had an address handwritten on the back. He looked down at the address as if to confirm the number then stepped toward Frank and handed it to him. Frank saw the address was in Rome.

Frank said, "So what is at this address in Rome and what are we supposed to do?"

"You are going to do what you do best, you are going to kill the two men at that address and bring me a case they have."

George asked, "What's in the case?"

"None of your business, but it is full of money, nothing illegal, just money from a prior business transaction that didn't work as planned."

Frank asked, "Will they be expecting us?"

"In general, I am sure they would be suspicious of anyone that knocked at their door, but they aren't expecting you."

Frank knew that this was a setup, in fact he thought to himself that this could be the address that Jerry's family was being held at and Edwin in a sick and twisted way was going to let that end badly.

Jerry also thought the same thing and figured that this had gone on long enough. Jerry calmly pulled out a gun and shot Edwin, a good thing for Edwin that it was a stun gun. Jerry pressed the trigger a few times to see Edwin writhing on the ground in pain.

Frank stated the obvious, "I guess that ends the charade, Jack, we have Edwin incapacitated, Jerry hit him with the stun gun. The address he wanted us to do a hit at is Via Alessandria n. 5, in Rome, apartment number 4A."

Jack spoke to Frank, "Copy that you have Edwin incapacitated, I will relay to Langley. The address you have is where Jerry's family is being held, Mark's ETA is about 10 minutes."

Jack relayed the situation to Bowles at Langley. He asked what they should do with Edwin. He was surprised that Jerry didn't shoot him with a real gun, but was grateful that Jerry followed orders to take Edwin alive if possible.

Bowles said to Jack, "Have Frank and the boys secure him, and then take him to the Safe House in Rome. You need to stay where you are right now to monitor Mark and be the center of communications for his current operation. We think that Mark is about 5 minutes out now.

Michelle Banks was starting to worry. She knew that her husband was meeting with Edwin, she also knew that he had a bad temper and was super protective of her and their family; he would be even more so if he knew she was pregnant with his first son. Michelle was dragged back into the present, literally, by her girls; they needed to use the bathroom again.

Michelle asked John Doe, "Can we use the bathroom; the girls need to go again?"

"Alright, but don't try anything funny."

Michelle and the girls entered the bathroom. She looked at the window again, it was too small for her, but one of her girls could fit through it, though she doubted there was anything to hang onto on the other side of the window.

The girls went to the bathroom. They were about to leave when Michelle heard a noise at the outside door. Michelle was standing in the tub as she grabbed Susan and dragged her over the side of and in to the large bathtub. As she reached over and grabbed Emily, everything went black.

Mark reached the building a little ahead of schedule, 10 minutes left till 6:30pm and the missed call. He had his bullet proof vest on, two guns, ammo, and his flash bang grenade. He was ready and standing around the corner from 4A. He talked to Bowles through Jack, "I am in position and ready to breach the hostage location. Please confirm green light on this operation."

William responded, "Mark, you have the green light. We see the hostages alone in the bathroom, you should move now."

"Affirmative, I am going in."

Mark reached the door, hung a small C4 charge from the door knob, stepped sideways along the wall about 5 feet, and rotated the detonator switch. The door swung in on its hinges. Within the half second after the blast, Mark had already removed the pin from the flash bang grenade and now tossed it in the opening. Less than a second and one half later it went off.

Mark rushed in through the door. He spotted his first bogey in the kitchen area of the small apartment. He dispensed with him with two taps to the chest. Mark saw blood, so he knew he wasn't wearing a vest, but it was a good thing that he was because the other bogey had recovered from the flash bang and shot Mark in the chest. The shot didn't penetrate the vest, but caused what would become a bruise the size of a softball. Mark's body absorbed some of the power behind the bullet and this threw him to the ground.

The gunman, thinking he had his man, now turned his gun on the bathroom door, putting a few rounds through the door, then finally taking on the actual door knob. Mark recovered quickly and was able to finally take down the last bogey with a few shots. The man had complete surprise in his eyes. As he was falling, he dropped his gun.

The gunman's final shots made the bathroom door swing in, the screaming of girls could be heard. John Doe saw that the woman was on the floor with blood around her not moving body, he took one last look at Mark and coughed out through bloody teeth, "You lose." Mark put one more shot through John's forehead and he slumped to the ground dead.

Mark got to his feet; he was fine with the exception of feeling like he got kicked by a mule and more than likely had a broken rib or two. He rushed over the short space to the bathroom door. There he saw Michelle on the floor, motionless and her two girls in the bath tub screaming for their Mom to get up. Mark talked to Jack, "Two bogies down for good, Michelle has been hit and is lying uncons- cious on the floor, she is bleeding pretty bad, get an ambulance her fast. Also let the locals know that they have two to pick up with bags. I am going to see if I can stop the bleeding."

Jack called the ambulance and told them to hurry; he gave the description of the victim. He asked which hospital they would take her to and relayed the information to Frank. Frank told Jerry and saw his face go white.

Bowles told Jack that he had arranged for a charter flight to take them all up to Rome and that it was ready now. Jack relayed the in- formation to Frank so that they could go directly there with their prisoner. Jack and Luke were going to collect Bianca, James and Elizabeth and head to the airport as well.

The flight would take less than an hour. Bowles still didn't know who to trust in Italy, so he was flying in some CIA Officers from France and Germany, to meet Frank and George in Rome at the safe house with Edwin.

Mark waited for the ambulance, he was able to slow the bleed- ing and found a weak pulse, and he relayed this to Jack. Jack told him they were all coming to Rome and would be there within an hour and a half or so. Mark also said to tell Jerry that he would take the kids to the hospital and wait for him there.

The ambulance came and took Michelle. Mark gathered the grieving kids and told them that he was a friend of their father's. He was going to take them to see their mother. The local police arrived and made Mark get on the ground; they may have even shot him, were it not for the two men that arrived from AISI, Italy's equivalent to the US FBI.

They sent the two police officers away and secured the area. They talked to Mark and reminded him that he should not leave the country and that his release into his own custody was already approved by their supervisors, but that the CIA could not just do whatever it wanted to do while in the sovereign nation of Italy.

Mark told them that he was taking the girls to the hospital and that he wouldn't leave Italy. Mark hoped for his sake that William Bowles had enough clout to get him out. One of the big operations that the CIA did in Italy in 2003 resulted in 23 CIA officers in trouble for kidnapping a suspected Muslim Terrorist. Mark was also hoping that he had diplomatic immunity, he probably did or he would be inside of the police car going to the station right now.

Jerry talked to one of Michelle's doctors while in route to the hospital. The doctor said, "Michelle would be fine and was now in stable condition. She had been shot in her back, while lifting one of her girls to safety in the bathtub. The bullet went through her back and stomach, missing all bones and vital organs; she also had a lot of blood loss from her miscarriage."

Jerry lost his breadth, "Did you say miscarriage?"

The doctor replied, "Yes, we are sorry we could not save the boy, I assumed you knew. Michelle is stable now and should recover over the next week or so. She should be conscious by the time you get here." The phone clicked off.

Jerry said out loud to no one in particular, "Michelle was pregnant with a boy, he didn't make it, but she will be fine. I am so sad and happy at the same time."

Then Jerry wept, for he still had his wife of 8 years, his two girls and all of them would be good, except for his unborn son. He had always wanted a son. Of course they had been trying, but he hadn't known about him until just now.

Chapter 20   Vacation Ended

Luke talked with Frank on the plane ride to Rome.

Luke asked, "What do we do now? I think it is time we go home. Vacation is over."

"Yes,… that it is."

"We all talked and still want to help our country. Are you going to help train us?"

"No, I am not a trainer, in fact, I am no longer a field officer, I am the new acting Station Chief for Italy. You will be contacted by the CIA a few days after you arrive back home. They will go over all the legal and training issues with you fully. The review process should be shortened, considering your assistance with the CIA on this operation.

After all, they already know how you will behave under fire, literally. Not many people, unless they have served in the military, have the experiences you and your family has. You are all heroes."

Luke and Bianca talked about their family on the plane ride back to the States. The kids seemed none the worse for wear. James was still excited about learning hand to hand combat and insisted on wearing sunglasses all the time.   While Elizabeth said that she wanted to help her country any way that she could. In fact, the whole family felt patriotic fervor.

They had a very successful vacation while helping stop a ring of counterfeiters that were supplying terrorists with funding.

The ride from the airport back to their home was silent with the exception of Luke softly snoring. The Wards were excited to finally be home.

After the limo driver had deposited their bags in the foyer and left the drive, Elizabeth noticed a piece of paper on their kitchen counter. She called out, "Mom, Dad, you need to see this."

Bianca responded, "What is it, what is wrong?"

"There is a letter here from William Bowles of the CIA"

"Oh my God! How did they get in here?"

James stated as a matter of fact, "Mom, we are spies now, they do stuff like that."

Luke reached out and took the paper from Elizabeth, then read it.

"He said that we did an excellent job helping our country and that we will be a great asset moving forward. He also mentions that we will be going to Washington, D.C. for additional training and talk about our future assignments next week."

James said for the second time in the last couple of weeks, "We are a SPY FAMILY."

A month later the Wards were settled into their rental house in Washington, D.C. Bingo, their dog was just as happy with this new house and yard as he was back in Illinois.

The twins were starting at a new high school, kind of a bummer because they didn't really know anyone, but it was just temporary anyway, they were all moving to Paris soon.